D0981497

PRAISE FOR
THE ABYSS SURROUNDS US

"An intriguing fantasy world full of floating cities, ruthless monsters, betrayals, and unlikely friendships."
—*Publisher's Weekly*

"[A] fresh and fascinating look at a lawless future."
—*Kirkus Reviews* (starred review)

"[A] fantastical world of ruthless pirates; lovable, deadly creatures; and dynamic characters."
—*School Library Journal*

"This is a solid, well-crafted, new adventure story with an interesting, unusual hook."
—*Booklist*

"*The Abyss Surrounds Us* is highly original and addictive."
—*SLJTeen*

THE
EDGE
OF THE
ABYSS

THE
E·D·G·E
OF THE
ABYSS

EMILY SKRUTSKIE

flux
Mendota Heights, Minnesota

First Edition
First Printing, 2017

Book design by Bob Gaul
Cover design by Laura Polzin
Cover images by Zdenek Krchak/Shutterstock Images; Dieter Hawlan/Shutterstock Images; elwynn/Shutterstock Images; Peter Wollinga/Shutterstock Images; pick/Shutterstock Images; ZaZa Studio/Shutterstock Images
Map by Llewellyn Worldwide Ltd. art department

Flux, an imprint of North Star Editions, Inc.

Library of Congress Cataloging-in-Publication Data
Names: Skrutskie, Emily, 1993- author.
Title: The edge of the abyss / Emily Skrutskie.
Description: First edition. | Mendota Heights, Minnesota : Flux, [2017] | Summary: Eighteen-year-old Cassandra Leung struggles with her morality and her romantic relationship with fellow pirate Swift Kent as she and the Minnow pirate crew work to take down wild sea monsters, dubbed Hellbeasts, who are attacking ships and destroying the ocean ecosystem.
Identifiers: LCCN 2016055131 (print) | LCCN 2017004788 (ebook) | ISBN 9781635830002 (pbk. : alk. paper) | ISBN 9781635830019 (hosted e-book)
Subjects: | CYAC: Science fiction. | Sea monsters–Fiction. | Pirates–Fiction. | Chinese Americans–Fiction. | Lesbians–Fiction. | Youths' writings.
Classification: LCC PZ7.1.S584 Ed 2017 (print) | LCC PZ7.1.S584 (ebook) | DDC [Fic]–dc23
LC record available at https://lccn.loc.gov/2016055131

Flux
North Star Editions, Inc.
2297 Waters Drive
Mendota Heights, MN 55120
www.fluxnow.com

Printed in the United States of America

To Tara, for making me dunk Swift in Chapter 19

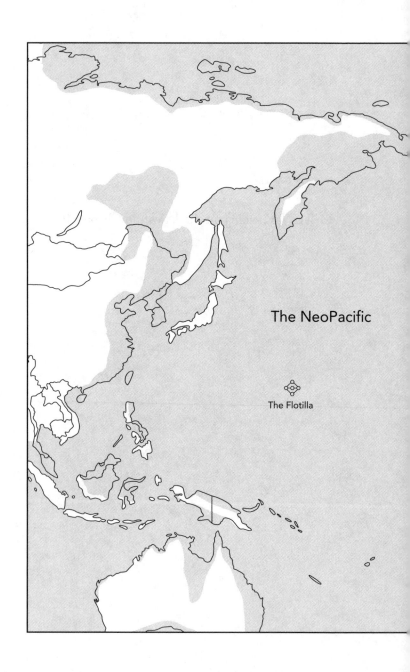

The NeoPacific

The Flotilla

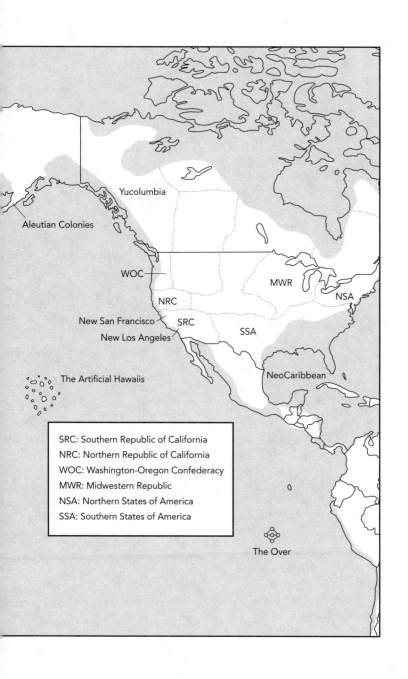

Yucolumbia

Aleutian Colonies

WOC

MWR

NSA

NRC

New San Francisco

SRC

New Los Angeles

SSA

The Artificial Hawaiis

NeoCaribbean

SRC: Southern Republic of California
NRC: Northern Republic of California
WOC: Washington-Oregon Confederacy
MWR: Midwestern Republic
NSA: Northern States of America
SSA: Southern States of America

The Over

1

By the third week in the ice, I've decided I like it down here. The bottom of the world is vicious. Merciless. Cold.

It's everything I need to become.

It's summer in the NeoAntarctic, but I wouldn't be able to tell from the feel of it. My breath fogs in front of me as I stand watch in the *Minnow*'s navigation tower, bundled in one of Varma's coats. It reaches past my knees. Over at the instrumentation panel, Lemon's curled into a ball, staring drearily at the readouts.

It's been three weeks since the night I turned my back on the world that raised me and gave my allegiance to Santa Elena. Three weeks since we abandoned Bao, the pirate-born Reckoner I reared, and fled for colder waters, where neither he nor the Southern Republic of California's ships would chase us. Three weeks since the ship's inker branded me with the captain's mark. Three weeks since I could look Swift in the eye without an unforgiving fury burning through me.

I know she was under orders from the captain when she snuck into my family's stable and pumped a lethal dose of cull serum into my favorite Reckoner. I know she didn't know me then. She had no idea what I would come to mean to her. But every time I start to let the idea of Swift into my skull, I see the ragged holes in Durga's skin where her keratin plates tore off. I smell her rotten flesh. I remember being five years old, pretending I was a Reckoner pup as I tussled with her in a kiddie pool barely big enough for the two of us.

Finding out the truth of what happened to Durga didn't just hurt—it tore through the way I'd already grieved her. Suddenly every night I'd spent curled up and crying in a nest of towels on the *Minnow*'s trainer deck felt insufficient. The truth made it hollow. The truth forced me to start over. Durga died in agony, and *Swift* was the one who made sure of it, and I know, deep as marrow, there's no going back to the way things were.

I haven't said a word to Swift since I came back aboard the *Minnow*. It's been surprisingly easy, mostly because the captain's been keeping me too busy to have time for anything else. I knew it would take a lot of work to turn a Reckoner trainer into a pirate trainee, and Santa Elena hasn't skimped. She's been running me three times as ragged as the other four kids she's taken into her "talent development program." Every conscious moment is another chance for her to shape me into someone worthy of succeeding her.

Today, that means iceberg watch. Eight straight hours of iceberg watch.

It's working, though. I'm getting stronger every day. Nothing will ever compare to the power of a Reckoner beneath my feet, but there's firmness in my muscles that wasn't there a month ago.

Lemon stirs. A slender hand reaches out of her parka to pull up a piece of data. Her eyebrows furrow, and she purses her lips, leaning closer.

"What's up?" I ask, but Lemon, as usual, says nothing. I turn my gaze back out to the sea, to the ridges of ice that crest out of the waves. The waters are calm enough that we've dropped anchor, so all I have to do is make sure nothing wanders too close.

The closest berg is a hundred yards away. Bullet holes pock its side. The captain stopped objecting to ammo wastage a week ago, and since then, nearly everyone has taken a few potshots at the ice to pass the time. There isn't much else for the crew to do while we wait out the aftermath of... the incident.

I don't know what else to call it.

I pull Varma's jacket tighter around me, hissing through my teeth as I press my hips against the railing. One hour until my watch ends. One hour until I can descend into the ship's warmth and join the other trainees in the mess.

Well, most of the trainees. Swift takes her meals in her room these days.

I flinch. This is the problem with iceberg watch—it's too quiet, and it's giving me too much time for my thoughts to wander in dangerous directions. I rap my knuckles against the instrumentation panel to get Lemon's attention.

"Hey, how about that one on the northeastern horizon? What do you think it looks like?" I ask, raising one sleeve to gesture toward a towering iceberg.

She keeps her eyes fixed on the data.

"C'mon…" I squint, trying to make out the berg's contours against the pearly sky. It splits at the top like a great jaw unhinging, and a ridge creates an ellipse of shade that could pass for an eye. Wind and water have sculpted the ice, making it narrow and sinuous.

My stomach clenches. I try to forget what I've imagined, try to see something else, anything else. But there's only one thing my mind jumps to, one thing I've been hardwired to see when I look out at the ocean.

"I see a serpentoid Reckoner," I say, praying that Lemon doesn't notice the slight hitch in my voice or the way my spine's gone stiff.

There's a beat of emptiness, filled only by the creaking of distant ice and the low whisper of sea wind.

Then Lemon says, "Cetoid."

A short laugh bursts out of me. I've been trying to get her to play this game for days, but Lemon saves her voice for only the most important things. "It's too narrow to be a cetoid," I say, shading my eyes with a hand and peering closer to try seeing what she sees. "Maybe if it were rounder, but—"

A tug on my sleeve stops me midsentence. I look down

and find Lemon's petulant black eyes still fixed on the monitors.

"Cetoid," she repeats. She points.

Impossible. I move around behind her to get a good look at the screen. My fists clench in my oversized pockets. Lemon edges away from me as I lean closer. Her fingers fidget over the keyboards. She hones the output until I can see it clearly.

A massive, plated body. Furiously pumping flukes. There's no question about it. There's a cetoid Reckoner in these waters. A cetoid Reckoner with no companion ship in sight.

And it's headed straight for us.

2

I'm halfway down the ladder by the time Lemon's voice snaps over the all-call. "This is navigation. We've got an inbound cetoid Reckoner on our instruments. Await further instructions."

Beneath me, the main deck is abuzz. The crew comes pouring out from the warmth of the lower levels, leaning over the railings, hoping for a glimpse of the monster on its way. But something far more dangerous is stalking through our ranks, and as I jump from the ladder, I nearly crash headlong into her.

"Cas," Santa Elena says, catching me by the shoulders. Even with a massive winter coat softening her, the captain gleams with wicked edges. Her teeth flash bright against her warm brown skin, and her eyes shimmer with a challenge. "I have a feeling we'll be needing your expertise."

I'm still not used to the captain chumming with me,

but it's so much better than being in her crosshairs. The fact that she's stopped calling me "Cassandra" is just the beginning of the benefits that come from being one of her precious chosen protégés. It's strange to think that she was my greatest enemy less than a month ago. Now, under her tutelage, I might just survive these seas.

Surviving *her* is another matter entirely.

Santa Elena steers me toward the aft of the ship, her fingers twisted in my jacket's baggy shoulders. The chaos of the main deck fades, and I let the quiet focus me, knowing the captain's mind is already ten steps ahead. Even with this impossible monster on the radar, Santa Elena's unflappable.

I draw a few deep breaths to clear the last of the panic from my head. I need every inch of my wits if I'm going to make the right calls. "It's probably drawn by the noise the engines are making," I say, eyes dropping toward the rumble beneath our feet. "Can we spin them down? It'll get cold, but it'll give the beast less of a target."

Santa Elena nods. She plucks the radio from her belt and raises it to her lips, her breath fogging the plastic. "Captain to engines. Bring us down to minimum spin, but don't let us go all the way cold. We might need to move at a moment's notice."

But quieting the ship down might not be enough to get this beast off our backs. "Best bet is to send out the herding dogs," I tell the captain, jerking my chin toward the nearest Splinter dock. "Head the beast off with a smaller, quicker target. Cetoid's brain will get latched on the puzzle, giving us a chance to draw it away."

"And if it doesn't get drawn away?" Santa Elena counters.

I swallow. Dread churns in my stomach, but I crack a weak smile. "Got a harpoon?"

A minute later, I'm clambering into a Splinter on the starboard side of the ship. I lean over the needleboat's outer edge in time to catch Chuck dropping into her own Splinter on the deck beneath me. She flashes me a thumbs-up as she settles into the narrow white ship's cockpit, then starts to braid her waves of inky hair. I return the gesture, sit back, and pull the safety straps over my shoulders.

"Cas will take point, for obvious reasons," Santa Elena's voice announces in my earpiece. "If she gives an order, you follow. Understood?"

"Understood," I reply immediately.

"Understood," Varma says from one of the port side Splinters. I can almost hear his smile.

"Understood." Chuck's voice comes loud and clear through the earpiece, soft and distant from below.

There's a pause, and somehow that pause kills me even more than the familiar voice that mutters, "Understood."

Murderer. Poisoner. I swear I smell Reckoner blood. The venom sinks into my thoughts before I have a chance to steel myself against it. I grit my teeth and clench the controls. There are bigger things to worry about than the girl in the Splinter on the other side of the ship. I focus on the task at hand. I cut through the chaos and hone in on the only thing that *should* matter, the truth of what I saw on the monitor.

There should only be one free-swimming, unbonded Reckoner in these seas, and he's not a cetoid. Half the reason we fled south was to ditch Bao—we retreated to cold waters to keep him from following us.

But cold waters are nothing to a cetoid, and somehow this one is fully grown. Its size on the monitor put it at nearly the same length as the *Minnow* itself. It shouldn't exist.

Bao wasn't supposed to exist either, but Fabian Murphy's greed found a way around that. The IGEOC agent stole Bao—Bao and so many others—from the stables that trusted him, and he pawned those pups off to pirate buyers hoping to raise the beasts for themselves. Santa Elena was the first to realize she needed a proper trainer to do it, so she went through the trouble of kidnapping me. But as long as Fabian Murphy's dealings are unaccounted, no Reckoner in these waters is completely impossible.

"Splinters away at my mark," Lemon announces over the all-call. "Three. Two. One."

The snap of pneumatics launches me violently sideways. My needleboat sails in a neat arc over Chuck's as we both drop. It plunges into the still, icy seas, sending up a spray that winches my muscles tighter as it ghosts over my face. I bring my Splinter to life with a twist of my wrist. On my left, Chuck revs her engines to match.

Being a pirate trainee is mostly pain. Mostly backbreaking work. But I kinda like this part.

I let the Splinter fly, and it leaps forward like a coiled spring, pouncing across the water. With Chuck on my tail, I round out in front of the *Minnow*, letting the stern of the needleboat kick up a wave that nearly plows over Varma as he crosses my wake.

I ignore the third boat at my rear and set my sights on the distant horizon. "Lemon, give me a heading."

"See that big berg? Looks like a serpentoid Reckoner?"

So she *has* been paying attention. I scoff.

"Point yourself right at it and keep going."

I cut across the waves, glancing back at the *Minnow* to gauge my heading. Its patchwork figure rears against the gray skies, and a glow of pride sings through me. The ship's a survivor. I joined up as a trainee because I was desperate for protection and desperate for someone who could teach me how to survive these oceans. At the start, I never wanted to be the captain's successor. But I can't deny the way my heart swells at the sight of the *Minnow* and the thought that, if I earn it, someday it could be mine.

Four months ago, I'd have wanted that boat at the bottom of the NeoPacific. My whole life up until that point had been devoted to crushing piracy, to wielding the absolute power of Reckoners against ships like this one. That was before Bao. Before the truth about Murphy. Before…

"Cas," Santa Elena snaps in my earpiece as we streak out into the NeoAntarctic. "I've armed Swift with the weapon you'll need to take it out, just in case."

My heart shrivels.

"Anyone else feel a chill?" Varma deadpans.

Chuck cackles into her comm. "You know, I didn't think it could get any more frigid down here. You two had better watch it. Might freeze us in place."

"Hey, could be handy against this freak Reckoner," Varma shoots back.

"It's not a Reckoner," I mutter, surprised at the sudden wave of defensiveness that rushes through me. "Reckoners are trained. Reckoners aren't wild."

"Fine. Varma, what do we call it?"

"Santa Elena."

"What do we call it that won't get us gutted?"

"Oh, I don't know. You do the honors, *rani*."

"Stop flirting," I snap.

"Someone's gotta," Varma retorts.

"A hellbeast," Swift says.

Silence. My hands tighten on the controls. I drop my gaze to my lap, taking in the feeling of the Splinter's engines rattling through my bones.

"Yeah, sounds about right," Chuck says.

It's the last thing I hear before the sea erupts in front of me.

I wrench the Splinter's wheel, sinking into the surge of water as I swerve to avoid the plated snout that explodes out of the waves. A hellish shriek rings out as the monster releases a blast of fetid air from its blowhole.

"Split!" I scream and whip my head around to make sure that all three Splinters have steered clear of the bus-sized maw that snaps down with a vicious *crack*. The Hell-beast—Swift's right, that's exactly what this thing is—twists, its massive eye rolling in its socket as it points itself right at Varma's retreating tail.

It's definitely not a Reckoner. A Reckoner wouldn't attack without signals. Something about us is driving this beast into a fury, and with no way to communicate, there's nothing we can do to calm it. It slides underwater, speeding after Varma with a few pumps of its flukes.

"Watch your keel!" I shout. "Cetoids ram from beneath." I gun my engines, taking off after the Hellbeast.

Varma's the best Splinter pilot we have, but he's nothing compared to the monster's speed. Its dark shadow closes the distance in seconds. The sound of Varma's heavy breathing echoes in my ear.

"Swerve *now*!" I yell.

Varma twists the Splinter so hard that he nearly rolls it, just as the cetoid's snout rockets out of the waves. This time I see more than the gray hide, the keratin plating, the powerful flukes. I see the scars raking its skin. I see the broken ropes hanging from hooks embedded in its flesh. I see the metal ring wound through its blowhole.

Someone tried to keep this beast. Someone failed.

I check over my shoulder and find that Chuck and the other Splinter have regrouped at the base of a massive berg.

"You two, get on my tail," I call, setting my sights on the Hellbeast's shadow as it twists around and sets its sights on the hum of my engine. "Varma, circle wide. These things can't turn fast. That's our advantage. Use it."

"Got it," he grunts, rounding out on the other side of the monster. A building scream behind me heralds Chuck's approach, and I throw down the hammer. I tug the wheel, sinking into an arc that sets me flying past Varma. We circle, and the Hellbeast slows, unsure which Splinter to go after.

"Keep circling," I holler. "It's getting confused. So long as we keep moving, we can keep it guessing and keep it slow."

"Cas," Chuck says. "The *Minnow* can't make tight turns either. And we're not fast enough to outrun this thing."

I close my eyes, just for a second. Just long enough to let her words sink in. There's only one way to escape this monster. I swore when I joined the *Minnow*'s crew that I would never kill a Reckoner, but this is different. It has to be different, or we're all dead. *It's not a Reckoner*, I tell myself. *It's a Hellbeast.*

"Swift?" Her name feels like a forgotten language on my tongue. The last time I spoke it aloud, she was strapping my armor on me. We were saying our goodbyes, neither of us knowing that I'd be coming back. Neither of us knowing that it would take a single sentence from Santa Elena to make me hate her. Neither of us knowing what it would mean when we kissed like we had nothing left between us.

"Cas?"

"*Finally*," Varma mutters under his breath.

"What exactly did Santa Elena give you?"

The shriek in my ears builds as her Splinter sidles up alongside mine. I keep my eyes fixed on my hands, watching the tendons pulse in my wrists. One glance confirms that the cetoid is still turning on the inside of our circle, still trying to get a lock on one of our boats.

I lift my eyes to meet hers.

"You're going to hate me even more for this," Swift says, her voice hollow, and hoists the weapon sitting in her copilot's seat.

It takes me a second to fully register what it is and what it means. The familiar, brutal lines. The heft and weight of the thing. The captain lifted it like it was nothing the day she used this rocket launcher to drive four shells into Durga's already-decaying body.

This is a sick joke, I want to scream, but that's not it.

This is a test.

Santa Elena's found an opportunity to further my training. She wants to test my mettle. She wants me to work with the girl who ripped my life in half and use the weapon that finished what she started. Santa Elena wants to see if I'm cut out for command. She's telling me to show her that I can overcome the hatred that's been paralyzing me for the past three weeks.

"Fuck the captain," I groan, not caring that she's probably listening in on the line.

The corner of Swift's mouth twitches upwards. Just barely, just enough that I know I'm not seeing things. And weirdly, unfairly, inevitably, it makes me feel a little surer of myself. Sure enough to start coming up with a plan.

"On my mark, I'm going to break away," I announce, checking to make sure the cetoid is still spinning after our tails. "It'll give chase, and I need you three to be on its rear the very instant it locks on to me. Chuck and Varma, hang back, swing wide on my tail, just make sure it stays on its mark. And… you." A blush builds in my cheeks that has no right to be there. "You stay on its tail like it's on your line."

"Cas, what are you planning?" Varma asks.

"Cetoid's most vulnerable point is its blowhole. You blow it up, the animal's drowning, either in seawater or in its own blood. It's a small target, and we're only gonna be able to hit it when the beast is right at the surface. Don't miss."

"I won't," Swift says, and I hate how much I believe her.

"You're using yourself as bait?" Chuck asks, her tone incredulous.

I grin, my fingers tightening on the controls. "If no one else is volunteering," I say with a shrug, then yell, "Now!" before any of them have a chance to reply. With a brutal yank on the controls, I spin out of the circle and throw down the hammer. The Splinter leaps forward like a horse from the gate, bucking up against the waves.

"It's on your tail," Varma confirms.

I glance over my shoulder, trying to catch a glimpse of the Hellbeast's shadow, but I come up empty. "I'm blind," I shout, trying to wrestle down the itch of fear building in the back of my throat. "I can't see it at all—someone's gotta let me know when it's about to surface."

"Watch your front!" Chuck yelps, and I swerve just in time to avoid the iceberg in my path. I squint against the icy air, acutely aware of the way my heart is pounding. *Is this what leadership is?* I wonder, bending lower over the controls. *Being scared shitless all the time?*

The whine of the Splinter's engines blocks out any static on the comm, and the water spraying off my hull is scattered into fine mist by the wind. Tranquility settles over me, and for a moment my head feels clear.

"Coming up now!" Varma shouts, just as Chuck screams, "Cas, *swerve*!"

But I can't. I know I can't. Everything relies on Swift lining up that shot, and if I deviate from my path, so will the cetoid. She needs a perfect target, one that she can't possibly miss.

I hold true.

The swell of water behind me marks the Hellbeast's approach, and I brace myself as the rear of the Splinter lifts. "Swift!" I warn.

"Cover your ears," she replies.

I rip my hands from the controls and clap them over my ears just as I hear a slight *puff* from over my shoulder. The world tilts. The cetoid's plated snout snaps upwards, sending the back end of my Splinter spinning into the air.

And then the blast. The noise of it crushes into my skull, and the heat washes over me as the Splinter jerks forward. I scrabble for something, anything to grab onto. The restraints snap taut against my chest, choking the breath out of my lungs.

The Splinter's nose points straight down. The realization hits me with eerie calmness. *I might not walk away from this.*

The waters beneath me flush red and thick just before I hit them. Ice floods my veins, blackness floods my vision, and then blankness floods my mind.

3

I wake to bright, artificial lights overhead. My head throbs when I try to lift it, and I squeeze my eyes shut. There's a coldness sunk into my core that the coarse blanket pinning me to the bed does little to help.

The room isn't familiar, but the motion beneath me lets me know I'm on a ship, and the distant rumble of the engines makes it clear we're on the move. Some sort of antiseptic clots the air, and I wrinkle my nose, coughing against the smell.

"Finally," a familiar voice on my left breathes.

I turn my head, gritting my teeth against the dull wave of pain that judders up my neck. Slumped in a chair at my bedside is Swift. Her hair is rumpled, her eyes hooded—she looks like she hasn't slept in days. As she sits up straighter, she seems to realize the strangeness of her position and she averts her eyes, staring at her hands instead.

"What happened?" I groan. Part of me wants to rage, to revolt, to kick her out of this weirdly clean room. The other part knows I'll be lucky if I have the energy to sit up straight.

"Well, I hit the blowhole like you asked. The beast went down, but it hit you hard, flipped your Splinter right over. After a few seconds, it was clear you weren't getting out of the wreck on your own…" She trails off, looking even more uncomfortable.

"And?" I prompt.

"And I jumped in after you." Her gaze meets mine, her bright blue eyes burning with a challenge.

I purse my lips. Just over a month ago, I was snarling at her through a closet door, claiming that she never once tried to save my life. I was wrong then, and I'm wronger now. "Shouldn't have done that," I grumble, rolling my head back toward the wall.

"No one else was volunteering," she says, the ghost of a smile on the edges of her mouth. "Besides, captain would probably skin me if I let her new favorite trainee sink to the depths." The cold, clear resentment in her voice makes me wonder if I imagined the smile. I don't want to think about what it means if I did.

I bare my teeth at her, then brace my elbows against the bed. A spasm of pain crushes into my head, but I fight against it. *This is nowhere near as bad as the broken ribs*, I remind myself, then switch to a mantra Santa Elena taught me that gets me through rough mornings in the Slew. *All of this is temporary. All of this is temporary.*

"You probably shouldn't—" Swift starts, but she falls silent when she sees the look in my eyes.

I tilt my head from side to side, testing my range of motion as I shuffle backward against the pillow. Swift moves like she's about to adjust it for me, but then thinks better of it. "So I take it I've been knocked out, but where the hell am I?" I ask, glancing around the room. There's a grab bag of medical equipment scattered across the counters and another bed pressed against the opposite wall.

Swift shrugs. "*Minnow*'s infirmary."

"We have an *infirmary*?" I hiss.

She shrugs again. "Last time you needed it, you weren't crew."

I roll my eyes, but somehow even that hurts, so I close them and lean back, sinking into the pillow. The familiar rumble of the *Minnow*'s engines grinds against my skull, but it's not wholly unpleasant.

Swift draws a breath, and immediately my hands tense into fists. "Look, as long as we're talking…"

"Don't ruin it," I warn.

That gets the barest hint of a chuckle from her, and a pang rushes through me that has nothing to do with the pain in my head. I'd forgotten how much I like hearing her laugh. My body hurts plenty, but it hurts even more to be around her, to be this close, knowing there's no way for us to go back to the way things were.

"Cas," she starts. "I just don't understand why you're still punishing me for something you forgave the captain for months ago."

The insides of my eyelids suddenly become very interesting. I keep my breathing shallow, but my pulse is rising as I grasp for the right answer. "I'm always going to hate the captain for what she did. But I had three months on this ship to learn how to hate her properly, three months to figure out how to carry the weight of it, to keep it from destroying me." I open my eyes and meet Swift's. "I'm still trying to figure out how to hate you right."

She deflates, just slightly. Her gaze drops to her hands, and her mouth falls open like she's about to retort, but no words come out. There's this broken, twisted thing between us, and even though part of me is committed to the hatred that simmers in me, another part wants to reach out, to see what's left to fix. It would never have been easy, and it never will be after all that's happened.

But maybe part of me wants to try, and it's getting harder to deny it.

"Hey, want to see something cool?" I ask.

Swift's head jerks up.

I grit my teeth and lift my right leg, wriggling my foot until it comes free from the blankets. Someone's taken the liberty of dressing me in sweatpants, so I extract my arms and yank the cuff of the pants back.

Marked on the inside edge of my right ankle is a little black fish.

"I was wondering where that was," Swift mutters, leaning forward to examine it. I tense up as she presses against the edge of the bed, but if she notices how her proximity affects me, she doesn't comment on it. "Not exactly subtle, is it? The captain approved?"

"Explained it to her well enough." When Santa Elena brought me to the ship's inker and asked me where I'd have my loyalty branded, I told her without hesitation. I came onto this ship a prisoner, the weight of my position constantly dragging on me like a ball and chain. *If I'm going to call this ship home*, I told her, *I want my ink to remind me of where I started.*

Santa Elena respects that.

Swift leans back, her fingers flying to the nape of her neck where her own Minnow rests. I know she's thinking of the story she told me that night under the stars about the man with the sword above his neck, the reason she chose her nape as the tattoo's place. A reminder of the power she holds, of the cost of her choices, of the danger that looms over her every day she serves under the captain.

The danger we share now that I've signed on.

"It's a good spot," she says after a moment, letting her hand fall back into her lap. "I think Varma just put his on his face because he could."

I snort, collapsing back into the pillows again. "I don't do meaningless tattoos."

"Wait, does this mean you have another tattoo somewhere?"

"No," I snap. My head throbs, and I wince. Lying, for some reason, feels so much more difficult with a head injury. But Swift doesn't need to know about my extra sessions with the ship's inker—not even Santa Elena knows about them. I don't even want to think about the circumstances it would take for Swift to see the tattoo. "How long was I out?" I ask, trying to push aside the thought.

Swift scoffs. "The water didn't even take you out—just disoriented you. You were lucid when I dragged you out of the sea, but you were... well, you were going cold, and you'd inhaled so much water—shock response or something. Reinhardt pumped some nasty stuff into you once we got you back on the *Minnow*. Said it'd make you sleepy, but it'd toast you right up."

"You know what I mean," I grumble. Whatever Reinhardt gave me must have been powerful stuff, because my memory ends the moment I hit the water.

"We've been underway for about two hours now."

I scowl, picking at the edge of my blanket. "Underway" means we're not hiding anymore. It means that the appearance of the Hellbeast has sparked some new impulse in the captain, biting at her heels, forcing her to get the ship moving again. "Where are we heading?"

"There's an island stop and fuel-up in our future. Captain wants our tanks full in case we run into another one of those things."

The idea that there could be more creatures like that in these waters sends a chill through my already-frozen veins. Even though my head screams not to, I have to think about what this monster was and what it means.

The Hellbeast had scars. It had ropes and metal in it, like someone had tried to train it. No IGEOC-supervised stable would ever do that to one of its charges, which means the beast had to have come from some other source.

From one source in particular.

Fabian Murphy, the traitorous agent who sold Santa Elena the unborn beast that got me captured, clearly had wider business in the NeoPacific. There's a logical enough conclusion to be drawn. This Hellbeast was one of the pups Murphy sold, but the pirates who tried to raise it didn't know what they were doing. The beast got loose. The beast got mad. The beast went out for blood.

But it's the size of the thing that scares me more than all of that. To get to that size, it would have to be devouring the oceans' stock of neocetes. The Reckoner industry is regulated to make sure that stock never depletes. If there are more of these monsters, it isn't just the industry at risk—the entire biosystem could be destroyed. It would take decades to reverse that kind of damage, and it would destroy the livelihoods of all of the NeoPacific communities dependent on fishing.

The Flotilla would starve.

My guilty conscience flickers to Bao. I released a Reckoner into the NeoPacific less than a month ago, thinking it would be an isolated incident. As a single monster, Bao's impact on the biosystem should be negligible. But what if he's part of a trend? What if he's hunting ships like the cetoid? I try to soothe myself with reasoning. Bao was properly trained—a Reckoner, not a Hellbeast. He only attacked if signals told him to. He had no wound, no vendetta.

Except he *was* wounded that night I turned my back

on the shore. He lost an eye in our fight against the SRCese warships. But he wouldn't…

Would he?

"Cas, you okay? You're zoning out."

I nod, closing my eyes. The lights are too bright, the thoughts in my head too overwhelming. There's a second smell underneath the antiseptic, one I'm all too familiar with, one that's creeping into my awareness the more I think about it. One of us smells like Reckoner blood. I'm not sure which.

Swift lets out a long breath. "Alright, well. Even if you hate me, I'm here. I'm…"

Somehow I feel what she's about to do before she does it. Her fingers barely get the chance to brush mine before I'm jerking my hand away. The motion sends a crackling pain through my skull, and my hand slams into the wall with a meaty thud. I double over, clutching my head, and it's somehow at this exact moment that Reinhardt bursts through the door, sees Swift with her hand outstretched, and *explodes*.

"You were supposed to radio me the instant she was up again!" the weasel-like medic screeches, swatting her over the head with his clipboard. Not for the first time, I wonder why such a high-strung man ended up practicing medicine. "She is in a fragile state and you of all people should not be harassing her like this!"

"Ow—Christ, old man," Swift yelps, raising her arm too late to defend herself from another blow that catches her on the ear.

Reinhardt seethes. "Don't 'old man' me, captain's pet. Out. Now. And don't let me catch you skulking around here until she's fully recovered."

"But—"

"Out, unless you're looking to occupy that other bed." He waggles the clipboard threateningly, and Swift shoves herself out of the chair. She rushes through the hatch without another word of protest. Reinhardt slams it behind her. He lets out a sigh of relief, sagging against the door. His beady eyes turn toward me. "Cassandra, so good to see you up. How are you feeling?"

With the last ounce of energy in my body, I flip the medic off.

4

Santa Elena allows me exactly one night of bed rest before she drags me back to my duties. My morning starts with the captain bursting into the infirmary and telling me, in no uncertain terms, that I have ten minutes to get my ass down to the Slew. My head throbs as I stagger down to my bunk, throw on fresh clothes, and make my way down to the hold. My stomach's gotten slightly better, but it still twists at the thought of the workout that awaits.

When I enter the Slew, relief sweeps over me—Swift isn't here yet. A few crewmembers mill about on the mats nailed down to the floor of the ship's hold, but Varma is the only trainee in sight. He waves and grins wider when he sees me. "Gave us a scare, shoregirl," he says.

"Would have been one less in the running if you had the sense to let me drown."

"I think you're forgetting the girl with a rocket launcher who started calling the shots the moment you were out."

I scowl, and he claps me on the back.

"Let's get to work, grumpy."

We go through a series of warm-ups that force me to grit my teeth and swallow back my nausea. Back on shore, I was a morning person, but I absolutely was not an exercise person, and little has changed since I gave the captain my allegiance. Varma is the perfect workout partner—his infuriating optimism is the ideal fuel for my rage. My frown mirrors his smile as we take turns doing pushups, planks, and all sorts of other torturous exercises.

"You're lagging," Varma comments in the middle of a curl-up set that gives my stomach's durability a run for its money.

"I will vomit on you," I snarl back.

Lemon wanders in by the time we're halfway done and starts her own routine. No matter where on the ship we work, the captain insists that we keep fit. It's smart of her, sure, but I can't help but resent it when it's this early in the morning and my head hurts this much.

"Captain said you're not sparring this morning," Varma tells me after a particularly cruel set leaves me lying flat on the ground, an arm slung over my face to block out the light. "Said you're to report directly to her when you're done warming up."

"Then I'm done warming up," I tell him. Part of me wants to snap at him for not telling me sooner, but with the way my stomach's churning, I'm afraid a little more than cruel words will come out of my mouth. I raise my hands so that he can yank me to my feet. Varma may be insufferable, but he's always kinder than he needs to be, and I'm not one to pass up that opportunity.

I hail the captain on my radio and receive instructions to report to the navigation tower, so I clamber up through the ship, not exactly hurrying. When I reach the main deck, I pause. It's the first time I've been out in the open air since yesterday, and I'm stunned at the warmth already seeping into it as we plunge northward into the Southern Hemisphere's summer. The wind tosses my hair, sweeping it back out of my eyes, and I lean into the salty breeze, one hand on the rungs that will take me up into the navigation tower.

No matter who I am or where I go, there's nothing that can strip away the way the sea takes my heart. It's the one constant that's kept me grounded as my life has been pulled up by the roots and turned inside out over the past months. Every time I look out over the ocean, no matter where I stand, I feel right.

A flicker of motion at the fore of the ship catches my eye. Swift's perched on the barrel of Phobos, the biggest gun we have, looking small and insignificant against its massive bulk. She stares out at the waves, kicking her legs, probably waiting for the Slew to clear. I mount the ladder, and her gaze swings to me. Even from this distance, I can see her eyes narrow. She knows I'm headed for the captain.

I start climbing.

When I finally reach the top of the tower, I'm greeted by the unfamiliar sight of Santa Elena hunched studiously over the communications panels in Lemon's usual seat. Yatori's at the helm—the old man passes me a brief nod before turning his attention back to the controls.

"Captain?" I ask, and Santa Elena's head jerks up.

"Good to see you out and about, Cas," she replies. Her eyes are hooded and bleary, and immediately I understand. The captain's just as rattled as the rest of us by the Hellbeast's appearance. "Talk to me."

"What about?"

"This Reckoner. What was it doing out here? What does it mean?"

That same defensive urge twinges through me. "Hellbeast, not Reckoner."

She raises an eyebrow.

"A Reckoner is a trained animal. This one was completely wild. They're not the same thing."

"Hellbeast. Kinda like that."

"Swift came up with it," I blurt.

Her wicked grin wipes the dullness from her eyes. "Heard you two finally got to talking last night. How—"

"Captain, you called me up here for a reason?"

Santa Elena rolls her eyes, sitting up a little straighter. "That I did. Go on."

I tell her. First what I know for sure—that the beast was kept, that the beast was abused, that the beast broke loose. Then what I suspect—that Murphy played a hand, that it might not be the only one, that the existence of more puts the entire ocean at risk.

When I finish, the captain has her eyes closed, her lips

pursed tight. I know better than to interrupt her as she thinks. Fear creeps up my throat as I wait, insistent and unwelcome. I've sworn to do my part to right Murphy's wrongs, but Santa Elena has her own priorities. It would be easy for her to decide this isn't her problem. She's just one woman with a boat, an ocean to hunt, and salaries to pay—it might be that there's nothing she *can* do. And as her loyal trainee, I'll be expected to sit back, follow orders, and watch the NeoPacific go to hell around us.

I want to believe the captain is just. That her selfishness and cruelty can take a backseat for bigger things. But a little voice in the back of my head warns me that I knew exactly what I was getting into when I took her brand on my ankle.

Finally she leans back over the communications board and says, "The way you pitch it, seems we need all the help we can get."

Something loosens inside me like a muscle going slack. "Help, Captain?"

"I don't suppose anyone's mentioned the Salt to you yet?" From the way she says it, I just know the word is a proper noun.

"Never."

Santa Elena shrugs. "It's hardly surprising that pirates don't care much for each other. We can barely share hunting grounds, let alone cooperate. But we're not foolish enough to think that any of us can go it alone when things get rough. There's a network in place, rarely used, but viable." Her fingers fly across the controls, twisting knobs and bringing up information on the displays. "In emergencies, our reach spans the NeoPacific. I'd say this qualifies as an emergency."

The *Minnow* has been so isolated in the past six months that I assumed it was the natural order of the pirate world, never talking to our brethren. But the directory Santa Elena pulls out of the ship's records has hundreds of ships, each with its captain marked in red beneath its name. I lean over her shoulder, skimming the list for ones I might recognize. A large number of the entries are struck through with a damning red line. I don't have to ask to know what that means.

Santa Elena tugs the microphone to her lips. "This is Captain Santa Elena of the *Minnow*, hailing on all Salt channels, over."

There's a long silence. Then, "This is the *Kitefish*, we read you loud and clear. What brings you to the Salt, over?"

Santa Elena taps the data on the display and nods to me. I move in next to her and flick through the listings until I find the *Kitefish*. The red text beneath its name reads—

"Am I speaking with Captain Darius Omolou, over?" Santa Elena asks.

"No ma'am, only his communications officer. Is this captain-worthy, over?" His voice is deep and smooth, with a hint of an accent that I can't pin down.

"Get him on the line and tell him it's urgent, over."

The words are scarcely out of her mouth before a new voice rises from the dashboard. "This is the *Kettle*, over." This accent I know right off the bat—it's almost laughably Irish.

Santa Elena sits back in her chair, one hand covering the microphone. "Strap yourself in, Cas. It's about to get very, very chaotic."

What follows is a whirlwind. The navigation tower rings with a tumult of voices as what seems like every ship on the list reports in. Everyone tries to talk at once as they attempt to unearth why Santa Elena has called on them. She has to shout to get the full story out, her voice cutting through the chatter on the channel.

When she finishes explaining the implications of the Hellbeast's appearance, there's a brief beat of silence before the Salt erupts into discussion. Through some of the shouts and mutters, I catch what sounds like other encounters. Pirates claiming to have seen shadows too large for any neocete or whale. Some who say they found rotting carcasses washed up on atolls. And, perhaps most disturbing of all, several who confirm that the NeoPacific's stock is depleting. Some of the captains dispute the claims, hurling insults and wild accusations, and there's no consensus to be reached with this many people talking over each other.

As Santa Elena listens, she slumps lower and lower in her seat, a sour expression settling over her features. Finally she's had enough. The captain sits upright and slams her hands on the station so forcefully that the Salt goes silent. "Anyone with any stake in the future of these oceans, listen up. I'm setting course for the Flotilla. This mess is only sorting itself out if the Salt convenes in person. Let's make it something easy to remember. Christmas Day is five days away, for those of you not counting—I expect to see your boats tied to that raft by then. Agreed, over?"

I never thought I'd hear a group of pirates agree unanimously on something. Today's the day I'm proven wrong.

After she signs off, the captain turns around to face me. "Welcome to the larger world of piracy," she says, spreading her arms. "And you thought shore politics were complicated."

My brow furrows. "But why... why are they all coming? Why would they drop everything just to respond to your call? What—"

She cuts me off with a wave of her hand. "There are systems of loyalties and favors in place between nearly every ship in the Salt. Each of us owes, and each of us is owed. You'll learn the ropes soon enough."

"In five days?"

"In five days. Yatori," she calls to the helmsman. "Set a course for the Flotilla."

———

I'm in the middle of sorting my laundry when a knock on the door interrupts me.

I roll my eyes. I know that knock too well, and if Swift thinks I'm answering the door for anything she has to say, she's fooling herself. My fingers winch tighter in the t-shirt I'm holding, and I toss it on the pile of Lemon's clothes where it belongs. Ever since I joined up, the other crewmembers have pitched in a few things apiece to give me enough to wear. Tonight, I'm sorting it all into piles based on its prior owner. Lemon's the closest to my size, so her pile is second biggest after the ones I borrowed from Swift, back before—

She knocks again, harder this time. "Cas, I know you're in there."

This feels familiar.

"Alright, if you won't answer the door, I'll just do this from out here."

I grab another t-shirt, this one too big to do anything but sleep in, and throw it on the Varma pile.

"Cas, I'm sorry. I know it's three weeks too late, but I didn't think you'd listen before. And now that you *are* listening, I'm probably going to fuck it all up, but I have to…" She trails off, gathering herself.

Something tells me she's been trying to muster the courage to do this all day.

"I could sit here all night and say nothing but sorry until you know for sure it's true. I'm sorry I ruined your life, I'm sorry for the part I played in trapping you on this ship. I never meant for any of it to end up like this, but I'm sorry it did."

My hands shake. I clasp them together and lean back until my head collides with the edge of my bunk. Nothing she's saying changes the hurt. Nothing she's saying excuses what she did. Durga's keratin plates rotted away from her skin, and she fought through incomprehensible pain to defend the *Nereid*. Swift did that. But I can feel myself crumbling anyway, little by little, like a cliff face eroded by the sea.

"I wish I didn't have to be doing this through a fucking door," Swift groans, and there's a thud—what sounds like a boot.

Wanting is a disastrous thing, and in the coldness that's consumed me in the past month, I'd almost forgotten what it feels like. But the sensation can't be ignored any more than a festering wound. The fire of it devours me, and I run my hands through my hair as if that will do anything to help. How can I feel like this? How can one person be pulled by two forces so equal and powerful, both inspired by the same source. How can I hate her, but at the same time—

"Cas, you know how I feel. How I feel… well, it started the day I saw you hatch Bao, and it's never going to get any better. Believe me, I've tried. It'd make both of our lives easier if I didn't feel like this, but I do, and it ain't changing." She pauses. "I'm talking to myself out here, aren't I?"

There isn't a word for what I feel for her, and maybe there isn't a word for what she feels for me. Maybe it's stupid to even try to label these things. Words won't do.

And it's that thought that pushes me to my feet, that brings me to the other side of the door.

"Cas?" Swift breathes. She must have heard my footsteps. "Look, if you want your space—"

I don't even want her to finish that dumbass sentence. I wrench the door open, taking only a fraction of a second to enjoy the shock on her face before I grab her by the collar.

She lets out a slight "uh" just as my lips slam over hers, and then she's crumbling, her defenses shattering as I drag her into my room.

My body's a live wire. Heat. Electricity. Energy. We collide with the back wall, and the sudden jolt seems to wake something in her. She goes from an incredulous participant to the starving girl I know she is. Her hands find my hips, yanking me into her, and *god, it feels so good.* It feels so good to stop caring about all the reasons and rationales. All the hurt and history, all the blame, all the things that made me cold—they aren't gone, but they aren't standing in my way anymore either. The knot of worry and fear and anxiety that's been living at my center for the past month melts away under her rough hands.

For the first time in a very long while, I don't feel one bit numb.

But something makes Swift hitch, as if her mind's hit a snag or it's finally caught up to what's going on. She pulls away, rolling her head so that her forehead presses flush against mine. "Cas, what are we doing?" she whispers.

I don't have a good answer for that. All I can do is meet her gaze, as out of breath as she is, and wait until she realizes that I can't justify pulling her in here with anything other than *I wanted to.* I watch it register in her eyes, watch her understand that her apology was the start of something, not its end, and that the part of me that hates her is still alive and well.

Then I see the moment she decides none of it matters. Her eyes go soft, my stomach swoops, and she leans in and brushes her lips over mine. We've never kissed like this before, never slow, never delicate. It's so strange that I almost reject it, almost tighten my hands on her shoulders and yank her down into a *real* kiss. Swift and I are supposed to be all clash and burn, but maybe we can be something more than that, and it's that thought that stills me as I kiss her back, soft and sweet and tender.

She smiles weakly when we break apart, her hands slipping from my waist. "I... honestly didn't think that would ever happen again," she says.

I shrug. "Foresight's never been your strong suit."

"Oh, fuck off," she groans, laughing and stepping back. My hands slide off her shoulders. It feels worse, having her farther away. The distance makes room for the hatred, and the farther she gets, the more I want to push her back. Swift catches my eye, and she must see the conflict threatening to boil over inside me, because she glances back at the open door, every bit of it a question.

Stay or go? Try or quit? In or out?

"Hey, guess what?" I blurt.

"What?" she asks, rightfully wary.

I grin. "Captain's put us on a course for the Flotilla."

The way she lights up banishes every atom of hate inside me. It's impossible to despise her when that glowing, honest smile cracks through. Swift usually gets to see her family only once a year, when the *Minnow* makes berth at the Flotilla at the end of the summer hunting season. Now it seems she'll get to see them early. She covers her mouth with one hand as if to clamp down the uncontrollable glee rising out of her.

I hesitate, not sure whether to pat her on the back, to hug her, to keep my distance.

Swift answers that question for me, reaching out and snaring me before I can get a word in edgewise. We sway back and forth as I wrap my arms around her, listening to my heartbeat get slower and slower as I settle into the *rightness* of it. Even though the itch at the back of my spine urges me to pull away, to make her the enemy she's supposed to be, her embrace grounds me in something unshakeable.

"Swift?" I mutter into her shoulder.

"Yeah, Cas?"

"Get the door."

5

Waking up next to Swift again is terrifying.

In the past month, I've dreamt about it. Some mornings, I've snapped awake shuddering from a nightmare where we'd gone back to the way things were like nothing had changed. I've spent countless early morning hours lying in bed, paralyzed with fear and trying to convince myself that it would never happen, that I was too strong to let it happen.

When my eyes slide open to find Swift's Minnow tattoo at the end of my nose, I choke back a scream.

Slowly I remember the apology. The kissing. The look of pure joy on her face when I revealed that she'll be seeing her family soon. It made me forget all about hating her. I remember the breathless moments after the door closed when we collapsed into my bunk. We didn't dare move. We didn't dare speak. In the dim light, the wonder in her eyes was the last thing I saw before I drifted off with her arm slung around my waist.

Was that really all it took?

I frown, taking stock of the way we've settled. Her fingers are twined in mine, locking my arm over her waist. Her t-shirt has ridden up enough that my forearm is draped over bare skin, and I feel the ridge of her newest scar tucked against the crook of my elbow. My knees rest on the back of her thighs. If I try to disentangle myself from her, I'll wake her up for sure.

If I don't, I'm going to do something we'll both regret. In the morning light, I can't stand being this close to Swift. I can't believe that I let my guard down like this, that I dragged her into my room, that I asked her to *stay*. I need to get out of here. I need to get *her* out of here. I need—

Swift twitches beneath my arm. Her fingers curl tighter in mine, and her eyes slide open. She lifts her head, peering down at our hands, then glances back over her shoulder. "Hi," she says, her voice cracking.

I try to smile, try to act natural, but I can't sell it. I wriggle my fingers, dislodging myself from her grip. Swift tightens her lips, but at least she doesn't complain. I turn my back to her and sit up, my eyes falling on the piles of unsorted and sorted laundry carpeting my floor. If it hadn't been for Swift, I'd have gotten it done last night. The thought irks me. I've always prided myself on how much more put-together my room is compared to hers.

A brush of fingertips at the base of my spine shatters my thoughts, and I stiffen. "Look, Cas—"

"You should go." It's so much easier to say when I don't have to look at her.

The mattress creaks as Swift crawls to the foot of the bed, where her discarded boots lie. She doesn't even hesitate, doesn't try to protest. "You're right," she says, low and defeated. "I don't… I don't think we're ready for this yet."

"We" is putting it kindly. We both know it's me who needs convincing, that I'm the one who can go to bed one way and wake up another. And "yet" is optimistic, but I'm not about to take that from her. I watch her pull on her boots, my head a jumble of words I can't quite string together and thoughts too undercooked to share.

She listens at the door before she opens it, a far smarter move than I would have given her credit for. In the fragile state we're in, the last thing we need is needling crew, gossipy trainees, or, worst of all, the captain herself butting into things. Once Swift is sure no one's in the hall outside, she slips out, shutting the hatch delicately behind her.

The moment the latch clicks into place, I lean forward, bury my head in my hands, and groan.

———————

The next day is a dance. First around the Slew, around Varma's suspicious eye. I'm back to sparring today, and the captain's been merciful enough to pair me off with him. I focus on dodging his gangly limbs and blocking out the grunts and yells from the next mat over, where Chuck and Swift are squaring off.

"Heads up, shoregirl," Varma shouts, and I stagger back as his foot swoops past my head. "You're spacey today, huh?"

"Head injury," I snap, probably a moment too late for the truth.

"You're blushing." He sidesteps me as I lunge.

"We're fighting."

"You're willingly in the same room as Swift."

I don't have an answer for that one.

Varma lights up when he sees my scowl deepen. "Chuck!" he shouts.

"Yeah, *lelemu*?"

"Have you noticed anything else odd on this fine morning?"

"Oh, plenty!" Out of the corner of my eye, I catch Chuck dodging Swift's swing, grabbing her by the elbow, and twisting her into a hold.

"Such as?" Varma's roguish grin doesn't falter as he blocks a flurry of blows from me. I take it back—I'm starting to resent the captain pairing me off with him. At least I can get within arm's reach of every other trainee on the ship.

"Well, I woke up early, first of all."

"Highly unusual," he quips. Varma aims a lazy kick at me, and I easily knock it to the side.

"And so I decided to check in with my workout buddy." Said workout buddy thrashes in Chuck's grip, trying to dislodge Chuck's thick arm from around her neck, but there's no moving the enginesmith trainee once she's latched on to something.

"Who, no doubt, was still asleep, as is her habit." Varma and I have the good sense not to engage, our own sparring match forgotten as we watch Swift writhe.

"One would think."

"But?"

"But imagine my surprise when I opened the door and found that dear Swift's bed was as cold and empty as our captain's black heart."

Swift's eyes bulge, and she lashes out with her unrestrained hand, grabbing Chuck's mane of hair. Chuck shrieks, her head snapping back, and Swift manages to twist free. "Lay off, you jackasses," she spits, crawling to the edge of the mat. Her eyes flick up and find mine, daring me to do something.

So I whirl and punch Varma in the gut before he can do anything about it. He collapses on the mat, wheezing in mock indignation. "Save me, Chuck," he gasps. "Their love is too fierce and powerful for my weak, scrawny—"

Swift storms out of the Slew before he has a chance to finish. Chuck shrugs when the hatch slams behind her. "Cas, want to tap out?" she asks.

I grit my teeth. "How about you two have some fun together, and I'll catch up later." I turn on my heel and march right out after Swift.

I find her perched on Phobos's barrel, curled up and staring down at the waves rushing past. The wind breaks over her uneven hair, tossing the longer strands across her face and ruffling the shorter bits. She keeps her eyes fixed on the sea as I approach.

"They were being dicks," I start, leaning against the gun's mounts.

"It isn't fair," Swift growls. "They bunk together basically every other night and they don't get any shit for it."

"Because they're impossible to embarrass."

"I'm not—" She bites down on that last word. Even Swift has to admit that it's way too easy to get a rise out of her.

Silence grows between us—a calm hush rather than an unhappy tension, surprisingly. I've fought her with silence for so long that I'm not used to enjoying it. But for a moment it's just her above, and me below, and the waves beneath the both of us, and I'm not opposed to any of it.

"Thanks for backing me up at least," Swift says at last.

"I'm on your side." The words come so fast that they have to be true, and it jolts me to my core. I'm glad she can't see my face from up there.

"Even though you hate me?" Swift asks.

"Even though I hate you." But "hate" doesn't feel like the right word anymore, and I think she senses it too.

The dance continues into the afternoon. The crew scurries around the deck, the ship consumed by the chaos of making ready to dock at the Flotilla. We're not due into the floating city until tomorrow morning, but there's so much preparation that goes into it, from careful inventory of the ship's supplies to a thorough cleaning of the upper decks.

Last time we docked, I was locked away inside my bunk and I missed all of the work that went into making the ship "portworthy." Now I'm steeped in it.

All the sorting and counting numbs my mind, but I can't help being a little thankful for the task. Partly because I can fix my brain on it without my thoughts wandering. Partly because it keeps me away from Swift. Mostly because it's rigorous enough that I'm out like a light when I collapse into bed that evening.

I wake to Lemon's voice ringing through the ship, announcing that we're three hours out from the Flotilla. No further instructions come from the all-call, and I find myself perched on the edge of my bed, staring at my still-unsorted laundry, when a knock at the door startles me so much that I nearly topple headlong into a pile of Varma's shirts.

"Yeah?" I shout, gripping the mattress for balance.

"Got your allowance for shore leave," Swift replies.

There's a moment of hesitation on my part, a moment where I consider telling her to leave it there, telling her I'll come get it later, or even telling her that I can't take a salary that was bought with blood. The first two excuses are weak, and the third is hypocrisy. "One sec," I tell her, and spend the next several scrambling around as I throw on clothes.

When I open the door, Swift thrusts a canvas bag at me. "Captain's giving everyone a little extra to keep us occupied while the Salt convenes." There's a strange hitch in her voice, as if something about pirates gathering puts her on edge. Maybe it's something to do with her mother—for all I know, she could be on one of the Salt crews.

I take the bag from her and turn it over in my hands. Marked on the fabric in a blocky, childish scrawl that's unquestionably Swift's handwriting is the word "CASS."

"You don't know how to spell my name," I say, my voice flat. Swift bristles, and too late I realize that she thinks I'm making a jab at her illiteracy. "No, I didn't mean—" I stutter. "Just, you don't even know this about me."

Her lips twitch into a sneer. "What's my last name?" she asks.

The question is like a kick to the stomach. There's nothing I can add to the harsh, empty space between us. We know so little about each other, but I'd never really thought about it until this moment. Swift leans against the doorframe, her eyebrows raised, waiting for an answer I can't give.

"My name's spelled with one S," I blurt.

"Kent," she replies, then snatches my salary out of my hands. Swift pulls a marker out of her pocket, rips the cap off with her teeth, and crosses out "CASS" with three quick strokes. She braces the bag against the wall next to the door and starts writing. I stare at the floor, wondering what other important pieces of information I've never thought to learn. What other parts make up Swift Kent that I've never absorbed. What other parts of me she's missing.

When she finishes, she tosses the bag to me.

Written under the crossed-out scrawl is "CASANDRA LUNG."

I can't help it—I snort, clenching the fabric tighter. "I— You don't— My father's family is from Hong K—"

But then I see that Swift's about to burst, her cheeks red from holding back laughter. I slump, pushing my hair out of my eyes. "You should have seen your face," she cackles.

"Give me that." I snatch the marker away from her and scribble over the abomination of a name she's written. "C-A-S L-E-U-N-G," I spell out, scrawling each letter in an exaggerated, loopy font. The marker feels strange in my hand—I think it's been four months since the last time I held one.

"Satisfied?" Swift asks when I'm finished.

"Satisfied."

"Can I get my marker back?"

I hand it to her.

"Do you want to come with me when we dock?"

My breath hitches on the grin that takes over my lips before my mind can catch up with what she's just said. "Uh, yeah, I guess," I tell her. Because I have nothing better to do with myself on the Flotilla. Because I like her home and her family and the way I see her when she's around them.

Because I may not know much about Swift Kent, but I'm never going to be able to deny that I want to.

6

The last time I walked the streets of the Flotilla, I was hand-cuffed to Swift. It feels strange to be at her side as an equal, wearing a pistol and a radio on my belt as we weave through the crowds that throng the Flotilla's docks. Santa Elena's docked the *Minnow* in a far less privileged position than the last time we came. In fact, it seems like the captain wants our ship as out of the way as possible.

I wonder if that has anything to do with the fact that we don't have a Reckoner in tow anymore.

Swift leads the way across the swaying docks, up the rickety stairs that lead to the upper levels of the floating city, and across the massive, spindly bridges that span the gaps between the rusted metal towers. Some of the homes and shops are lit up with sparkling lights in preparation for the holiday ahead. I can't help but marvel at this place every time I see it, even though Swift hates my admiration. Swift looks at it and sees the scrap. I look at it and see what the scrap has become. The Flotilla is a miracle, a perfect marriage of architecture and salvage.

The journey to the top of the towers is long and complicated, and I keep making wrong turns or missing the moment that Swift abruptly swerves onto a different path. Somewhere along the way, Swift slips her hand in mine. Somewhere farther along the way, I stop minding that it's there.

We arrive outside the Kent household just before noon to find Teresa and Eva tossing a ball back and forth on the path out front. They shriek when they see Swift, which brings her father, Saul, crashing out the door with little Rory on his heels. Pima, the youngest of Swift's half-siblings, rests in a sling on his chest. Swift drops my hand to catch her sisters, grabbing one with each arm as she tries to hoist them up onto her hips. She barely has Teresa off her feet when her father intercepts the three of them with a big bear hug.

He catches my eye over her shoulder. "Well, this is new."

I shrug, trying to clamp down on the smile edging out of me. "Circumstances change."

"And *you*," he says, drawing back and laying his hands on his eldest daughter's shoulders. "This is new too. What brings you back so soon?"

"The Salt is convening."

Saul's face darkens. "Is it—?"

"No, no. Nothing like that. Just a minor ocean-wide

crisis." She puts on her brave smile, the one she wears when something has her genuinely worried. I've come to know it far too well. Her father seems to recognize it too, because he pats her reassuringly. "Oh, and there's this," Swift says, pulling out her salary bag and foisting it over to her father.

Saul takes it, his brows furrowing. "Santa Elena must be rattled, giving you this much for shore leave."

"It's some real end of the world shit, Dad," Swift says.

"Language, girl."

She grimaces, her gaze dropping to Pima. "You don't care, do you, little nugget?" Swift clucks her tongue as Pima's plump brown fingers grab for her hair.

I pull away, and no one notices. Swift needs time to catch up with her family, to celebrate this rare gift the circumstances have given her. I don't want to intrude on it, but's that's not the only reason I leave them and go wandering down the creaking, uneven path.

The truth of the matter is I can't be around Swift's family right now. Not when I've turned my back on my own and everything they stand for. Not when I can never go back to them. Every single day between that morning when we were all together for the last time and now feels like a weight on my shoulders. I try to keep my spine straight under the load, but then I remember the way my brother, Tom, grinned and pulled my ponytail, the way my mother hugged me, the way my father quietly reassured me that I wouldn't have to take the little blue pill he pressed into my hand.

One of the little girls laughs behind me, and I buckle,

catching myself on a rail, my sweaty hands sliding along the rusty surface. A blast of sea wind tugs my hair out of my eyes. I square my shoulders, my back turned to the Kent household. I can't let anyone see how much this hurts.

I grasp for something to distract myself and latch onto Swift's apprehension. Something about the Salt scares her, and if I'm smart, I'd better be as wary as she is. What does a gathering of pirates entail, anyway? My mind skips to the movies I've seen, the old-school scallywags gathering in rum-soaked halls to make loosely trusted alliances. But somehow I doubt that's how these things actually work. All I know is that one pirate ship on its own is dangerous enough. With dozens in the same place, maybe Swift's right to be scared.

I nearly lose my footing when the radio on my belt crackles to life. "Trainees, report to the Town Hall. Swift, show Cas the way—I know she's with you."

I turn around, and Swift's eyes lock on mine. I can't tell what scares her more—facing the Salt or how far away I got without her noticing.

———————

Swift explains the Town Hall to me as we pick our way down the winding stairs. Ordinarily, the building serves as a meeting place for the Flotilla's leaders, but on the rare occasions that the Salt convenes, the hall serves as the main gathering place. It's positioned in the city's center, where it seems every road and ramp converges. The building fronts down here are a little more polished than the ones in the towers—if they're made of salvage, the construction does a great job of hiding it.

The Town Hall looks like it could be made of concrete. It's a squat, square building at the base of one of the tallest towers, and it gives the impression of a cornerstone holding up the entire Flotilla. Swift leads me through the vaulted front door, brushing past some of the *Minnow*'s crew and dozens more people who look like pirates from other Salt crews. "Captain should be in the main chamber," she says over her shoulder. She looks like she's about to cry.

"What's going on with you?" I hiss in her ear as we dart across the foyer and into a massive room built like a council chamber. Desks line the floor, all of them facing a pulpit at the front, and Santa Elena lounges at the edge of it, deep in conversation with a huddled group of people. The other three trainees have beaten us here, all of them lined up attentively at her shoulder.

"It's not important," Swift snaps, just as Santa Elena notices we've arrived.

"Took you two a while," the captain says, beckoning us forward. She grins wide, but there's something theatrically insincere about it that puts a hitch of hesitation in my step. It reminds me of my first days on the *Minnow*, when she paraded me in front of the crew in her throne room. "Captains, I'd like you to meet Cas, my newest bid."

Five unfamiliar faces turn to scrutinize me, and I scrutinize them right back. The captain introduces each of them in turn. Kaede Kurosaki, captain of the *Water Knife*, who acknowledges me with a stiff nod. Darius Omolou, captain of the *Kitefish*, who bares his teeth in a way that could, in some circles, be interpreted as friendly. Eddie Fung, captain of the *Crown Prince*, who looks kind of young to be captain of anything. His attention glances off me and goes right back to Chuck, who returns his smile with a nervous one of her own. Then there's John Mallory, captain of the *Kettle*, who's grizzled and worn in a way none of the other captains are. And Erica Weis, captain of the *Sunburn*, a young woman who, with her bleached blond hair, dazzling smile, and bright, tanned face, looks like she stepped off an SRC beach just minutes ago.

"This is your replacement for *Code*?" Captain Kurosaki asks, a harsh cut in her voice.

Santa Elena grimaces. "There were… unforeseen complications with Code. Complications that had only one outcome."

"Code would have been useful on any crew—no complication is an excuse for executing him when we had an arrangement—"

"You run your crew. I'll run mine."

"You'll hold your promises, Santa Elena, or you'll have the *Knife* to answer to."

A sour look flashes across Santa Elena's face, but she stows it before it has a chance to settle. "You have your pick of my crew, Kurosaki—make an offer." I glance at the other trainees, but none of them seem alarmed that the captain has just offered to trade them off to another boat.

"The helmsman's boy?" she asks, her eyes flicking to Varma.

"Varma's too valuable to affiliate with anyone," Santa Elena shoots back, and some of the captains in the knot sag with relief. "He stays a free agent until one of you can actually make a competitive offer."

"You insulting the quality of my crew?" Captain Kurosaki snaps.

"Edena's promising, but she's nowhere near Varma's level." Santa Elena passes a nod to a stout girl standing at the other captain's shoulder. "If you're swearing only her to me—"

"Edena was weighed against Code."

"And Code betrayed my confidence so badly that I bled him into the sea."

"That's a slight on his value, not Edena's."

Santa Elena bares her teeth. "And what do you judge to be the value of my new blood?" she asks, clapping a hand on my shoulder and drawing me forward. My stomach drops as every eye sweeps me up and down, taking in my faults and failings and very few strengths. I feel like a cow at auction.

"Scrawny," Captain Omolou starts.

"Gun belt's too high on her waist," Captain Weis adds. I bite back a scowl—I only wear it that high because my hips are so straight that it'd slide off otherwise.

Captain Kurosaki's lips are set in a thin line. "And how long have you been on a crew?"

Santa Elena's fingers stiffen on my jacket, and I know

exactly the answer she wants me to give. "Been on the *Minnow* four months." The grip on my shoulder loosens.

"And your specialty?"

Santa Elena's nails dig into me, a clear message that if I don't hold my tongue, she'll rip it out in front of everyone here. "Cas has yet to settle—she's only a month into her advancement," she says. "Perhaps it's best we let the matter rest for now. Come back to it in a few months."

"I wanted that boy," Captain Kurosaki mutters.

"Not enough to mourn him," Santa Elena notes, and surprisingly the two of them share a savage grin. "Come here, Edena. I want to hear about how your training's going." Santa Elena loops an arm over the other captain's trainee, leaving me blinking in the center of the gathered pirates as they wander off across the chambers.

This explains a lot. For one thing, why the captain keeps five trainees when she only needs one successor. This is how the bonds of the Salt are forged. Captains promise their crew to one another, sculpt them into valuable tools, and cut off the ones they don't need. I glance around the room, wondering how many of the young crew in the growing crowd are promised to the *Minnow* in exchange for Santa Elena's allegiance. How many are old trainees whom she's already cast off? And—

"Swift," Captain Weis says, all but glowing as she waltzes around to us. "How's things? Lessons? Guns? Anything to report?"

Swift stiffens, her cheeks flushing. "I, uh… I took down an SRCese quadcopter with the 86-West on the fore."

Captain Weis shrieks. "Holy *shit*! That's incredible—that's my girl!" She slaps Swift on the shoulder. "Tell me about it. How'd you run up against quadcopters? What kind of artillery were they packing?" She talks a mile a minute, bouncing up and down on her toes the whole time.

"Typical chuggers. Used Varma to bait it out front, then unloaded. One shell."

"That's all it takes if you do it right! Oh my god, I've got to show you the *Sunburn*'s new arsenal—you'd *love it*!"

Swift's lips bend into a smile, but her eyes are strained—she still looks flustered and frightened.

Captain Weis takes a step back and, for the first time, notices me standing there. "Hey newbie!" She sticks out a hand, and I shake it. "Sorry about the belt thing—didn't mean to neg you on your big debut."

"Not a big deal," I mumble.

"But of course it is! You gotta make that first impression, otherwise what use are you to your captain?"

"I don't… I didn't…"

"Cas, c'mere." Swift yanks me by the elbow. "Captain, we'll catch up later. I just remembered… there's a thing…"

Before I can protest, she yanks me out of the meeting chamber and down the tiled hall. There's no dragging my heels with her—she whips me into an empty office and shuts the door behind us.

"Why didn't you tell me?" I snap.

"Tell you what?"

"Any of this! The captains' trading game. The fact that she's trying to pawn me off—"

"Cas, it's not like you would have been handed over right then and there. It's just a promise."

"And you're promised…"

"To Captain Weis, yeah. If Santa Elena decides I won't succeed her, she's grooming me for a position on Weis's boat."

"Then the other trainees…"

"Varma's not promised. Santa Elena likes to hold that over other captains. Omolou has a claim on Lemon, and Fung has Chuck—an Islander princess for an Islander prince."

"And Kurosaki had a claim on Code."

"Yeah, she's *pissed*." Swift leans back against the room's desk, which looks like it hasn't been touched in months. She runs her hands through her hair, tugging on the shorter strands. "Look, you don't have anything to worry about right now. And I've been psyching myself out all day, but the worst of it's over—doesn't seem like Weis is interested in trying to collect yet. We're gonna be fine, okay?"

Just as her stress starts to fade, I finally understand why it was there in the first place. Captain Weis is Swift's failure incarnate. The future she'll be signed away to if she fails to succeed the captain. She seems like a nice woman—over-whelming, granted—but Swift's spent five years clawing for the *Minnow*, trying to scrape enough to support her family. Nothing less will do, and even the idea of it is enough to make her nerves go raw.

I cross my arms, drawing my lips tight. In the past month, I'd lost sight of everything I was supposed to be doing aboard the *Minnow*. I chose to stay for a reason—I wanted to find a way to expose Fabian Murphy, to end the corruption of the Reckoner industry, to do some good in the world after all the harm I've caused. But I never counted on having to do it under a different captain, one who might not understand the injustices that we've both wreaked upon the world. And I've spent four months getting to know Santa Elena and the way she works. With the future of these oceans at stake, I can't afford to let that go to waste. The prospect of being traded away freaks me out almost as much as it does Swift.

A bang on the door jolts me out of my thoughts. "Swift? Cas? You decent?"

Varma.

He pauses, no doubt trying to figure out whether our silence answers his question. "Captain wants you back out on the council floor. Got some, uh… networking to do."

Swift catches my eye. "Back into the fray," she says with a shrug.

7

The next three days are a whirlwind. Every morning, the captain drags me out of my bunk and across the raft to some new meet-and-greet with the other captains and their unpromised crewmembers. She trots me up and down the docks of the Flotilla until I know them as well as the biology of a Reckoner body. I never get to speak for myself at these meetings, and Santa Elena seems bent on keeping my shore origins a secret from the other captains.

It probably leaves them wondering *why* she's hyping me like this.

It leaves me wondering why she accepted me as a trainee in the first place. Like most everything she does, the captain's motives are beyond question, but that doesn't stop me from trying to come up with *something* as yet another Salt captain leads us through an awkward but polite tour of her boat. Does Santa Elena honestly believe that someone like me could succeed her someday?

And even if she does, do I? I asked for my position because I needed the captain's guidance, the captain's sculpting, to become the kind of person I have to be to set the things I've made wrong right. It was never about winning her seat, but all of this talk about my future has me realizing that maybe I need to have a plan in place. Swift's got the rest of her life on lock—either she succeeds the captain, or she takes up a position as a gunner on the *Sunburn*.

The rest of my life is a void threatening to swallow me, and it's that thought keeping me at the captain's heels. There's a whole parade of options waiting for me among the Salt, and maybe it's worth it to explore them.

"What are you thinking?" Santa Elena asks after the tour is over. She pulls me aside, away from the ears of our hosts. "Anything catching your eye so far?"

It shouldn't surprise me that the captain's allowing for my opinion in all of this, but it does. "I… I guess the *Kettle*'s been my favorite," I tell her. I try to push some enthusiasm into my voice, but the words still come out halfhearted. None of the ships have struck me as viable options. With the threat of Murphy's monsters looming on the horizon, an unfamiliar pirate boat is the last place I want to be.

Santa Elena's brow creases, her lips pursing. "Not a smart choice."

"How come?"

"I don't know if you picked up on it, but the *Kettle*'s an Irish transplant. Mallory brought it to these waters about twenty years ago, but all that time doesn't make up for the fact that he's out of his own ocean."

I frown. "That matters?"

"You'd be surprised," Santa Elena mutters, and for the first time I realize how much I've gotten used to her accent, the rounded vowels, the way her "t's" and "d's" muddle—not overt, but soft and present. I've never put much thought into where it came from, but from the way her eyes drop to the worn wooden boards of the docks beneath our feet, I gather she's familiar with the scorn that follows when you wander into waters that aren't your own. "The NeoPacific's huge territory," she says, "but the captains native to this ocean don't take kindly to sharing it with people who didn't start out here."

"So if Mallory offered, you'd turn him down?"

She smiles. "Not necessarily. Might hold out on it, see if we can coax something out of Kurosaki once she sees you're competitive. I'd rather get her back on my side."

It's my turn to stare at the ground. After Captain Kurosaki turned her nose up at me when we first met, I haven't been keen to challenge her opinion. My sentiments were confirmed when I got my first glimpse of the *Water Knife*. Kurosaki's boat is a marvel, a dual-hulled skimmer that looks like it could outpace anything that swims or sails these waters.

And strapped to its bow is the skull of a serpentoid Reckoner.

I can still feel every single one of those razor-sharp teeth prickling my skin at the thought of Kurosaki's boat. Only one serpentoid of that make has fallen in these waters, and I know exactly which Reckoner that skull belongs to—Uli, a snake beast that once escorted ships on the Southeast Asian trade routes. He was a product of our neighbor stable, the Ofilis, and one of my earliest memories is watching from a hillside with my father as Uli took down a pirate raiding party trying to destroy their facility. He was killed three years ago off the coast of the Philippines. All Reckoner deaths hurt, but taking this much sick pride in killing them—it sends my stomach churning. There's no respect for the beast in celebrating his death the way Kurosaki does. I don't tell Santa Elena, but I could never serve under a woman who treats her kills like that.

"Don't look so glum," she says, cuffing me on the side of the head. "Tomorrow, when the Salt gathers in full, we're going to let your big secret loose, tell 'em what really makes you special. And then there won't be a captain here not bidding."

The next afternoon, the council chamber in the Town Hall is filled, half with pirates and half with their noise. Christmas Day has come at last, and so has the rest of the Salt. Under the thunderous drone that echoes through the massive chamber, I find my place along the back wall with the other trainees. Swift slumps against the wall next to me, her eyes squeezed shut and her shoulder pressed into mine. She's exhausted, but she's been spending the past few days up in the towers with her family, and the effects are notice-able. Even the presence of Captain Weis a few rows ahead of us isn't enough to stress her out when she's this content.

I've been up there a couple times to visit, but I can never stay for more than half an hour. Partly because the captain's been keeping my schedule packed. Partly because of the dark look Swift gets in her eyes every time the con-versation turns to the way the captain's trying to sell me. But mostly because I still can't handle the sight of a happy family.

At the head of the room, Santa Elena stands on a plat-form with a knot of other captains, watching as people gather. Above her, a projector screen glows to life, the time-piece in the corner just minutes away from noon, when the gathering will start in earnest. The captain's pose is stiff and authoritative, her easy charisma dampened by the swell of the room around her.

It's not helping my nerves.

The clock flicks to noon, a buzzer sounding it off, and the room goes quiet. Santa Elena steps up to a podium that's been rigged with an ancient-looking microphone. "Brethren of the Salt," she thunders, and her voice echoes out above, distorted and crackly through the speakers. "As you've no doubt heard, there's trouble brewing in our waters." Her emphasis on the last two words sends a wave of scathing mutters through the crowd, but the captain pays them no mind. "A week ago, my crew encountered a beast in the NeoAntarctic, the likes of which we've never seen before. A monster with no bond, a beast spat from the depths of Hell itself. And this Hellbeast came after us with the voracity of a trained Reckoner."

The mutters in the crowd take a turn for the incredulous.

"But you've no doubt heard this by now. And, if our crews have been gossiping as usual, you heard how we painted the seas with the Hellbeast's blood."

I tense, and Swift's eyes flick to me.

"That's not why we're here. That Hellbeast was the start of something larger, something that's been stirring in our seas since this summer." Santa Elena's voice is grim. "If there are more of these beasts in our waters, our lives are at risk. Not just at their hands, but at the hands of their appetites. They could devour the NeoPacific's biosystem, and if they're allowed to, every fishing-dependent community would starve. This one included," she says, gesturing broadly as if she can encompass the Flotilla with a sweep of her hand. "But I've got someone here who can help us sort through this threat and determine exactly what we need to do about it."

Now it's Swift's turn to go stiff, her expression locking up as she tries to mask her resentment, her jealousy. But somehow that makes me bolder. I shove off the wall and stride down the aisle, keeping my chin held high the way Santa Elena taught me. All eyes are on me as I step up to the captain's side.

It feels right.

Santa Elena steps to the side, guiding me to the microphone with a hand on my shoulder. She passes me a quick nod. We worked on this speech last night, but whenever I tried to rehearse, it had felt forced. A performance. Now, here in front of the Salt, my voice comes out loud, clear, and true. "My name is Cas Leung. I'm a trainee under Captain Santa Elena of the *Minnow*. Before I signed on to her crew, I was a Reckoner trainer."

Now they know, and they don't like it one bit. The room erupts in outrage, some of the captains bolt out of their chairs, and others already have their pistols out of their belts. Cries for my execution echo across the chamber, but the only words that matter are the two in my ear as Santa Elena bends close and whispers, "Hold fast." She nudges me to the side, pulls the microphone to her face, and bellows, "EVERY PERSON IN THIS ROOM WHO DARES CALL THEMSELF PIRATE, SHUT YOUR FUCKING MOUTH AND LISTEN TO THIS GIRL!"

The room stills.

I press forward against the podium, swallowing back the sensation of my heart in my throat. Any one of them could have a pistol on me. Any one of them could shut me up before I've said what I need to. I try to make my next words as big as I can, as big as the captain's. "I know you don't trust me, but I'm on your side," I start, my eyes skipping from face to face as I search the crowd for someone who doesn't look like they want to kill me and wear my skin. "I've sworn my allegiance to Santa Elena in ink and blood, and I'm going to fight for these waters whether you like it or not. Now if the datamaster would be so kind—"

The projector above me flares, bringing up a slide of

images, statistics, projections. Pictures of ichthyoid Reckoners lunging out of the water, of ravaged neocete carcasses, of shadows beneath the waves so large that they make my head spin. Someone's even managed to photograph the silhouette of a simioid. The shadowy outline of the sea ape's form sends a shiver down my spine. My love for Reckoners draws a firm line at the viciousness and near-sentience of simioids, and the thought that there could be unregulated ones roaming the NeoPacific frightens me more than any captain in this room.

I clear my throat. "This is the data we've gathered as a collective. The Salt's roots are spread wide through these oceans, and a lot of you have seen something happening over the past months. It's enough to warrant action. We need to organize and start hunting down these beasts so we can prevent—"

"Why do you have a Reckoner trainer on your ship?" I glance down at the council floor to find Captain Kurosaki on her feet, her arms folded as she stares down Santa Elena.

"Not relevant—" Santa Elena starts.

"Last time you were in this port, rumor has it you had a Reckoner bonded to the *Minnow*. Where's that beast now?"

Santa Elena doesn't falter. "Dead," she says.

But our captain isn't the only one who can smell a lie. The whole room knows the moment the word leaves her lips, and suddenly Kurosaki is standing on a desk, shouting, "Is that what this is, then? Covering your ass while you let a killer beast free in our waters? Wasting our time, pulling the

Salt together to wipe out your mistake before it comes back to bite you?"

Santa Elena bares her teeth. "As if everyone else in this room is blameless. I'm not the only one here who purchased a pup off Fabian Murphy, and you know it."

"But you're the only one who's confessing."

And now there's blood in the water. Santa Elena's blundered and every captain in the room is making sure we know it. She tries to talk them down over their yelling, the speakers crackling and snapping as she shouts about keeping the larger issue in mind, about making sure we're acting as a unified body, but it's nothing against the rising tide of wrath that overtakes the chamber.

The captain's eyes go wide, but none of this is surprising me. People can take sides in any war, but nothing brings them together like their hatred of a hypocrite.

"Captains, we need to calm down," she repeats, but it's like kicking a hornet's nest. Shouts fill the room, and fists shoot into the air. Some of the trainees are springing from the back wall, running to their captains' sides in case they're needed. I search for Swift in the chaos. She's still pressed up against the back wall, the other three trainees at her side. Their eyes are on the captain.

Her eyes are on me.

I push forward, nudging the captain out of the way. "Please, would you just *listen*!" I shout over the crowd. "Monsters like these were created to wipe you out. Don't let them do what they were bred for just 'cause my captain made a bad deci—"

Santa Elena drags me back from the microphone before I can get anything else out. "This isn't working," she mutters in my ear. Her hand is on the gun at her hip. I hesitate, then slip my hand onto my holster. I didn't come into this room ready to fight my way out, but from the way it's looking, I might have to. Suddenly I'm grateful for the training bouts she's put me through. Suddenly I'm terrified I'll forget everything I've learned so far, or that it won't be enough.

The captain moves, just a step. Just enough to get in front of me, and now I'm remembering that day in the Slew when Varma told me anyone who fights the captain comes out in pieces. I wonder if that applies to other captains.

With the noise swallowing the room, barely anyone notices when the doors fly open and Lemon staggers in, breathing raggedly. I watch through the gap beneath Santa Elena's arm as she rushes to the trainees on the back wall and shouts something over the roar of the crowd. Everyone within earshot of her goes stiff. When she's done talking, Swift taps her on the elbow and points to the front of the room. Her lips form the word "*Go.*"

Lemon doesn't hesitate. She sprints through the stew of the council chamber floor as fast as her twiggy legs will take her, vaults onto the stage, and swings around the podium.

She never speaks unless it's critical. Today, she screams.

"There's a cephalopoid Hellbeast within sight of the Flotilla, and it's going after a civilian ferry." She pauses, then adds a flat "Merry Christmas."

8

Santa Elena is off the stage in seconds, with me and Lemon tailing close in her wake. The captains who were clamoring for her blood just seconds before do nothing but stare as she sweeps up the aisle. The whole room is deathly quiet. They recognize. They know.

There's only one ship in this ocean that's brought down a Hellbeast before.

And we're going to do it again. This isn't just a rescue— it's proof. We can show the Salt exactly why they should be listening to us. Show them our commitment to cleaning up this mess. We can win their loyalty and save the people they've fought so hard to protect.

If we can just take down this monster.

"*Minnow* crew to me," Santa Elena commands. "Any-one who dares get within this thing's range is welcome to tag along and help with the rescue, but if you get in my way, I will make no distinction between you and the beast."

We sprint for the docks, the captain at the head of our little pack. The news must already have swept these streets, because everyone who dives out of our way looks at us like we're running straight toward our deaths.

Which we very well might be. But Santa Elena's shoulders are squared, her strides long, no hesitation in any movement she makes. If it's to the death, so be it. With the Salt and the entire Flotilla watching, we can't afford to be anything less than unflinching.

We charge up the gangplank and onto the main deck, Santa Elena shouting orders over the clamor of the crew. "Swift, get your gear. Varma, you're piloting for her—I want both of you in the starboard Splinter in two minutes tops. Lemon, get to navigation immediately. I need your eyes peeled—put Yatori on course for the beast. Chuck, in the aft Splinter. You're running defense for Swift and Varma. And you." Her eyes fall on me, full of life, ready for a fight. "You stick to my side like glue."

The ship springs to action around us as we stalk across the deck. I do my best to formulate a strategy. If I had Bao, it would be so simple. Cephalopoids don't get plated—their flesh is tender, easy for a terrapoid beak to slice. But I don't have a Reckoner to set on the beast, and the fact that there's a civilian ferry in the mix means that any move we make has to be calculated. No blind shooting, no blowing things up. This monster has to be taken out with precision.

And I have absolutely no idea how to do that.

Santa Elena strides to the fore of the ship, pulling her radio from her belt. "All under-fifteens on this boat, report to me on the main deck," she snaps. I whirl around just in time to catch a handful of deckhands scampering up the ladder from the lower decks. There are five in total, including the captain's ten-year-old son. I only recently learned his name is Alvares.

"Everyone here?" Santa Elena asks, counting them off on her fingers as she checks, because these kids can and will lie about anything. "Alright, I want you on the raft for this one. No excuses. You five hold down our docking space and wait for us to get back, got it?"

They all nod, even though it's plain to see they'd rather ride into battle with us. Satisfied, Santa Elena shoos them with a flip of her hand. Before they all trot off down the gangplank, she snatches Alvares by the shoulder, pulls him into a tight embrace, and mutters something in Spanish into his wild curls as he beats his arms in protest.

I hug my arms tighter around myself, trying to forget that I still have a mother.

When she lets her son go, she lifts the radio again. "Yatori, cast off," she orders, and pneumatics scream just as Alvares leaps off the gangplank. The docking arms retract, the *Minnow* snapping free as the plank lifts, and finally Santa Elena's eyes come back to me.

"Navigation tower," she says, and I follow her there.

By the time we're up the ladder, Yatori has us clear of the docks, the ship sinking into a slightly aggressive pace as we prowl wide around the Flotilla. I see the ships converging before I see their target—so many bows, all pointed in one direction. Something kindles in me, a spark of hope that maybe the pirates can unite over this after all.

Then I take in the attack.

From a distance, it almost seems like everything's fine, like the ferry's just stalled. But there are pulsing tentacles as thick as SUVs snaking up the sides of the hull, their colors shifting wildly in the afternoon sun. They vacillate between the deep blue of the sea and the white of the ferry's hull, but there's an undercurrent of black that tells me something clear as day. This animal is frightened out of its mind.

"Splinters away on my mark," Lemon announces, but I block out the rest of her countdown as we careen toward the Hellbeast and its prey. I have to figure out a way of beating this thing, or at the bare minimum some order I can pass along to the captain, who's watching me expectantly with a taut smile on her features.

"I…" I stutter, and something dark flashes in Santa Elena's eyes. She's relied on me, and I haven't let her down so far. "We have to bait it away from the ferry, first thing. Can't do anything about it when it's that close to civilians."

The captain nods, then leans over her radio as the two needleboats streak out in front of the ship. "Circle close, but not too close. See if you can get the beast's attention, but don't you dare let it snag you."

Something sure settles inside me as I watch my orders take shape. "Tell the other Salt crews to hang back. Keep the *Minnow* itself at a safe distance—we have no idea how fast this thing might move once it's loose."

As Santa Elena radios in my instructions, Yatori pulls the ship up, setting us into a lazy circle just outside of the beast's easy range. The Splinters weave back and forth as they dart in close, turning so fast that their spray kicks up against the Hellbeast's arms. One tentacle detaches from the ferry, waving experimentally back and forth as it stretches out after the whine of the needleboats' engines. Varma and Swift dart in again, their hull flashing past the loose tentacle just outside of its reach. Chuck circles wide on the other side of the ferry and then charges back, screaming within a hair's breadth of one of the tentacles still attached to the ship.

It loosens, a touch of reddish pigment flushing into its coloration. But as it falls away, I notice something very wrong with the ship in the monster's grasp. "The hull's cracked," I breathe.

Cephalopoids have a knack for shattering ship hulls. Their favorite method of attack is to find a hold that allows them to crush and crush, each minute winching their muscles tighter until the rivets holding a ship's hide together peel back, or its beak finds a weakness and tears through the metal, or the pressure of the suckers rips the ship open like a can of biscuits. Even without training, this monster figured out exactly how to take down the ferry.

And the very second it relinquishes its quarry, the boat will start to sink.

Santa Elena reads the situation, blinking quickly. She adjusts a dial on the radio, then says, "This is the *Minnow*, hailing on all Salt frequencies. The ferry's hull is cracked.

The instant that beast lets go, I need every daring ship inbound to start running evac immediately." Part of me is thrilled that she hasn't forgotten the civilians. Another part reins it in—with the rest of the Salt focused on evacuating the ferry, there's no one to stop the *Minnow* from taking all the glory.

A few affirmations snap out from the radio, but the captain's eyes are already back on the Splinters. She sets her hands on her hips, and I step up to her side, trying to see what it is she's seeing. Is it the patterns Chuck and Varma carve as they feint right and left, urging the Hellbeast to stretch itself farther each time? Is it the way Swift sits in Varma's gunner seat, bristling for orders to shoot? Or is it the beast itself that has her attention?

It has mine. Not because of the threat it poses, but because of the black pigments that swirl across its shifting skin. Cephalopoids are complex. They're smart. They can be frustrated and wrathful, and that's what I'd expect from a monster like this.

But this thing's just scared.

A poor, lonely beast, severed from the purpose it was bred for, caught up in a world it doesn't understand completely, latching on to the first bit of instinct that comes to it—I can't avoid the irony as I look down on the monster that reflects myself back at me.

Which is, of course, when the captain's hand lands on my shoulder. "Cas, a strategy would be mighty helpful right about now," she hisses. "At the bare minimum, talk me through what we're doing here."

My jaw clenches. This Hellbeast isn't violent like the other one was, and even if it were, a cephalopoid is a whole different can of worms. All Reckoners are nigh impossible to kill when they're being controlled by trainers, and even without lights and noise to direct its motions, this cephalopoid is smart enough that it won't go down easily.

"It's not aggressive," I start. Santa Elena lifts an eyebrow. "What I mean is… We took down the cetoid Hellbeast in the NeoAntarctic because we were able to bait it into Swift's line of sight." I leave out the part where I nearly got myself killed in the process. "And that cetoid had a weakness. The blowhole was a single target—a design flaw, I guess. Cephalopoids don't have something like that. Only way to take them down for sure is destroying their brain, and to do that, you have to get past eight arms and a bone plate."

"A rocket wouldn't do it?"

I shake my head. "Wouldn't come close. Cephalopoid flesh is designed to absorb blows like that."

Down below, another tentacle peels off the ferry, whipping out so quickly that it nearly upends Chuck's Splinter. She cuts hard across the waves, struggling to keep the boat pointed straight. The captain grips my shoulder tighter. "So what do we do?" she asks. "How do we kill it?"

We don't, I want to tell her. *We bait it away, save the people, let it live.* It's scared. It doesn't deserve this. But the company I keep would never accept something like that. If we're going to convince the Salt to follow us into battle against the Hellbeast threat, this creature has to die.

"If I had Bao, this would be a lot easier," I grumble. "I don't… I don't know."

Her hand slips from my shoulder, her eyes hardening. The captain's disappointment crushes me like a weight. I find myself astonished that her good faith means that much to me, that it hurts this much when it's gone. Suddenly I know exactly how Swift feels. Santa Elena lifts the radio again, snapping it back to the *Minnow*'s private line. "Seems our new blood's run its course."

"Orders?" Varma asks. Below, his Splinter swerves, bleeding off a bit of speed as he teases the edge of the Hellbeast's reach.

"Stay alive. Peel the beast off the ship. And after that, I'm open to suggestions."

My heart's in my throat. I drop my hand to the pistol on my belt, my fingers sliding into the grip as if I can squeeze an answer from the gun. Something to win back the captain's favor, something to make sure the animal doesn't suffer. A clean death.

A burst of yells snaps through the channel, and I lunge forward, leaning against the window as I take in the scene. The cephalopoid has detached. Red pigment flushes across its skin as its arms splay after the Splinters. A worrisome stream of bubbles spurts from the cracks in the ferry's hull, and Santa Elena twists a dial on the radio and shouts, "Salt crews, get in there *immediately*."

The ships at our back plunge forward, and Yatori twists the wheel. I steady myself against the glass as the *Minnow* bucks, its engines catching. We set after the Hellbeast, which in turn sets after the Splinters. Varma and Chuck weave their paths together, drawing the beast on, and I can barely make out Swift in the gunner seat as she lunges upright and slings the rocket launcher over her shoulder.

That's not going to work, I want to scream at her, but even if I did, it wouldn't keep her from firing the first shot. The shell slams into the cephalopoid's tentacles, the thunder of the blast rolling over the waves. But when the smoke clears, the damage is nothing but surface level, and the cephalopoid is still coming.

"Don't waste your ammo," Santa Elena growls, but doesn't bother putting those words through the radio channel. Swift reloads the rocket launcher, keeping it poised, but she holds back before firing, looking for her opening.

She's not going to get one—I can tell her that much.

I'm so focused on watching the weapon in Swift's hands that I nearly miss the moment the cephalopoid's attention shifts. Its alien eyes flick backward, spotting us on its tail, and suddenly its speed flags. And we keep hurtling toward it.

"Yatori, swerve!" I yell, just as one of the beast's tentacles lashes out, the suckers on the tip sticking to our hull with a wet slap. The helmsman yanks the ship portways, the deck lurching beneath our feet, but it does little to shake the monster's hold.

"Gun it!" Santa Elena shouts. "I don't want that thing getting another arm on us."

The engines roar, and the *Minnow* plunges forward, yanking the Hellbeast like a pull toy. It flares its arms, dragging us back, and the ship swings sideways. Santa Elena and I scrabble for handholds, and Yatori clutches the wheel with all his might. Lemon hugs the navigation panel, her cheek smashed against the instrumentation as if she's listening to the computers' processes.

"Splinters, distract it," Santa Elena grunts into the comm. "Shoot it. Bait it. Get it off us."

"No." The word snaps through the comm with calm authority, with every ounce of potential Santa Elena's carved into her. Underneath the groan of metal under stress, Swift's voice fills the navigation tower. "Chuck, get clear. Varma, get out of the boat."

What the fuck does she think she's doing?

Part of me knows exactly what the fuck she thinks she's doing. I catch the moment Santa Elena's surprise over being defied melts into a hungry look. The radio goes untouched. Instead the captain leans forward against the window, waiting to see if her work has wrought something worthy.

I scan the waves, searching for their Splinter, but all I find is Varma's head bobbing up and down as he treads water, abandoned in our wake. The Hellbeast slaps another tentacle on our hull, and a primal fear curls through me so powerfully that my lips start to tremble. It occurs to me that I've never been on the losing side of a Reckoner attack. I've never felt what these pirates feel when they run up against a beast designed to obliterate them. I've never looked down at a monster rising from the waves and known I was about to die.

Which is what I'm stuck on when I hear the scream of

her engine, too high for the cephalopoid to detect. Its rage is focused on us, sharp like a knife, and it scarcely notices when Swift's Splinter comes roaring around our keel.

The rocket launcher sits in the seat beside her, the seat she once occupied. I stare, thunderstruck, as she guns the engine, bending low over the controls. The waters froth around her as the cephalopoid's tentacles rise out of the water, reaching for our hull, but she pilots with a single mind, the Splinter on an arrow's course.

An arrow's course set right for the Hellbeast's eye.

Swift always knows where to put a killing blow.

Ice seeps into my veins, ice more frigid than the Neo-Antarctic we left behind. I take it in as if in slow motion, the moment the beast realizes what's coming for it, the moment she unsnaps her harness and leaps clear of the boat, the moment the needle-sharp bow of the Splinter plunges into the soft, glassy surface of the cephalopoid's eye.

I don't watch the Hellbeast die. It's a foregone conclusion, predestined by the momentum of the ship that rocketed through the monster's eyeball and up into its brain. I know what that will look like, and I don't want to take any part in it. What I watch, with my breath swollen in my lungs until they feel like they might burst, is the spot where Swift's head disappeared beneath the waves, far too close to the beast's tentacles for my liking. The ocean's surface is glassed over, decorated with the wreath of froth she left behind.

When she bursts from the waves, her uneven hair hanging in her face as she claws for breath, I can't help but sigh, not caring that the captain might catch it. Only then do I dare shift my gaze to the damage she wreaked.

Which is significant.

There will be no recovering the Splinter, even if it weren't embedded in the cephalopoid's brain. The hull has shattered from the impact, and smoke curls up from where the overheated engine cooks part of the cephalopoid's flesh. The beast's body is already starting to sink little by little, and its pigments have flushed white, marking it as well and truly dead. The ghostly tentacles lose their suction as the deadweight of the Hellbeast drags at them. They peel off the *Minnow*'s hull a sucker at a time.

And taking it all in, barely a speck against the mass of the monster she killed, is Swift, treading water, her breathing ragged through the radio.

She makes a strangled, surprised noise when the cheering starts.

It comes from the passengers on the ferry, even as they're helped across haphazard gangplanks onto the rescue ships. It comes from the pirate ships that prowl the waters around us, rising over the churn of their engines. It comes from the towers of the Flotilla at our back, and as I turn and shield my eyes against the sun, I pick out people with binoculars and cameras waving their arms from the heights of the floating city.

I glance back down just in time to catch Chuck wheeling her Splinter around, Varma already slumped and sopping in her copilot's seat. She skims up to Swift, who clambers aboard on unsteady legs, like all sense of the sea has been knocked out of her, like she can't believe what she just did.

Next to me, the captain chuckles. "Well, Cassandra," she says, her hands folded behind her back and her smile as sharp as the syllables of my name. "Maybe next time."

9

When we get back to our docking position, the five under-fifteens are joined by a crowd so massive that the docks have sunk several feet into the water. Santa Elena pushes her way to the front of the gangplank as it lowers, her shoulders squared, an electrifying grin on her face. She beckons Swift, who's still swiping at her soaking hair with a ratty towel. When she stumbles up to the captain's side, Santa Elena grabs her fist and thrusts it into the air.

Swift's knees wobble as the crowd roars in response. It occurs to me that being celebrated is a foreign experience to her, made even more alien by the captain's turn on her in recent months. But Santa Elena is nothing but thrilled to have Swift at her side today. "This girl just saved your entire raft!" she screams over the crowd.

An exaggeration, to be sure, but the people love it. Some of the crew begin chanting her name, and the docks take up the mantra until it seems like the entire Flotilla is rattling with the words "Swift! Swift! Swift!"

Santa Elena catches my eye and gives me a sly smile, as if to drive the point home. *This could have been you.*

———

I hate how good "hometown hero" looks on Swift. Not because I preferred her dull and lifeless, but because it hurts, watching her glow. It hurts to hate seeing her relieved. She's finally done being unnoticed, being uncelebrated, being out of the captain's favor. I should be happy for her, but all I feel is the bitter sting of Santa Elena's disappointment falling on me.

A tide of celebration sweeps the *Minnow* crew through the lower levels of the Flotilla, and there's no fighting it. We're escorted from bar to bar by shouts of praise, and every screen in the city seems to be rotating through footage of the fight, from the phones people pass around to projections in the heart of the Flotilla.

I keep to the edge of the festivities, watching from the shadows as Swift drinks in the moment her home finally notices her, as Chuck and Varma stumble after her, jeering good-natured insults that do nothing to dampen her mood. I watch her duck into the tattoo parlor. I watch her emerge with three bars across the inside of her right forearm. One for each of her kills, I realize, from the way her face falls when she spots me among her herd of admirers. One for the cephalopoid. One for the cetoid.

One for Durga.

She knows she's fucked up, but she doesn't know how badly until I turn around without a word and storm back toward the docks.

There's only one person on the main deck when I reach the *Minnow*, and I don't spot her until it's too late. "Cassandra," Santa Elena says, regarding me from the ship's prow. "Surprised you're back this early." From her tone, she isn't surprised at all.

I freeze on the gangplank, my hands shoved deep in my pockets, weighing my options. Evening is settling over the Flotilla, the dock lamps just starting to glow as the sun settles against the horizon. The captain looks like she was taking a moment for herself—do I want to interrupt it? Or should I be running for my bunk?

She answers that question for me with a flip of her hand that beckons me to her side. An order, not a request. "Let's talk about your progress," she says.

I join her at the rail and stare down into the harbor waters. Out here on the fringes of the docks, the ocean's waves aren't broken up—they rise and fall chaotically, creaking the docking arms holding the ships in place. Everything feels jointed, uneven, at odds with the rhythm of the sea, a constant reminder that the Flotilla wages a ceaseless war against the forces of nature.

The captain's hand lands on my shoulder. It used to feel like it belonged there. It doesn't anymore. "What do you want for yourself in the end, Cas?" Santa Elena asks.

I shrug, half-hoping it will dislodge her. "A place in the sea."

She nods. "That's what you told me the night you asked to join my crew. It hasn't changed?"

I blink, trying to decide how much to give away. I've never told her upfront about my desire to bring Fabian Murphy to justice, to right the wrongs he's caused, but I think she's probably deduced that there's more to my shifting loyalties than having nowhere left to go. "I still don't know what side I'm supposed to be on," I tell her, and the truth feels so good that I give her more of it. "Neither of them feels right. On shore, I was supposed to set monsters on people who had no choice but piracy. But I can't pretend that you guys are completely just and moral either."

"That's fair."

And because we're being truthful, and because we're alone on the ship, and because I can't stop thinking about it after my catastrophic failure today, I turn to her and ask, "Why'd you take me on in the first place?"

Santa Elena smirks. "Well, first of all, because you aren't scared of asking for what you want. That's an absolutely essential skill when it comes to leading a boat like this. And I've seen how ruthless you can be. When you were training that pup. When you took down the SRCese ships on our tails. The way you've been handling Swift." She counts off each of her points on her fingers, then taps her sharpened nails against the deck railing.

I roll my shoulders uncomfortably, wondering just how much she knows about how I've "handled" Swift.

"But above all that, I accepted your proposition because it felt like legacy."

"What do you mean?" I ask, my mouth dry.

"The spot you occupy. The boy who had it before was so much more like you than you know."

I grit my teeth, and a trickle of nausea creeps up my throat. The boy who had it before was a soft-spoken navigator with electric green eyes and a grudge against Swift. He tried to get me, her, and the monster in my charge killed. And Santa Elena executed him for it.

The captain catches my consternation and gives me a soft smile. "I'm the only one on this boat who knows what Code was before he came here."

"He came here in slavers' chains—that's what Varma said."

She nods. "That he did. And I drove the hardest bargain I've ever done to buy him. Slavery doesn't sit right with me for… obvious reasons, but I couldn't shoot the men who sold him to me—you have no idea what kind of mess that would stir up. The most I could do was get that shivering twelve-year-old out of their hands and leave them as light of purse as possible. And once I had him freed, he told me exactly how those circumstances fell on him." She draws a deep breath, closing her eyes. "Do you know what a lightrunner is, Cas?"

"Smuggling ship. Ultra light, ultra fast." In the time since the Schism that divided the world into smaller territories, smuggling has flourished almost as much as piracy. There's good money in slipping illegal goods past state borders, but to do it, you have to be quick enough to make the crossing without getting caught.

Santa Elena nods. "Takes a skilled hand to control a ship like that. It was Code's mother's trade, and Code was learning from her when their craft ran into a pirate net. They killed her immediately, of course. Looted the ship's cargo, which included the boy helping run it. And when a kid gets taken from a trap like that, he goes straight onto the slave market."

The chill of the night works its way into my veins.

"Code hated pirates, naturally. I put him on deckhand duty, had him work side by side with the new girl I'd picked up on the same stop." The captain winks at me, in case it wasn't clear that girl was Swift. "But he was biding his time, waiting for his opportunity. Sound familiar?"

I grimace.

"One night, the little devil crept up to the navigation tower and started pulling every trick he knew. If Yatori hadn't caught him, we'd have been dead in the water in minutes. But Yatori took pity on the kid and struck a bargain with him. Code would apprentice for him, and he wouldn't tell me what Code had just tried to do." Santa Elena pauses. "He told me, of course. And after that, I started watching Code more carefully. Started seeing the potential in him. Yatori trained him well, and by the time he was fifteen, I knew I wanted him in the running. So he was the first to get promoted when a slot opened up."

I flinch, imagining what befell Code's predecessor.

"She died in a raid, Cas. Don't get ideas." I try not to let her see the spark of delight that seizes me when she uses my nickname, but the captain sees everything. She pats me on the shoulder. "Change is coming to the NeoPacific. We're making these waters anew, and at the end of all of it, I'm confident you'll find something to ask for. But until then, I need you at your best."

I nod. *This* is the captain I threw my lot in with. The woman who saved a terrified slave boy and gave him a shot at her crown. The one who shouted down a room full of pirates to make them listen to me and planted herself between me and their fury when it all went south. The one who's leading our desperate bid to save these oceans. And Santa Elena deserves more than what I gave her this afternoon. I brace myself for her disappointment, trying to swallow the bitter taste in the back of my throat. "I'm sorry—" I start, but she cuts me off with a sharp look.

"You failed today, Cas. You're lucky Swift was there to save us all. If we're going to go up against the Hellbeasts, we need your expertise. We need you to be better than you were with the cephalopoid."

Do I tell her? Do I confess that even if I could have come up with a strategy to save the monster, I would have hesitated to call it out? She swore when I came on this ship that she'd never make me kill a Reckoner, and even though we've decided the Hellbeasts are separate animals entirely, these indirect kills have started weighing on my conscience.

Santa Elena sighs, staring down at the inky waters, her face lit by the last glow of the setting sun. "Look, I can't have Swift destroying a piece of expensive equipment every time we need to take down a beast. We're down to three Splinters, and it's going to take a significant chunk of the hoard to replace the ones we've lost. Swift got lucky the first two times, but I'm not giving her a third chance, no matter how good she's getting at it. If we're really going after the Hellbeasts, she isn't going to be our hunter. You are."

My ears ring, my fingers crimping tight around the railing. "I can't do that," I tell her. "I'm not that good with weapons, and even if I could point them in the right direction, it's just plain *hard* to kill a Reck—Hellbeast."

She laughs, the empty space of the deck reflecting the noise back at her. "Trust me, that won't be an issue. You aren't going to be killing them the way Swift does—you'll be doing it with an old friend."

It takes me a second too long to catch her meaning.

Santa Elena gives me a wicked smile. "There's a monster in these waters that comes when we call. Might as well put him to good use."

I can't name the mix of emotions that wash through my blood. It's joy, it's nostalgia, it's fear and pain and panic. It's all of the above but none of them in full, each tainted in some way by the others. Santa Elena's giving me a chance to redeem myself.

We're going to get Bao.

10

It takes me days to adjust to the idea that I'll be a Reckoner trainer again. I spend most of them on the *Minnow*, too pissed at Swift to venture onto the Flotilla, which reeks of her territory. But it isn't pleasant, being trapped on a ship with nothing but your thoughts.

And I have so many thoughts.

After the cephalopoid attack, sentiment in the Salt has swung in our favor. Santa Elena commands the crowd now, and already Salt vessels are setting out on the hunt. I tell the captain in private that those crews are likely underequipped to kill a Hellbeast, much less fend one off.

She agrees. She sounds pleased about it.

There's one beast in the NeoPacific that every Salt captain has been warned not to attack. Word went out over the channels that anyone who spots a terrapoid with one eye should radio it in and mark its location. Santa Elena's been spreading a similar message among the ferry captains and other ships that make berth at the Flotilla, promising a cut of the *Minnow*'s stockpile to anyone with information that leads to Bao's whereabouts. The captain seems optimistic, but it's been five days since the hunt began, and still there's been no sign of him. It's a wide, wide ocean, after all.

I'm glad for it.

I'm not ready to go back to that life. I haven't set foot on the trainer deck since the night I took down the SRCese ships and turned Bao loose, and the thought of having to return fills me with an uncanny mix of dread and longing. It's like a phantom pain, like part of myself has been cut off. I'm still whole. I'm still everything I need to be. But the empty space of what once was can't do anything but hurt when I remember it's there. Back before, when I was raising Bao for Santa Elena, I could play the part of trainer because I knew it was all a sham, knew no *real* Reckoner could be raised from a pirate ship. But to be standing on that deck and earnestly preparing a Reckoner for a battle I believe in—it feels too much like accepting where I stand.

And I'm still not sure if I accept where I stand right now. Every time I try to think about it, I end up burying my head in my hands and wanting to scream. It wasn't supposed to be like this. My life was set from birth—I'd raise and train Reckoners, stay on the shore's side, work the job I was born to do. Joining the *Minnow* was like throwing away the first seventeen years of my life, and at the time it felt necessary. It felt right. But if I survive the Hellbeast crisis and carry on with the pirates, I'll be preying on the weak.

I'll be killing in the name of greed, and the first seventeen years of my life have made sure that I'll never be able to justify that.

Every day we go with no news, my heart lifts a little bit. Let him be dead. Let him be an ocean away. Anything to keep me away from the place I unquestionably belong.

The *Minnow* is desolate with the entire crew on leave. Apart from a rotating guard, no one sticks around the ship when they have an entire floating city to enjoy. And without other people around, the boat's boring as hell. After my past as a Reckoner trainer was revealed, interest in my prospects dwindled among the Salt. Santa Elena's all but given up on trying to promise me to another captain, leaving my schedule horrifically empty. I find myself running laps around the main deck, doing extra sets of exercises in the Slew—anything to keep busy. Worst of all, I start to enjoy it.

On the fifth day, I finally cross the gangplank, fed up with my own bullshit. The Flotilla's too big for it to be entirely Swift's, and my salary bag's been tucked in one of my drawers for too long. I stuff some bills in my pocket, dress in the clothes that fit me best, and set off into the city.

I start by walking the well-worn path between the docks and the city center, stopping only when I reach the Town Hall's steps. Some vaguely familiar faces lurk around—other Salt crews and trainees whom I've met during the whirlwind tours a week ago. They give me nods, but thankfully no words.

Running a hand through my hair, I glance between the roads and pathways and up at the bridges that span the towers above. The only other route I know in this city leads to the Kent household, and I'm aiming to go anywhere but there. I consider what else the floating city has to offer.

Then I start following my nose.

It isn't long until I find what I'm looking for. There's an alley just two blocks away from the Town Hall where the seven red flags of the Chinese Commonwealths are strung between the buildings and the heavenly smell of pork and scallions clots the air. The first of the bills in my back pocket goes toward siumai, which I order in my best Canto as the shopkeeper smiles patiently. I climb to the upper levels of the alley and find a corner stoop attached to a boarded-up apartment, where I sit and dig in.

Hina, the *Minnow*'s cook, does her best, and I commend her for that, but after months of meals designed to appeal to every palate on the ship, it's pure bliss to wolf down food that is so thoroughly *mine*. I eat so fast that I nearly make myself sick.

When I look up, my eyes immediately find the sign. It's garish, a mess of fonts, words tumbling together in every language spoken on this raft. It takes me several seconds to pick through them and find the English.

"Uplink Café: Devices for rent."

The bills in my back pocket are a firebrand. I jolt to my feet, my fingers crumpling the plastic container left over from my food. I pitch it in the nearest recycle, still staring at the building across the bridge. It pulls me like a magnet, its open doors beckoning, its dark screens an invitation.

The last time I was on an uplink, it was aboard the

Nereid, the night before the *Minnow* struck. I've never had time to think about how I could reconnect, and Santa Elena keeps tech on the ship limited to avoid any tracebacks to our location anyway. But now I have nothing but time, and plenty of cash to spare. It had never occurred to me that I could simply rent a computer on the Flotilla and I'd be able to see everything I've been missing.

It's too great to pass up, too terrible to tackle, but I'm across the bridge and through the door in seconds. Before I know it, I'm set up at a station with an ancient-looking monitor attached to a computer that's slightly newer, but not by much.

It takes me a few seconds to remember my passwords, my fingers rusty on the keyboard. With shaking fingers, my siumai churning in my stomach, I pull up my mail.

The first thing that catches my eye is the disastrous 1,457 blinking in the corner, marking the unread messages that have accumulated since that day in August. A cursory glance reveals heaps of junk, including overexcited e-mails from college recruiters who haven't gotten word that I'm A) not interested in higher education and B) kidnapped/gone rogue/*whatever* it's appropriate to call my current situation.

A quick search shows me exactly what I feared I'd find here.

The first unread message at the bottom of my inbox is dated August 11th, the day the *Nereid* fell. The subject line is empty, as my mother tends to leave it, and the body is quick and to the point: "Updates on Durga's condition?"

The next: "Are you okay? Distress call reported, but no details attached."

The one after has a subject line that reads "REPLY IMMEDIATELY" and says, "I understand it might be chaotic out there and I know it must be hard with Durga gone, but we need you to confirm you got out of that mess alive."

The next message is from my brother Tom, two weeks later. I don't question the gap. I was dead. Killed in action, or else by a little blue pill I was supposed to swallow in case of capture. They didn't know that Santa Elena had managed to take me alive, that I was two weeks into raising a Reckoner on a pirate boat.

But Tom wrote anyway.

I don't know why I'm doing this.

Cas,

You've been dead for sixteen days. I guess it would feel more real if there was a funeral or something, but we never got your body. We don't even know how it happened. The ship's security footage shows you being marched onto that pirate ship, and that's the last I'll ever see of you. Mom and Dad have been trying their best to help me process it (even though I don't think they've fully processed it themselves) and they suggested I started writing things down. But writing it out isn't working when I just want to talk to you, so I guess I thought…

I dunno. This is stupid. But I already feel a little better, and I think when I hit send it's going to feel even better than that, so I'm going to keep on telling you everything I want to tell you, and you're never going to read it, and you're dead anyway so what's the point?

God, okay. If you were alive, I'd tell you that it was my first day of sophomore year yesterday. And everyone was telling me they were sorry and looking at me like I had a hole in my head which, I guess, isn't too far from the truth.

I took your morning shift. It only seemed fair, and it makes me feel like I'm with you, even though it also makes me feel like the walking dead. But I see why you like it. Liked it. The sunrise over the cliffs is pretty neat, and it's kind of nice to hang out with the Reckoners when they're just waking up. Right now we have Ophelia from the Jewel of Blue in for her one-year checkup. She's only had one encounter—she chased off a raiding ship before they'd even fired an opening shot. I think it's the teeth Mom gives our ichthyoids. People are so scared of sharks to start with, so when you send one the size of a yacht after them, they tend to freak. Ophelia's growth is a little worrisome though, according to Dad. At a year, she should be pushing seventy meters, and she's barely fifty. We're having her trainers monitor her diet to see if she's hunting enough to get proper nourishment.

I know you'd like hearing about the Reckoners. I guess there's no better time to tell you than this—you're the trainer I wanted to be. I was so fucking jealous the day I saw you going out on your first mission, and I wanted to be that. I wanted so badly to be the one shipping out on that boat. And now, even though you're dead, I kinda still want to be that guy. You're one of the industry heroes now, you know? People think you're the shit, and I want to tell them about that time that you went to show Amanda Hallbrook the Reckoner pens and one of the cephalopoid pups got hold of her and you tried to fight the thing off her by whacking it with a net and screaming. Like, that's the story people should be sharing about you, because you're my dumb sister and not some fucking war hero.

I can't believe you're dead. I dunno. I'm sending this anyway.

Love,

Tom

I'm crying. Of course I'm crying. My brother thought I was dead, and it hurt him so much, and I was so caught up in the *Minnow*'s world that I never spared a thought for my family's pain. He *lost* me.

There are more messages. I skim through them, tears still pouring down my cheeks, hunching low over the keyboard so the monitor blocks my face from the other patrons in the café. I move my lips as I read, as if I can coax the sound of Tom's voice out of the words he's written to me. Every week he writes, walking through his pain as he tells me about the Reckoners, about school, about everything I'd hear at the dinner table if I'd made it home this summer. But he writes to dead me, the idealized version of his sister who died a hero. In every letter, he remembers the flaws that round me out, that make me human, but never the flaws that make me worse. Maybe it's a side of me he never saw when I was on shore.

The thought of what he's about to find out brings the tears harder and faster than before.

Finally I reach the day—November 12th—when Fabian Murphy discovered me on the Flotilla, and of course there's mail from Tom to match. Its subject line blasts, "READ THIS FIRST," and its body begs me to delete everything he's sent in the event that I'm successfully rescued from my pirate captors. He tries not to be optimistic, but he fails horribly. From the way he writes, the pursuit will have me home the very next day.

On November 17th, his tune changes. He doesn't quite believe the reports that are coming in, even though he's seen the footage with his own eyes. He mulls over the way I leaped off the back of the pirate ship, the way I called Bao, the way I set him on the quadcopters, like he's searching for some coded message that will make it all clear. In his eyes, I could have been forced into doing what I did, and from the way he describes Mom and Dad's reactions, they believe the same.

Then November 25th rolls around, and there's no ambiguity about what happened that night. Everyone saw my choice as plain as day the moment I turned Bao on the pursuit boats. Tom sends a single message. From the time-stamp, I'm not sure if he stayed up late, woke up early, or wasn't sleeping to begin with.

(no subject)

What the fuck, Cas?

I wish I could explain it to him, but I can't even explain it fully to myself.

Astonishingly enough, he keeps writing. There are six messages between that night and now, the most recent from the day after Christmas. I skip the others and open his last one first.

CAS

I don't get it. I'm honestly stumped, Cas. I know you. I know you'd never in a million years join up with fucking pirates, so what is it? Stockholm syndrome? Brainwashing? Secret twin? Cloning? I've got theories, and I hate all of them.

I've stopped caring that you might actually read this and everything else I sent. It's all collateral in case you decide you want to start sharing some of your truths with me, because god knows I've shared enough of mine with you at this point. You're the only person who can make this all make sense in my head, okay? And if you really aren't a brainwashed secret twin clone with

Stockholm syndrome, you've got to be checking your inbox at some point.

So just tell me why, if you get the chance. If you've read the rest of the messages I sent, you'll know you owe me that much.

—Tom

I lean all the way back in my chair, pressing on my swollen eyes until I see stars. He's right. He's so right. My family deserves to know why I did what I did. I need to own up to my actions, to let them know that it's nothing to do with them, even though all of our lives are so wrapped up in the Reckoner industry that it has everything to do with them. I've considered so many times what my behavior must look like from shore, but this is different. That was speculation. This is the reality. Now I know for sure what I did to them when I turned my back on the shore.

And it fucking hurts.

There are no other messages from my family. I double check, just to be sure. For a moment, I flip through the older messages in my inbox, trying to remind myself what "normal" used to be for me. There are old homework assignments, essays for schoolwork that will never be relevant to my life if I let myself get sucked into the world of piracy. There are industry newsletters, filled with articles discussing the undergrowth of the most recent crop of Reckoners—just as Tom reported with Ophelia—and speculating about a food shortage. Even on shore, it seems the effects of the Hellbeasts are being noticed. None of the articles report any observations of the rogue monsters, but then again, Hellbeasts aren't likely to come near escorted ships. But it confirms that the problem runs deep, that the effects of Fabian Murphy's illicit dealings have already carved a bleeding wound into the NeoPacific's biosystem.

I'm so absorbed in connecting dots that I nearly piss myself when a chat window pops up. My brother's face peers at me from the avatar, his hair slightly longer, parted different, already a new person in the four months since I saw him last.

All he has to say is, "Cas?"

My fingers twitch, driven by impulse as I slam down the key that closes the window. But before I can relax, the chat pops up again. "Cas, is this you?"

I bite down on the urge to close it, weighing my options. What can I possibly say to him now? Now, when the Hellbeast threat is far more urgent than the choices I've made, when I can't even come up with the proper words to justify what I'm doing. I shift the cursor over my online status. I'm a click away from going invisible when a ringing sound blasts from the monitor's speakers and a video call snaps onto the screen.

I'm not ready, I'm not ready, I'm not ready.

I deny the call, bile rising in my throat. *Later, Tom. Later, when I've figured the rest of this out.* But the very act of shutting my brother down pushes me over the edge—suddenly I've gone from crying to outright sobbing, the noise loud enough to startle some of the patrons around me.

There are thirteen minutes left in my session, and there's no way I can use them in this state. I cover my mouth with one hand, trying to choke back the pathetic sounds hiccupping out of my throat, and log out of my account. My chair clatters backward as I shove myself up and make for the exit.

I push my way through the door, and the sunlight washes over my skin. I blink through the tears, running one hand along the railing of the bridge that spans the towers' levels as I try to feel my way toward a place where I can pull myself together. Somewhere secluded, somewhere no one from the *Minnow*'s crew can find me. If the captain saw me now, she'd never let me hear the end of it.

I haven't cried like this since the days after Durga died.

And just as that thought is settling in, I stumble around the corner and run headlong into Swift.

11

"They told me I might find you around h—," Swift starts, before the emotional train wreck I've turned into stuns her into silence. Before I have a chance to turn and run, Swift's hands shoot out and lock around my elbows. She peers down at my splotchy face.

Santa Elena's trained me well enough that I'm able to stare right back at her, but it's something I can only hold for so long before another sob rises out of me. I flinch, shrugging out of her grip to wipe uselessly at the steady stream of snot and tears flowing down my face. I should be furious with her, furious that she's seeing me like this, but all I can think is that I'm glad. I'm so glad that I don't have to ride this thing out on my own.

I don't resist when she pulls me into a hug, the two of us sagging against the wall. The heat of the sunbaked, corrugated metal bites into my side, but I ignore it, pressing my face into her jacket so that no one else can see the mess I've become.

"What happened?" she asks, her voice low in a way that makes her chest resonate against mine.

"Family," I croak, and her fingers tighten on the back of my shirt.

"Hey, let's not do this here," Swift mutters against the side of my head. "Come on. I know a place."

We keep our heads low as she guides me up through the Flotilla's wandering streets. Even so, some of the people we pass recognize Swift. They wave or call out, and Swift deflects them with apologetic grins or tips of the hand that isn't glued to my shoulder. She's probably doing it to shield me from prying eyes, but part of me suspects that she's trying even harder to avoid setting me off. I don't bother telling her I'm too torn up to put any effort into hating her.

The city grows beneath us as we spiral upward into the towers. I know the paths she's leading me down, but I don't start to balk until we're halfway down the familiar walkways that lead to her house. Seeing her smiling father, her pack of loving siblings, or even her ornery grandmother is the last thing I need right now.

"It's okay," Swift says when she feels me tense up. "They aren't there." There's an edge of a smile in it, something she's holding back, something she knows this isn't the time for. Instead she steers me around the building and out onto another familiar path. "After you."

The last time we did this, we were chained together. This time, I pick my way down the rooftops carefully, my shoes slipping on the metal. My eyes sting and burn from the tears, and I have to squint to make sure I don't slip off the wrong side and plunge to the city's base. I can feel Swift's hand hovering inches from my back, ready to grab me if I misstep. It goads me forward, and I make the last jump a little faster than planned, stumbling as I land in the little alcove.

There's no better place to break down on the entire Flotilla. No windows. No people. Just the back ends of shipping container houses, a little plastic bucket, and Swift Kent standing over me like a guard dog.

I slump back against one of the walls, pressing my hands into my face. "I don't know why you're even bothering…" I start, but I can't even finish that bullshit sentence. Swift cares about me, no matter how much I shove her away. The question isn't why she's bothering. The question is why I let her bother.

Swift crouches next to me, her eyes fixed on the horizon. We've managed to avoid eye contact for the entire climb up here, and I take a moment to appreciate it, appreciate her while it's my turn to look. Her hair continues to grow out in a mess, the shaggy, formerly shaved side now long enough to curl around her ears. Her eyes match the color of the sea. Have they always done that? My gaze drops to the jacket sleeve that covers up the three slashes of ink on her forearm. We haven't spoken since she got them.

"Look, you don't have to tell me anything if you don't want to," Swift starts, rocking back on her heels until she topples onto her ass. She rolls backward, folding her arms behind her head as she stares up at the dappled clouds above us. "Whatever helps, I'm here. And if me being here doesn't help—"

"Quiet," I tell her, and she follows orders. I roll my head back, trying to pull shapes out of these clouds the way I did with the icebergs back in the NeoAntarctic. I can all but feel the moment when her eyes shift to me and she starts to drink me in.

It must be a bitter drink. My face is splotchy and red, and even though my tears have tapered off, my eyes are still swimming in them. There's a thick line of snot trailing down over my lips.

Good. I want her to be repulsed by me. I want her to see me for the pathetic, sniveling creature that I am. A traitor to my family and everything they stand for. Uncertain, in the running for a job that requires absolute certainty. A Reckoner trainer and a pirate trainee that can't stand existing in the same body.

But when I drop my gaze to her, she stares back with no disgust, no condescension, no superiority. There's only concern and something else, something I don't dare name.

I hold the look until my swollen eyes won't allow it anymore. With the heel of my palm, I swipe the welling tears away, scoffing. I switch my gaze to the horizon, guilt seeping into my bloodstream. There are Hellbeasts swimming these seas, attacking innocents, devouring the biosystem until there's nothing left. We're facing bigger problems than my own inconsistent heart—and yet here it is, demanding attention it doesn't deserve. "I did something kind of dumb," I start.

She nods, like that's to be expected.

"I never should have looked—it wasn't going to do anything but this." I gesture to my messy face, then make another attempt to clean it off. My hand won't do—instead, I lift the hem of my shirt and bury my nose in it. As I try my best to rein in the snot and tears, I explain what I found in my inbox through stuttered sentences, fighting back against myself until I'm worn down and talking through what just happened in a flat, emotionless voice.

The whole time she nods. Offers prompting when I need it. Waits when I'm too overwhelmed to speak. She's being exactly what I need, and it makes me want to shove her off the roof.

Finally there's no more story left to tell, and we're left with the silence between us, punctuated only by the empty noise of sea winds whispering through the Flotilla's sub-levels and the groan of the floating city's structure. For a moment, it's nice. Me and her, the city beneath, a star of humanity in the endless blue around us. For a moment, I let myself forget what's happening, what's happened, what might happen.

"I'm sorry," Swift says finally. She sits up and folds in on herself, first with her arms, then with her spine, until she's just a curled-up ball of girl. "I wish I knew something to say that could help," she mutters into her elbows.

I nod, squeezing my eyes shut. This shouldn't be allowed, my own useless pain passing along its favors to her.

I want to get away from it, not wallow in it, and I can feel her dragging me down. There has to be some way to change tack. "You know, it was my birthday a month ago," I blurt.

"You're shitting me."

That gets a laugh—a small one, but I can't take it back. "December 1st. Five days after I officially turned pirate. No one knew. No one wished me anything."

"And you turned…"

"Eighteen, jackass. You can't spell my name; you don't know how old I am—"

Swift swipes a handful of dust at me, a wry smile twisting her lips. "You absolutely can't talk when you didn't even know my last name until a week ago."

"Fine. When's *your* birthday?"

"April 7th. You throwing me a party?"

I snort to mask my lack of a comeback. I don't even know for sure if I'll be alive come April 7th. I don't know if I'll still be on the *Minnow*. I don't know if I'll hate Swift or if by then I'll finally—

"So my family's moved out," she says, mercifully interrupting that line of thought. "Turns out when you save an entire raft full of people, especially on Christmas, they want to do you all kinds of favors. Got them set up in a home— an actual apartment, not one of these shipping container shitholes—on the lower levels, courtesy of… well, everyone."

"You didn't save an entire raft."

Swift grins. "Don't tell them that. The apartment isn't even the best part." But even as she says it, her eyes flick to the ground. "There's kind of been an arrangement made. People with money were on that ferry. Enough money to be charitable. Enough money to make it so that my family's set. For the rest of their lives, they're looked after."

Oh. *Oh.* Now I understand her fidgetiness. I get why she sought me out in the first place after days of not talking. Swift's life is one long exercise in self-sacrifice. She signed herself away to Santa Elena at thirteen to put food on the table for her family when her sisters' mother walked out. Every note she's earned in the past five years went to supporting her father, grandmother, and four half-siblings.

But not anymore. If they're truly taken care of, Swift's life just got a whole lot simpler. In the span of a couple days, everything's changed. And now she has no reason to be a pirate anymore.

She's free. And it's scaring the shit out of her.

"This should be the best damn thing that's ever happened to me," she says, scoffing. Her gaze fixes on the distant horizon, on the span of the ocean that's now open to her. "It feels too easy, too fast—it feels like it's all going to go away if I blink. I can't just… disappear. If I walk out on them, my grandmother's going to be right, going to say that she knew all along I was just another rotten egg like my mother."

"You're not," I mumble, before I can think better of it. But she doesn't give me a second to regret it—that dazzling smile flashes out so bright that I want to avert my eyes. It's not even a full grin. It shouldn't have this effect. But somehow the wry tilt of her lips shines like the sun. "Oh fuck off," I groan.

That brings out the dopey grin. "You got any plans for tomorrow night?" Swift asks.

"Are you seriously asking me o—"

"It's gonna be New Year's Eve, Cas. Let me show you how we do it on the Flotilla."

12

This is a very bad idea.

When the first fireworks went off, it was barely dark. The sun had just settled under the horizon when they exploded into the sky, the sparks flaring like stars against the glow of dusk. They launched from one of the inbound ferries packed with revelers coming to celebrate the last night of the year on the Flotilla.

The Flotilla wasted no time in firing back. Now the air is thick with the flash of light and the sounds of bombardment. I've gotten so used to the noise that it barely fazes me each time a new firework bursts. It's fully dark, and the light of the explosions reflects off the NeoPacific's glassy surface. The whole city feels like it's wrapped in a cocoon of sound and color. The Flotilla's essentially fireproof—or so I've been reassured. And the fact that we're climbing to the top of the towers with explosives strapped to our backs isn't what's worrying me either.

It's that Swift's leading the way, and I kind of like it.

"Pick up the pace!" Chuck shouts from the rear of our procession. I glance over my shoulder at her and Lemon. Swift's somehow managed to loop both of them into this little excursion, probably to offset the awkwardness a little. Neither of us is really sure if this is a date. And mercifully, according to Chuck, Varma's off partying with a few other guys from the subcontinent.

I can't help but delight in how grouchy it makes her. Lemon shares my grin, her angular face glowing as another round of fireworks bursts across the night. We clamber up the narrow stairs, following the clatter of Swift's footsteps ahead.

"Move it, Cas. Quit ogling Swift's ass, I swear to god," Chuck yells.

Swift stumbles.

When we spill out onto the highest deck of the tower, we're met with a massive crowd. People press against the rails, leaning out over the precarious edge to watch the fireworks. On a normal day, this is the most desolate part of the city, farthest from the docks and everything that makes the Flotilla's heart beat. Tonight, it's the place to be. Floodlights powered by rumbling generators bathe everything in a washed-out glow, a speaker system blasts music, and a few dedicated vendors have pulled their carts all the way up to the summit. The rich smell of their food intersperses with the sweat of the crowd. They'll make a killing tonight.

Even though everyone's celebrating, we can't escape the tension that thickens the night air. The Flotilla's held out for decades, but the cephalopoid attack struck too close to home, and the people are rattled. Every burst of fireworks feels somewhere between a prelude to war and a statement of purpose. *We're here. We're alive. And we're going to light you up.*

Swift hoists a rocket over her head, and all eyes swing to her. A cheer goes up, and I keep my eyes anywhere but the ink on her forearm as she brandishes the firework. "Anyone got a light?" Swift shouts. I hear the edges of the captain in her voice.

Almost instantly, she's swallowed in the glow of lighter flames that puff to life around her. Beaming, she holds out the rocket's fuse, and someone reaches out to light it. The string catches in a flurry of sparks, and Swift lifts the rocket over her head by the stick, leaning as far away from the sputtering fuse as she can. The crowd swells away, some of them clapping their hands over their ears.

It takes off with a scream and a puff of smoke. Swift immediately drops the stick, shaking her hand furiously and swearing as only a pirate can. The rocket spirals up over us, the hiss of its ignition rapidly fading. And then it bursts. I squint as the flash of light sears into my retinas, followed closely by the thunderous blast. Violent orange sparks cascade down over us, and some people in the crowd shriek, swatting away the embers that fall.

The rest are already clamoring for more. Swift beckons the three of us forward, and we unsling our backpacks, which are stuffed with enough explosives to send this entire tower up in flames. Most of them were bought with my salary, since, as Swift astutely put it, "I'm just going to use it for self-flagellation anyway." The rest were gifts from shopkeepers who saw their hometown hero and insisted she take them as tokens of their gratitude.

We pass out the fireworks to whoever reaches out to take them. A little girl runs past, waving a sputtering Roman candle in a way that makes everyone jump a few feet back, and a few more rockets shoot out of the crowd, one of them careening dangerously close to one of the other towers. The music cranks louder, drowning out the explosions above as my backpack gets lighter and lighter.

Finally I'm all out. I pass the pack off to a scrawny-looking preteen who looks like he needs it and draw back to the railing. Lemon trails after me, her head bobbing slightly to the thunder of the bass beat. We break free from the crush of the crowd, and a wash of cool night air rushes over me. "Ain't so bad here, is it?" I ask her when we reach the edge of the deck.

Lemon keeps nodding, her eyes flicking back and forth as she tracks each new firework that launches.

"Yeah," I say, leaning against the bars until the railing bends slightly. "I like it here too."

A year ago, I never could have imagined this night. I spent last New Year's Eve at a boat party with my parents and the other SRCese Reckoner trainers. Tom and I were glued at the hip for the entire evening, too nervous to intermingle with the adults and too unfamiliar to hang out with the other industry kids. We'd shot off a few fireworks once we were clear of the Reckoners' lines of sight—we didn't want any of them to mistake the fireworks for signals. It had been a quiet celebration. I'd worn a cocktail dress and braided my hair.

And now I'm on a pirate raft, dressed in shorts and a tank top with pirate ink on my body. My hair's still too short to do anything with it. I'm surrounded by reckless explosions and the sheer energy of the Flotilla, and somewhere out there, the world might be going to hell.

A lot can change in a year. A year ago, I had been so confident that I was going to spend the rest of my life in the Reckoner industry. A year ago, I was brimming with excitement because this was finally *it*. It was finally *here*. The year I'd go on my first solo mission. The year I'd prove myself as a trainer. The year I'd be the person I was meant to be.

I can't help but laugh, looking at where I am now.

But maybe that's the thing about new years, about time. No matter what's behind us, the future's always widely, stupidly open. A new year is a fresh start, a chance to put the past behind us and strike out into the unknown. That's what makes it worth celebrating.

And just as the thought is settling in, Lemon mutters, "Chuck and Swift are getting into a fight."

I whip my head around, scanning the crowd for Chuck's wild mane, for Swift's uneven hair. I find them, lit by the glow of a food cart's signage, wrapped in a heated argument. I'm halfway through the crowd by the time I realize they're smiling even as they gesture and shout, but by then it's too late. They've spotted me.

"Cas!" Chuck yells over the thud of the speakers overhead. "We need a judge."

"An impartial one?" I ask, once I've pushed my way to their side.

Chuck shrugs. "One who can count, at least. You game?"

"What's the game?"

She grins, gesturing to the cart, which boasts an impressive host of Hawaiian dishes. The Islander owner eyes us suspiciously. "I want to see if this *haole* can keep up with me, so we're gonna eat spam musubi until one of us gives up or hurls."

Swift already looks queasy, but she only grins when I raise an eyebrow at her. "Please tell me you're not doing this to impress me," I groan.

Chuck slaps a bill down on the counter. "Just keep 'em coming," she tells the vendor.

"You got it," the man replies, passing over two nori-wrapped blocks. Swift takes one, Chuck snatches the other, and they both look to me.

"This is a horrible idea," I say with a smile. "Go."

Chuck's inhaled hers before Swift's even gotten a bite down. She swipes another off the counter, taking a second to savor the sight of Swift desperately trying to keep her musubi together as she crams it down her throat. Another follows, but it crumbles just as fast as the first, spilling down Swift's front. "Oh dear god in heaven," Chuck mutters, incredulous. "If I'd have known—"

"Shut up!" Swift chokes around a mouthful of half-chewed rice. She tries to stuff the rest of the musubi in. She fails miserably.

"Swift, I'm begging you. Retain your dignity, woman," Chuck says. She tries to take a bite of her second block, but she's laughing so hard that she nearly spits it right back out. "You can't win if you're wearing half of it."

Swift's eyes are lit with righteous fire. Bits of spam, rice, and nori are stuck to her chin, and the closest part of the crowd has started to take notice of the competition. Some of them seem to be considering betting.

Swift meets my gaze. "Congratulations," I tell her. "This is the weirdest thing I've ever had a girl do on a date."

She thrusts her fists in the air and shouts, "I give up!"

"Oh come on!" Chuck yells, reaching for her third musubi. "You weakling! I thought you'd have more fight than this."

Swift's triumphant grin is nori-speckled and shit-eating. "At least I've got a date."

Chuck's furious stare snaps to me, waiting for me to deny it and leave Swift looking like an idiot. But Swift already looks like enough of an idiot on her own, so I simply shrug and say, "She ain't wrong."

"Unbelievable," Chuck deadpans, but she can't stop herself from smiling a bit. She turns to the vendor, who's already laid out the rest of the musubis she paid for. "I'll just… uh, package the rest of these to go."

Swift wanders away, picking at the food still stuck in her teeth. I'm not sure if she wants me to follow her, but then she glances back over her shoulder and tilts her head just so. I stuff my hands in my pockets and sidle up to her. "You missed a spot," I tell her, even though she hasn't, just to watch her pluck furiously at the crevices in her incisors.

She lifts an eyebrow at Chuck, who's now trying to bait Lemon into eating one of the musubis. Lemon holds it at arm's length. Swift shrugs. "Lost the battle," she says, her eyes shifting to mine. "Won the war."

And now it's dangerous. I feel like I'm on the edge of a chasm, leaning forward, ready to jump. No bottom in sight, no idea how far I'll end up going, no idea whether I'll come out alive in the end. Do I trust Swift? Do I need to trust Swift for this to happen, or can that come along the way? Maybe I'm thinking too hard about all of this.

"Cas?" she asks, nudging me with her shoulder, because of course I've zoned out.

Before I can answer, someone shouts, "TEN!"

The countdown has started. Projections around the city flicker to life, replacing the glow of the fireworks with numerals that tick back one by one. The seconds until the New Year hurtle past, and all the while I'm staring at Swift's face, trying to decide, trying to figure out the answers to questions I haven't even asked yet. The towers scream in unison, "THREE, TWO, ONE!"

New year. New start. And it's like the first time all over again. I don't know who moves first, but somehow we're lunging for each other, somehow Swift's arms are around my waist, somehow mine are around her neck, and when our lips meet it's just like it used to be.

There's just me and her, and the rest of it falls away.

All around us fireworks burst, the explosions rattling in my chest and in hers. I see flashes of light through my eyelids, feel the shock of the sparks that fall on my bare shoulders. I press my body as far against her as it will go, my lips urging hers open. This is right. This is what we're supposed to be doing. The ink on her arm doesn't matter as much as the fire between us, and the entire NeoPacific isn't enough to put it out.

I think she feels it too. Swift draws back from the kiss by just an inch, her hands still on my hips, her thumbs running experimentally under the hem of my tank top. "So," she breathes, the word lost in the chaos of the celebration.

"Happy New Year, huh?" I let one hand trail down her neck, her chest, her stomach, until my fingers hook into her waistband. There's an implication hanging in the space between us, one I'm not rescinding, one she's still trying to process.

Swift leans forward until her lips brush my ear. Her hands slip lower on my back. "Think we can make it to the *Minnow* without you deciding to hate me again?"

———

We do.

It isn't smooth, but I don't think it's ever meant to be. We fumble through the steps, laughing at ourselves every time an awkwardly placed elbow hits the wall of her bunk, every time a stubborn piece of clothing takes extra tugging to get loose. This isn't the first time she's done this. It isn't for me, either. But that doesn't make it any less significant, any less overwhelming, any less *everything*.

There's hesitation. There are pauses. Questions muttered into the crook of her neck, breathed against the goose bumps on my stomach. *Is this okay? Does this work? Are we okay?*

And we are.

She doesn't notice the new ink at first, too distracted by the rest of me. It isn't until after that she gets a good look at my back, and her breath catches in her throat. "Is that…" She trails off, her fingers reaching over to brush the thin lines etched across my skin. "That's not Bao."

"No," I tell her. "It's not."

Swift takes a moment to drink in the inker's rendition of the monster she killed. Durga's form splays across my back from my shoulder blades to the crest of my hips. It's incomplete, some of it little more than an outline, but still I wear the weight of the Reckoner I lost on my back. I shiver as Swift's fingertips drag down my spine. She leans over me and presses her forehead against the ink, and for a moment we stay like that: utterly still, draped in silence, and all too aware of where we've been.

When I can't take it anymore, I roll over, and Swift's eyes lock on mine. "You'll never forgive me for her, will you?" she asks.

Here, like this, I can't lie to her. "I don't know," I say. "But you've got to believe that I'm trying."

And then I feel her smile on my lips as she presses down against me, and it's enough, it's all enough. Whatever's twisted and broken between us, it's not going to hold us back. And for the rest of the night, it doesn't.

13

I don't change my mind when I wake up to find Swift Kent in my arms. It's not like the last time—I'm not waking up to a nightmare. I'm waking up to my wildest dreams. Somehow we've worked it out. We've found our balance, found a way to move forward, and as my groggy brain wraps itself around this, a smile creeps across my face.

"What time is it?" Swift groans when I run my hand up from her hip to her shoulder.

"No earthly idea," I mutter, fixated on the Minnow tattoo at her nape.

She pushes herself upright, then promptly flops back down, but facing me this time. Her face is close enough that I feel the sigh she lets out against my forehead. Swift's eyes meet mine. "Uh-oh," she chuckles.

"Now what?"

Her hand snakes over the curve of my hip, her thumb

working in gentle circles on my ribs. "Fuck if I know." Her eyes slide closed, and she mumbles, "I'm too delighted to think straight at the moment."

I snort, and she pulls me closer, her lips brushing over mine as my body curves against hers. It could be sunrise. It could be noon. It could be we've spent days here, and I wouldn't care. Time only moves forward, and ahead of us is nothing but second chances.

———————

When we finally emerge, I find out it's close to noon. Swift goes first, to make sure the coast is clear, and then beckons me urgently out into the hall. I stumble after her, brushing at my shoulders as I try to get my clothes to sit in a way that doesn't broadcast what everything else about this situation inevitably does. There are footsteps above, voices muffled behind closed doors—the *Minnow*'s bursting with a constant awareness that makes me feel scrutinized no matter how few eyes are on me. But Swift's snuck around this ship for five years, and she moves with easy confidence down the hall. "I have to go check in on my family," she hisses when we reach my door. "I'll be back as soon as I can, and then… Oh, I don't know." She slips a hand around my waist and I lean up to kiss her as quickly as we can get away with in the open.

As I yank the door open, I watch her retreat down the hall, and I swear she's about to start skipping.

I change and shower in a daze, still trying to assure

myself that last night happened. Every so often, I'll brush a hand over my hips, over my shoulders, trying to imitate the way she touched me as if it'll convince me it was real. I keep catching myself grinning, to the point that I'm half-scared to go grab food from the mess, worried that everyone will see right through me.

Unfortunately, my stomach isn't giving me a chance to pull myself together.

Fortunately, the new year is on my side. When I get to the mess, nearly every crewmember in there is listless and hungover. My nervous energy doesn't blend in well, but my less-than-rested eyes more than make up for it. I grab a plate of eggs and slide into my usual spot at the trainee table, where Chuck is slumped over next to her own food and Lemon appears to have fallen asleep sitting up.

Chuck cracks open an eye when she hears the bench creak. "Please don't say a word," she growls.

"Did Varma ever show?" I ask.

"What did I just fucking say?" she snaps, then flinches. "And no. *Lelemu* stayed out with the subcontinent bros."

Right on cue, Varma bursts through the door of the mess. As always, he's beaming, and if he had too much to drink last night, it wasn't enough to drown out his Varma-ness. Once he's grabbed a tray, he sashays over to the table and plunks down on the bench across from Chuck. "Happy New Year, guys!" he says. "What'd I miss?"

Chuck glowers. I blush. Lemon, as usual, says nothing.

Varma shrugs, then starts shoveling eggs into his

mouth. He's about to speak around a half-chewed mouthful when the radios on our belts go live.

"This is the captain speaking," Santa Elena announces. "We have a lock on Bao's location, courtesy of John Mallory and the *Kettle*. They're tracking him for the time being, but it's uncertain how much longer they can keep their position. We have to move immediately. I'm giving you lot two hours to get your asses on this ship and ready to shove off, starting now. That's all."

"You've got to be shitting me," Chuck groans.

———

When we report to the captain in navigation, she kicks everyone out but me. She doesn't seem an ounce hungover—instead, Santa Elena paces the deck with a vivacity generally reserved for bonfires and lightning strikes. "Mallory's crew was shooting off a few fireworks last night, and it seems the light and noise called our little friend out of the depths. Should have thought of that a week ago," she says.

I stare down at the main deck, half-listening, trying not to look too often at the gangway. The ship tries to bustle, but ends up in more of a drag. I spot Chuck ducking to the railing and attempting to discretely vomit into the harbor. Swift hasn't shown up yet—or, if she has, she's managed to slip aboard without me noticing.

"Cassandra," Santa Elena barks, and I snap to attention.

"Sorry, boss."

A smirk flickers across her features. "Have you been down to the trainer deck and taken inventory yet? I don't want to shove off and find that we're missing critical equipment."

I shake my head. "We're down to one Otachi, but I should be able to get by with just that." My arms tremble at the thought of hefting the Otachi again. The laser projectors are heavy, but I'm more afraid of what I'll be conducting at the other end of them.

The captain scowls, folding her arms. "I don't like 'getting by,' Cas."

"We have the beacon. Unless we're going straight into battle, we shouldn't need anything more than that," I retort. I half-expect to get slapped for that kind of back talk, but Santa Elena looks impressed.

"You're the expert," she says with a shrug. "Here's hoping we aren't going straight into battle."

Her approval leaves a sour taste in my mouth. The last time someone trusted my expertise in Reckoners this much, I ended up getting an entire ship full of innocents raided. There's no telling how Bao will behave if we approach him. No Reckoner's ever been away from their signals for over a month. I have no way of knowing how much of his training his turtle brain has retained until I start trying to call him in.

Down on the main deck, a familiar figure has just slunk back over the gangplank. "I'll... uh—I'll check that trainer deck stock, make sure we aren't missing anything else, yeah?" I say, edging toward the ladder. The captain dismisses me with a wave, and I do my best to avoid seeming like I'm in a hurry as I cross the deck and clamber down.

By the time I reach the main deck, Swift's already starting to climb down to the lower levels of the ship. I glance around to make sure that neither Chuck nor Varma is in sight, then tail after her. Swift's waiting for me when I jump off the second ladder. For a moment, instinct takes over—I reach out to her before I can think better of it, but she catches my wrist.

Something's off. Her face is taut, her grip too tight. She's looking anywhere but my eyes. "Is it... your family?" I ask.

Swift shakes her head. Her brow furrows, a clear sign that she's struggling to put something into words. Something that has to do with me—I'm sure of it. "I... Sorry, I'm being..." she mutters. Her grip on my wrist softens. A weak smile flickers across her lips, but it vanishes just as quickly.

My heartbeat shudders a tick faster. This morning, everything felt right with the world. Now we're setting off to fetch Bao, now I'm supposed to be a trainer again, now the captain's counting on me, and Swift being unable to articulate is just the icing on the cake. My patience thins from an ocean to a puddle, and I lock my eyes on hers. "Spit it out," I say, and too late I hear notes of Santa Elena in the way my voice rings through the narrow hall.

Swift laughs like a bone snapping, sharp and fast. "There she is," she says, letting go of my wrist as she fixes me with a simmering glare. "The captain's favorite, back on top."

"I'm not... *You're*—"

"I had a leg up for a while, but I'm never going to be as valuable as a trainee who can command a Reckoner. Basic math, Cas. Even I can do that."

"Wait—"

But already she's turned her back and set off down the hall, her shoulders squared. This is all wrong—it's all backward. It's me who's supposed to be running away, stewing in unknowable rage. Swift is the one who's supposed to be tailing after me, trying to wrap her head around *why*. I'm supposed to be the one slamming the door to her bunk, and Swift's the one who's supposed to punch the hatch in frustration, who's supposed to yell things like "Come on" and "Really?"

My knuckles sting. "Swift, you can't just—"

"I'm not doing this now. Go away, Cas." Her voice is distant, muffled, like she's thrown herself down on her bunk.

"Why do you care if the captain's favoring me? I thought your family was taken care of? I thought you didn't need—"

"Fuck off!" she snaps, and suddenly she's right on the other side of the door. I press my forehead against the metal, feeling the vibrations of her voice as she shouts, "Even if they were taken care of—even if I knew that for sure— you think I would just drop everything I've been working toward for the past five years?"

"But I thought you were doing it for th—"

A slam rings through the door like she's just slapped it. "Of course I was doing it for them! But that doesn't mean I wasn't doing it for me too!"

I go cold. Colder than the NeoAntarctic. So cold that I can't fathom where this day started. Nothing but silence hangs between us, and even though the whole ship is bustling—or trying to bustle—for a moment, there's nothing but stillness in the hall.

"Cas, you always think so much of me. You always think I'm noble, that I'm doing this for good reasons, and I wish it was true, but it's fucking *not*, and you have no right to assume that I don't... that I'm..."

"You said you were trapped." My voice is hollow, cracked, low. "You made it sound like—"

"What was I supposed to make it sound like? Like I enjoy being on this ship? Like I genuinely want to be Santa Elena's successor? Tell me how that would have put you on my side."

"You—"

"The only thing I'm trapped in is your bullshit assumption that I'm on this ship against my will," she thunders. "I'm a fucking pirate. I'm a fucking monster. And some day, I *want* to be a motherfucking queen."

I don't have the words to counter her. I don't even have the breath to try. I sag against the door, my fingernails digging against a rivet in the metal. "I don't understand," I mumble.

"Stop trying to," she snaps.

A hand clamps down on my shoulder, and I almost scream. "I think that's quite enough of that," Santa Elena snarls in my ear. With a jerk of her wrist, she yanks me down the hall.

14

The captain doesn't let go of me until we're at the trainer deck door, and even then it's only to grab her key. I don't bother offering my own—it's on the ring at my belt, but every second she's distracted is more time for me to compose myself. My face is flushed, and I take a few quick swipes at my eyes, just in case.

I hate how right Swift is. How true everything she said has been. How I should have seen it coming, and how it blindsided me anyway. This world grew her. It shaped her. How could I expect her to be anything else?

"Unclench your fists, Cas," Santa Elena says as she shoves the hatch open. "Keeping loose keeps you on your toes."

I stare down at the threshold, uncurling my fingers. Over a month has passed since the last time I was here. There's a familiar smell about it, the brine of the sea mixing with the faint carrion stench unique to Reckoners. The three roll-up doors are all down—one starboard, one port, one aft. With no openings to the sea, the whole deck rattles with the thrum of the ship's machinery spinning below.

I step onto the trainer deck, and it's the opposite of everything I've feared. It isn't a war that rises inside me, but a peace between my two sides. Pirate trainee. Reckoner trainer. Here they coexist without a problem. Here feels like home. Here feels right.

But there are still pangs. The Otachi thrown down on the counter where I left it the night I turned my back on the shore. The bulletproof armor piled haphazardly next to it. The spot on the deck where Swift and I rushed to each other the moment we thought was our last chance. The spot by the aft door where Santa Elena cut Code open. I suppress a shudder before the captain notices what's going on.

She turns, her hands on her hips as she drinks in the deck, and in this moment I remember exactly why her Minnow tattoo rests over her heart. "I've had this ship for ten years," she says. "Every time I come down here, I feel like I've forgotten her somehow."

I cross to the panel with the door controls and bring the aft door rattling up with a press of a button. The stale air of the trainer deck washes out as a gust of sea wind rolls in to replace it, and I inhale deeply, closing my eyes. When I open them, I'm startled to find Santa Elena doing the same.

She flashes me a grin that wipes years off her face. "Nothing better than that, huh?"

I shrug, then move to the counter where the Otachi

rests. I roll it over so that the straps meant to bind it to my forearm are faced down, then run a nail along the laser's casing, searching for the indentation that will allow me to pry open the battery compartment. If we're heading directly for Bao, I have to make sure that we have enough juice to keep the signals coming.

When it becomes clear that Santa Elena isn't leaving the deck anytime soon, I speak up. "So... how much did you hear?" I pop the compartment open and pull out the batteries, then rummage around the counter for the charger, waiting for Santa Elena's answer.

"Enough." I glare over my shoulder at her, and Santa Elena rolls her eyes. "Swift's ambitious. She's making the most of her time on this boat, and honestly... honestly, if she keeps on going the way that she does, she'll be the one who takes over it when I'm gone."

My spine goes rigid. Santa Elena doesn't give away information like that lightly. It's bait, or a tool, or a weapon. I shove the batteries into their slots in the charger with far more force than necessary. "She has a family—"

"So did I, once," Santa Elena says, her voice gone soft. "Now I have a son and a ship. Did the rumors ever reach your ears?"

"You told me yourself. You took this ship with your son on your back."

"And did anyone ever tell you what happened before that?"

I shake my head.

Santa Elena inhales deeply, and when she speaks, there's

an edge in her voice like she's talking at knifepoint. "When I was younger, I was crewing on a ship in my own waters. And so was Marcus. I won't bore you with the details, but we wanted a life together. We left the NeoCaribbean behind and ended up settling on the Over, a floating city in the southern NeoPacific. It was good for a while. But this life never really leaves you."

She pauses, shaking her head. I hold my breath, waiting for the inevitable turn.

"Alvares was only a few months old when it happened. Marcus went down to the docks—he was working on a fishing boat, and apparently a pirate crew had taken their slot. There was an argument, and Marcus... Marcus didn't walk from that argument."

"I'm sorry," I tell her, but she shakes her head.

"It was ten years ago. When I found out, I went down to their ship with Alvares on my back and every gun in our house on my hips. I didn't ask questions. I shot the men who killed my lover. I flushed every last crewmember off that ship. I took what I was owed, and I set sail."

She stares at the deck beneath her feet, her back bowed as if the weight of the *Minnow* above is crushing her. A life for a livelihood. Blood for sweat.

"You can't shake off this life, Cas. Not when it shapes you." Santa Elena fixes me with a scathing look, like she's daring me to argue otherwise. "Swift is long gone. She's committed. The only way of saving her is making sure she reaches the top."

I gape. "You want to save..."

Santa Elena raises an eyebrow. "Swift could be the greatest captain these waters have ever seen. You saw how she handled that Hellbeast in the harbor—the instinct's there. But she needs shaping. She needs the right circumstances. Now that her family's settled, the world is hers for the taking."

There's something about the way she says it that curdles a hint of suspicion in me. My brow furrows.

Santa Elena notices. She smiles. "It took some convincing, some deals, some string pulling. But in the end, I think the investment will be worth it."

I feel as if I've stuck my finger in the charger. My blood boils, but I keep my voice even and low. "Does Swift know you're behind it?"

"No." The captain's hand drifts to the hilt of her pistol. "And she'd better not get any ideas. I need her focus on this ship, not on port. I don't want any of this coming to light unless it has to. But if she steps out of line, I'll remind her that it means putting her family back in the shipping container I pulled them from." She takes a step toward me, and I find myself shrinking back against the counter. "This is a critical point in her becoming. And you, Cassandra Leung, are the linchpin holding it all together."

"I'm not," I stutter. "She doesn't—"

"Swift thinks that you're the frontrunner. She sees you getting all the attention, and because she has the brain of a hypercompetitive jock, she thinks this means I value you more. And I'll admit, in present circumstances, I *do* value you more. But that value is related to the current crisis, not your prospects as a trainee."

"So tell her that."

The captain looms over me. "No." She lets the word sink in for a second, then continues. "You're a goad. You're the itch that keeps her working. I want to see how far she'll go to upstage you. *That's* your value as a potential heir, and no more than that."

Months ago, those words would have hurt. But under Santa Elena's hand, I've become accustomed to her methods. This isn't her using me. This is supposed to be her giving me purpose. And so I let my lips twitch upward, let my brows lower, let the determination settle over my face like it's meant to. "I'd like to see that," I say, watching Santa Elena's eyes light up like it's Christmas all over again.

"What do you know?" she murmurs, her shark smile out in full force. "You might give Swift a run for her money after all." The captain turns and strides for the hatch.

The moment she's out of sight, I wipe the falsehoods from my face and sag against the counter. My mouth's gone dry, and I feel like my head's about to explode. I glance down my leg and find the Minnow inked on the inside of my ankle. I chose this. I swore my loyalty and placed my brand. Santa Elena is my captain, and I'm supposed to obey her, to learn from her, to do right by her.

Even if it means trapping Swift in this world forever.

15

I sleep like the dead in my own bunk, then rise with the sun. We've been underway all night, driving a frantic pace to reach the *Kettle*'s marker. Instead of the Slew, I make for the trainer deck. Exercise can wait. If the seas are favorable, I'll have a Reckoner at my call tomorrow. I have to be ready.

The weight of the Otachi hangs heavy at my side as I stare out into the morning sea. The waves fly past beneath the edge of the trainer deck, kicking up a chilling spray that ghosts over my face. I try to relax, try to shift the device to rest comfortably, but it's impossible when I don't have the twin. My left arm feels empty and weightless. I'm an imbalanced, ungainly creature.

When I was ten years old and first learning to work the beacons, my father always warned me never to give a signal I didn't intend for a monster to complete. There's never a guarantee that a Reckoner will follow your next command.

If you order a Reckoner to kill, you'd better not be surprised when that's exactly what it does.

But even though part of me rebels, insisting on following the rules I grew up with, I twist the Otachi's knobs to the setting that would summon Bao if he were in range. No other beast in these waters would respond to this call anyway. I tighten my fingers in the triggers, and a brilliant beam of light cuts through the waves. A low tone rings out, resonating in the hollow of my chest until my teeth rattle.

I swing my arm left, then right. Surprisingly enough, my Slew mornings have done me some good—I wield the weight of the device far better than I did a month ago. I take a step back from the deck's edge and twist the dials again. It takes more than one try to get them onto the right setting.

When I lift my arm and pull the triggers, the *charge* signal blasts across the NeoPacific. I tense as if something's bound to surge out of the water and pounce after it. Nothing does. There's just spray and mist and the line of my beam disappearing into the clouded horizon.

I pull back again. Change the dial again. Lift my arm, pull the triggers, and let the *destroy* signal fly. The sound itches my skin and shakes my bones like I'm the monster meant to follow its call. My fingers still clenched, I lower my Otachi-clad arm until the laser shines against the deck beneath my feet.

Santa Elena thinks she's doing what's best for Swift. She thinks she can buy Swift's attention, distract her from her family, that she can make herself Swift's only option. She honestly thinks that even if Swift were to break free from piracy, it would come back to snare her in the end. That there's no escape from this life. I don't want to believe that's true for Swift. I don't want to believe that's true for myself.

Santa Elena's heart is the ship. And I'm going to scorch it.

"That can't be good for the floor."

I jump, instinctively squeezing my eyes shut as the Otachi beam slashes in an uncontrolled arc. I relinquish the triggers, take two seconds to breathe, then crack one eye open. "Jesus Christ, Swift," I groan, slumping against the aft door's track.

"Should've seen your face," she replies.

Then there's silence. A quiet moment where we regard each other. Her with her eyes still glazed from sleep, barefooted and dressed in nothing but a sports bra and sweatpants. Me in my wetsuit, caught burning holes in the trainer deck.

"Don't tell the captain," I blurt, just as she says, "I won't tell the captain." She chuckles before she can help herself, but then a pained expression flickers across her face. There isn't room for amusement in the tense space between us. The captain's secrets press against me like a knife to the throat. I try to see the good in keeping them. Like Santa Elena said, the world is Swift's for the taking now that she thinks her family's looked after. It could be the thing that makes her.

The silence settles again. My eyes flick to the tattoo on her chest, the wings of her namesake bird that curl down over her ribs. Its head is hidden now. It wasn't, this time yesterday.

"You're up early," I note, turning my back on her. I have to raise my voice over the churn of the engines beneath us. Their rattle fills the deck, frothing the water in our wake. The seas, still and clouded, are cut by the white of our path.

Even with all the noise, I still notice when she starts forward. "Couldn't sleep."

"And so you decided to come to the trainer deck?" She's right behind me. I duck my head, my breath caught in my chest as I wait for her reply.

"What did you and the captain talk about yesterday?"

Of course. I turn to find her staring me down, her eyes dark and intent. Swift folds her arms, and my fingers tense in the Otachi triggers. "None of your business," I tell her.

She doesn't buy it. Swift takes another step forward, her shoulders squaring, and I find myself pressing back against the door's edge. My hair ruffles back and forth, caught in the strange winds that suck back into the trainer deck from the *Minnow*'s slipstream.

A familiar sensation creeps over me, but it takes another breathless moment before I'm able to put my finger on exactly what it is. I'm *afraid* of her. Not in the fluttery, happy way of a girl with a crush. No, this is the fear that consumed me that August day, when she marched me onto the *Minnow* with a gun aimed at my back. Swift is dangerous. Swift is a pirate. Swift is not a good person.

But neither am I. If the captain's taught me anything, it's that. So I let my cruelness edge out into the open with the curl of my lips and tell her, "We talked about your prospects."

She studies my face, but I've spent far too much time around Santa Elena to let anything slip there. I'm a blank page, and Swift has never been very good at reading. "Did you, uh…" she starts, and breaks off as a hint of color creeps into her cheeks. "Did you guys talk about…"

It takes me a moment to catch her drift. "No, we didn't talk about how you and I spent New Year's Eve. Though I don't doubt she's guessed something by now."

"Ah. Good to, uh, good to know." She cracks a nervous grin that banishes all the menace from her, but I've spent enough time around Reckoners to know that monsters sometimes lurk beneath stilled seas. "Look, about yesterday—I don't want to let that lie. We need to talk, to come to an understanding."

I push off the wall, crossing to the counter on the other side of the trainer deck. "I think I understand it well enough." My fingers shake as I fumble with the Otachi straps.

Her hand slips onto my shoulder. I fight the urge to tense, turning my head so she can't see the emotions battling for control of my face. It's even more of a struggle to steady my hands enough to pull the Otachi off and set it gently on the counter. "Cas, I don't want to lie to you about who I am. What I am. What I want to be."

"You weren't lying," I mutter. "I just wasn't seeing—I was using a vision I had of you that wasn't complete."

"No, hey." Her grip tightens as if she's about to pull

me around, but she seems to think better of it. "This is on me—don't you dare shoulder it." Swift lets out a long sigh, and the back of my neck prickles. "Look, I got pissed because you don't seem to understand. I *want* this life. There's no way out of it, so I might as well want it."

"But your family's taken care of now. You have a way out." Not true, strictly speaking, but I need to hear that if it were, it would change *something*.

"To do what, Cas? Look at me." And this time she does spin me around, catching me by the shoulder with one hand as she uses the other to tilt my chin up with a touch. Her voice is low, urgent, as if she has a knife at my chin instead of her fist. "I've been raised for this. I can shoot a gun, but I can barely read or write. I can drive a ship, but I can't even cook my own meals. Maybe if things had gone another way when I was younger... I don't know. Piracy's the only thing that suits me."

I blink. "That's not true. That can't be true—there have to be other—"

She covers her face with her hands. "No, see, you don't get it! You're shore-raised! You're born from this stupid idea that you can be whatever you want to be when you grow up because your world doesn't have these *limitations*. And now you just waltz in and decide to play at being a fucking pirate captain, and the worst part is it's *working* for you. I've fought my whole life to stand on the ground that you just walked onto—"

"So did I," I mutter. "Just on the wrong side."

Swift goes still. Her wrath breaks down as she processes

my words. She reaches up and runs a hand through the longer side of her hair. "Look, even if I could—" Her voice cracks. "—could make a clean break, I don't want to be trapped on the Flotilla, or on some other raft, or in some dead-end island colony. And I don't have citizenship with any state. And I want to be able to see my family, and..." Her eyes flicker to mine, but don't stay long. "The future's fucked, huh?"

I nod, pushing myself up to sit on the counter. The weight of all of it lays heavy on my shoulders. I can see the way the paths fork out from where we are. It seems so certain that Swift will inherit the *Minnow*, and then what's left for me? To be traded to Captain Kurosaki or one of the other Salt crews? To get trapped in the same vicious cycle that has Swift bound forever to this life?

I let my head roll forward. All of this, because when Santa Elena let me go, I turned my back and came running right back to the *Minnow*. I could have gone home. Could have kept my head down about Fabian Murphy, could have let him play the industry and pirates alike, could have had a shoregirl future where anything was possible. I could have lied. Telling them that Santa Elena forced me to bring down the quadcopters would have been child's play after three months of playing Santa Elena's mind games. Maybe my family would have taken me back.

Now my future is washed red with the weight of the things I've done for this boat. Any future I have is colored by the past months, by the choices I've made and the traps I've stumbled into. And, I realize, as Swift's shadow falls across me, by the way my heart's been torn. Torn and healed and torn again.

Her hand slips onto my shoulder again, and my heartbeat quickens. "What future do we have? What's left for us at the end of this?" I ask. The three lines on the inside of her arm hurt to look at, but I do it anyway, because the alternative is looking in her eyes, and that feels so dangerous right now.

"I don't know," she replies. There's something about that truth that lightens the space between us. Maybe all we'll ever have is the moment when we're certain, the places where it works out, and all that's up to us is whether we move forward.

Swift leans in, her hips against my knees.

Is this the part where I'm supposed to reach for her, supposed to pull her gently by the back of the neck or else slide my hand up the wide curve of her hips? I don't know if I want to do that. I'm not sure if I should be doing that.

But if all of this is so fragile, I have to take what I can get. So I meet her gaze and lift my eyebrows, waiting for her move.

Swift crashes into me like a wave—rough, rolling, her fingers digging into my sides as she yanks me against her. I gasp, but the noise barely makes it out of my mouth before her lips are on mine. I try to kiss her back, but this isn't the kind of kiss that allows for that. Her teeth dig into my lower lip, and I bite back a groan. I like this. I probably shouldn't like this as much as I do. If we're going to fight, it might as well be like this, with just enough pleasure to balance out the pain.

But that doesn't mean I'm going to lose. I snare her by the waist, her skin searing my chilled fingertips, and squeeze until she yelps. Her cruel smile presses into my neck. I think she likes this game as much as I do.

Just as her pinch finds the zipper of my wetsuit, a crash and the clatter of footsteps rings out from the ship's interior. "Never a dull moment," Swift growls. She shoves me back, too rough to be playful, too gentle to be hateful. Before I know it, she's ten paces across the trainer deck, trying to pretend like she isn't responsible for the heat on my skin or the swelling in my lips.

There's room for three breaths, three chances to force my heartbeat slower, and then Chuck, Varma, and Lemon race through the trainer deck door. "I told you it'd be open!" Chuck shrieks, holding a familiar object over her head—the cobbled-together wakeboard she keeps stashed in a corner of the engine room.

Varma spins, throwing his arms out, and catches sight of Swift lurking in the corner. He stumbles over his own feet, and for a moment he looks like he's about to say something that's going to get his ass kicked. I can all but see the gears in his brain turning, but in the end all he manages is, "Oh good, you're here too!"

Lemon's already throwing down the bungee lines at the edge of the deck. She works with feverish intent as she ties them to the handholds. There's a slight hitch in the routine, a pause where she looks for the trainee who's supposed to be tying down the other lines.

I jump off the counter and step up to take his place. It takes a little fumbling to mimic Lemon's practiced knots, but eventually I get her slight nod of approval. Chuck tosses down the makeshift wakeboard. Before she can slip her foot into the bindings, I blurt, "First ride's mine."

Chuck blinks. "Have you ever…"

"I'm here to learn, remember?" I say with a shrug. "And besides, the trainer deck's *my* turf. I call the shots down here, right?"

She looks baffled, but then Varma claps his hands down on her shoulders, beaming. "Strap in, shoregirl," he says, resting his chin on top of Chuck's head. "We ain't reeling you in until you're limp in the waves."

As I strap my feet to the board, I catch Swift's glare, a contemptuous look twisted with a hint of amusement, like she can't believe what she's seeing. Too late I realize I've done it again. I've slid effortlessly into a place she's fought her whole life to claim. My heart sinks. As Lemon hoists the buoyancy vest over my shoulders, I turn to the sea and peer over the edge of the trainer deck. The froth beneath us looks vicious, cold.

Whatever punishment it has to offer, I hope it's enough.

16

In the late afternoon, the all-call snaps on. I don't even need to hear Santa Elena's words to know what's happening—the ring of the speakers warming up is enough to chill my blood.

We're near.

I stumble up to navigation in a haze. My limbs don't feel right, but part of that might be the beating I took while being dragged behind the ship this morning. I don't feel ready for this. I don't feel ready for any of this.

"Mallory gave us an update," Santa Elena says once we're all assembled in the tower. "He's kept the *Kettle* on Bao's tail, but it hasn't been easy. He says the Reckoner's acting erratic. They've had a few close calls so far."

"Clarify close calls?" Varma asks, his eyes flicking to the ship's controls as if he's already calculating how to steer us out of a potential path of destruction. Swift slouches beside him, staring at the ground. She was long gone by the time Chuck and Varma yanked me back onto the *Minnow*.

The captain looks grim. "Bao charged the *Kettle*. Mallory's report makes it sound like a posturing thing—they were able to outmaneuver him and he lost interest. But it doesn't bode well for what we're about to try."

"The *Minnow* can't go near him yet," I say, and Santa Elena nods.

"We're calling a league-wide berth around the beast. We'll keep on the outside of his range until we know for certain that we have him under our control. That part's up to you and Varma." The captain nods to him as he snaps to attention. "You go get the aft Splinter up and running." She turns back to me. "And you. Suit up."

I wear the armor. It's a struggle to put it on by myself, but I flounder and pull and tighten until it sits properly on me, its weight dragging at my already-sore limbs. I clap the Otachi onto my right forearm and pull the straps tight. The extra protection is meant to stop bullets, but considering what I'm about to go up against, I feel like I need every layer of safety I can afford. Finally I hoist the signal beacon with one arm, tuck my helmet under the other, and make my way up to the deck above, where Varma's already slumped in the cockpit of the Splinter.

Surprisingly enough, Swift's there too, doing some sort of last-minute maintenance on the needleboat's guns. She spins when she hears my footsteps approach, nearly whacking her head on the Splinter's pneumatic docking arm as she straightens and faces me.

Over her shoulder, Varma, who's terrible at faking anything, takes his best shot at disinterest.

I wish I could apologize. I wish I could tell her everything that the captain told me without getting gutted for it, because that's exactly what will happen if I topple over Santa Elena's carefully laid plans. My hand twitches forward, unbidden, driven by an impulse to grab her and bring her closer.

She gives an almost imperceptible shake of the head, and I can't read the hard look in her eyes. Is it *Not here? Not now? Not ever again?* Whatever she means, I keep my hands to myself until she brushes past, her shoulder skimming against mine in a way that can't possibly be an accident. I take a second to watch her retreat into the ship's interior, her back stiff, her gloved hands clenched into fists.

Swift pauses. She looks back over her shoulder, and *this* I can read, because I've seen it before. This is the look from the day the quadcopters attacked, the day we knew danger was near and it might be the last time. This is the horrible feeling of not knowing what to say, wanting to say everything, and maybe never having another chance.

And just like back then, we let it pass. She rushes into the dark of the ship, I turn to the Splinter, and there are no words.

When I slide into the cockpit next to Varma, he's absolutely still. His hands grip the wheel, his eyes fix straight ahead, and he curls in his lips as if he's sucking in any unfortunate words he might blurt. There's a slight tremor in his left eye, making the Minnow tattoo on his cheek jump.

"Spit it out," I snap, and he lets out a long, exasperated sigh.

"That was incredible. How do you stand it? I felt like I was going to *explode*."

I scoff. "You feel like that every time you go more than a minute without running your mouth."

He casts an exasperated glance skyward, bringing up the docking control with a swipe of his fingers. "You guys need to sort out your issues. Promise me you'll sort out your issues?"

I grimace and pull the restraints over my shoulders. The signal beacon is safely nestled between my knees. "That bit's not up to me."

"Wrong answer," he says, and jams down a button.

"*Wait, Lemon's supposed to—*" I shriek, but it's too late. The Splinter's pneumatics release with a pop, my stomach swoops, and we snap sideways, plunging into the NeoPacific and the *Minnow*'s wake. Varma howls as the spray blasts over us. I sputter. "I can't believe you," I groan, once I've finished spitting out salt water.

"Admit you deserved that."

"Drive, you maniac."

"Aye aye, captain," he shoots back, his teeth bared in a wolfish grin. With a few elegant twists of his wrists, he spins up the engines and sets us in a lazy arc around the *Minnow*'s hull. I pull my helmet over my head and clip it, then lean down and start fidgeting with the signal beacon. My earpiece hums to life, and beside me Varma tilts his head.

"Set course due directly east," the captain commands. "Mallory's instruments and ours have him wallowing just subsurface, probably feeding. We'll guide you in as you get closer."

Varma whips the Splinter around and guns the engines. I duck my head against the wind, squinting as we tear through the waves. The skies above us are heavy with clouds, a foreboding crackle of electricity in the air. The waters are rough, but Varma guides us through them with a steady hand. I close my eyes and draw a deep breath, letting the foul mood of the weather seep into my lungs. For the past month, I've never had to command anything larger than a handful of Splinters. To go back to having a monster at my beck and call, I'll need everything this storm can give me.

"Cas, you doing okay?"

I snap my head up to find Varma's concern fixed on me. "Just drive," I growl.

"Seriously, you know you can talk to me if you want to, right?" He reaches up to his earpiece and disengages the audio, leaving the silence between us and us alone. "I dunno if you've picked up on this, but we're friends."

"We're competitors."

"Doesn't mean we aren't also friends. And you fucking need more friends, Cas. This whole thing sucks if you try to make it through on your own."

My lip curls. "Why do you care—"

"Don't come at me with that Santa Elena talk. I care because you're another human being and your life kinda sucks right now. Do I need more reason than that?"

I take a moment to process it. To realize that Varma, smiling Varma who's always kinder than he needs to be, honestly wants to be my friend. And what have I done to earn it, apart from scowling and snapping at him? I roll my head back, clunking my helmet on the seat's headrest. "You're probably a better friend than I deserve," I concede.

"And you're a better pirate than I ever thought you'd be," he replies, a teasing edge in his voice. "Now tell me if you're okay so we can move past this."

I chuckle. "I'm alright. I'll be fine." After a beat, I ask, "How the hell'd you even end up a pirate, Varma? You're too nice to have been doing this for long."

Varma throws his head back, laughing. "Would you believe me if I told you I've been doing this for longer than any of them?" He slips one hand from the wheel and runs it through his wind-tossed hair. "Been bouncing around pirate crews since I was nine. Didn't settle on the *Minnow* until I was fifteen."

"And before you were nine?"

His grin sharpens. "Before I was nine, I was an idiot. Not that that's changed," he adds hastily. "But before I was nine, it was really my only defining feature. I grew up on the coast of South Quarter India—Chennai, to be specific. No parents. Ran with a gang of kids who liked to play a little game involving the trade ships docking at our port. Basically you'd go sneak onto the ship and you'd bring something back. Some little trinket to prove that you'd actually done it. One day, they dared me to hit this tanker..."

He breaks off, shaking his head, then draws a breath.

"The ship was about to leave, and usually we had a good sense for this sort of thing. But I got spooked by the crew, wedged myself in a crate, and got stuck there. The ship went out to sea with me aboard, and no one was the wiser."

My heart sinks as I picture the boy he used to be, tiny and terrified, a mess of gangly limbs stuffed into a dark corner.

"I got by slipping food from the mess when they weren't looking—I was pretty good at sneaking. But this tanker was unescorted, and it was just too *delicious* for a passing pirate crew to pass up. The good thing about tanker jackers is the haul's too big—they don't bother selling anything else they find on the ship. Or anyone. But taking said kid on as a cabin boy, they're not above. And so the legend began," he finishes with a flourish.

I let his words sink in, considering the weight of them. Here he is, the perfect counterpoint to all of Santa Elena's talk. Varma was simply in the wrong place at the wrong time. Life is nothing but a series of weird coincidences. Varma's coincidences led him here, and he chose to stay in the end. Or maybe this life really won't let him go, and he has no choice but to go along with it. But his piracy wasn't predestined.

It was all an accident.

I roll my shoulders. The armor still weighs, but something else has lifted. Accidents and coincidences—that's all that's brought me to this moment. That's what made me a trainer. That's what made me a pirate. And that's what will make me… whatever I'm supposed to be now.

Varma slips his earpiece back in. "Captain, you got a heading? We've been pointed at a horizon for an awful long while now." He gives us a quick burst of speed, skirting the swell of a wave. The ocean's getting even choppier under the watch of the darkening skies.

"Sonar puts him within a half-kilometer radius. Better light that beacon, Cas," Santa Elena replies. Her audio is faint, crackly, the *Minnow* at the very edge of our range. If this goes south, we're on our own.

"Calling him now," I reply. I lean forward, my hands shaking, and press the switches on the board. It's the simplest command there is, meant to make it easy to bring a beast in. The homing signal rings over the waves, its low tones matching the hum of the engine as Varma spins them down. We slow to a drift, moving only to keep the waves from rolling us. I hoist the beacon and hook it over the edge of the Splinter, settling it so that its lights flash out against the inky waters.

Now we wait. Now we pray. Varma's hands are tight on the controls, his skin drawn taut over his knuckles. I try to ignore it, try to let him focus on the driving. I fix my gaze on the swell and sink of the waves, searching for the shadow in their midst.

It's been a month. No Reckoner has ever spent that long away from its signals. The record goes to a serpentoid named Iago, whose companion ship sank in a NeoAtlantic storm. It took more than a week for a recovery boat to track him down and bring him in. He came when they called. I might not be so lucky.

The drone of the beacon shudders through my skull. I can barely hear the rush of the wind or the gentle roar of the waves over its noise. My earpiece hums. "He's on the move. Headed your way. Should be approaching on your starboard side," Santa Elena says. Her voice is low and tense—even from over a mile away, I can tell she's on edge.

Somehow I feel him before I spot the shadow, before the waves on our right begin to swell. It's like a magnet draws my eyes to the monster rising out of the depths. My heartbeat quickens, and my breathing goes shallow. Varma shifts next to me.

His blowholes breach the surface first, letting out a blast of stale air that sends spray nearly twenty feet into the sky. Next to rise is the harsh curve of his beak. Water sheets off him as he lifts his head, his massive reptilian eye fixed on the beacon's pulsing lights.

He's grown. He's grown *incredibly*. He's easily twice the size he was when I released him into the NeoPacific on that November night. In the Splinter, we're insignificant. Nothing but a blip on his radar, a blip that's calling to him in a way he used to understand. For a breathless moment, Bao simply watches us.

Then he charges.

17

If it were anyone but Varma piloting the Splinter, we'd be dead. He throws down the hammer and yanks the wheel, spinning us clear just as Bao's jaws come together with a crack like a thunderclap. The surge from his body crashes against our hull, and for a moment I'm blinded, salt water burning my eyes. I feel for the beacon's handles and wrench it up into the Splinter before the waves steal it.

Varma's just as blind as I am, but he flings us forward anyway. I sink back into the seat, blinking furiously as the Splinter accelerates. I should have worn my mask. Should have worn my respirator. Should have seen this all coming. We glance off Bao's side as more of him surfaces, and a strangled yelp bursts out of me.

"What's going on?" Santa Elena shouts in my ear. "Someone start talking."

"Aggressive response," I manage. "Handling it now."

"Cassandra, is he tame or not? Is he responding to signals?"

I flip the switches, silencing the beacon. "Give me a minute. Varma, get on his blind side, keep him turning." He hauls the wheel, bringing us around Bao's rear as the Reckoner lets out a guttural roar. From this angle, I can finally see the mass of scarred tissue where his right eye used to be, the wound he received on the night I abandoned him. His hide is peppered with bullet pocks, and his keratin plating shows the battle damage of a seasoned beast. With a few strokes of his massive forelegs, he's onto us again, his neck tilted at an uncanny angle to bring us into his line of sight.

This isn't posturing. He's genuinely out to get us. I reel, trying to understand his behavior. It's almost territorial, like we've invaded his space and disrupted his routine. But Reckoners—at least the Reckoners I've known—don't form any sort of emotional attachments to the oceans they inhabit. Their only bond is with their companion ship.

But in the absence of that bond, who knows what steps in?

"Cas, gonna need a plan really soon," Varma mutters through his teeth. Bao lunges forward, and he spins the Splinter out of his path again. The waves around us are climbing higher and higher, and I swear I hear thunder.

"Working on it. Stay out of his way, but keep us close," I tell Varma. I grapple with the beacon in my lap, wrestling it forward until I can drop it safely at my feet. This isn't the tool for the job. The tool I need is strapped to my right forearm. I heft the Otachi, my fingers flying over the dials.

"Are you signaling him again? It didn't work the first time, Cas!" Varma yelps.

In response, I tug the triggers, blasting the *stay* signal into the air. The lasers carve the low clouds above us, and for a moment—just one moment, but it's all I need—Bao hesitates.

It's in there. He's remembering. A spark of joy rolls through me, followed quickly by a rush of pride. I did my job—I trained him well. Before the feeling can settle, Bao shakes his head and lunges again. Varma veers to the right, checking over his shoulder as he tries to pin down Bao's blind spot. My stomach swoops as we plunge down over the crest of a wave, the restraints cutting into my shoulders as I twist to get a good look at Bao.

He isn't there.

"He dove!" I yell, straining over the edge of the Splinter. There's no sign of his shadow, no way to tell if he's coming up under us.

"Captain's going to kill me if we wreck this Splinter," Varma snarls. "And that's only if this jackass doesn't do us in first." He accelerates, but the waves are getting worse, cutting us off, slowing us down. "Cas, I don't know if we can hold out if they start breaking," he says with a worried glance at the ocean around us. The Splinter isn't made for these conditions—if the seas get worse, they'll swallow us.

I know what I have to do. A dark laugh builds in me as I reach down for the buckles on my restraints.

Varma tenses when he hears the snap of the safety straps releasing. "Cas, what are you doing?"

I stand, my fingers winding tight around the Splinter's edge. As I shrug off the shoulder straps, I spot the shadow carving through the bulging waves, the waters swelling around his massive body as he charges us.

"Cas, don't you dare—Cas, no!" Varma shouts, as if he can stop me.

"The second I'm clear, break right as fast as you can," I tell him. "Run like hell, and don't come back until I tell you."

"Cas," he pleads, but it's a little too late for that. I vault over the edge of the boat, tuck my chin against my chest, and hit the waves like a cannonball. The flotation in my armor reacts instantly, swelling so quickly that it forces a bubble of breath out of my lungs. I tumble head over heels, regretting not wearing my mask with every second I spend underwater. A rumble shakes my chest as the Splinter's engines cut past me, and even though my lungs are burning, even though I need to right myself and set eyes on the monster coming for me, I need to do this first.

I pull the triggers, shooting the homing signal into the depths.

As I surface, blinking salt water from my eyes, I suck in a breath and inhale a healthy dose of seawater as I do. I swallow back the urge to gag—that can come once I figure out exactly where Bao is. A wave lifts me up, and I tense, waiting for the crest, waiting for the moment where I'll be the tallest thing around. At its apex, I see him at the instant he pauses, still on Varma's tail, and turns his head toward the lights that call him. The Splinter skims away, Bao wheels, and as the wave drops me, I find myself in what might be the most regrettable position I've ever put myself in.

Bao comes in like a hurricane, every bit the monster he was meant to be. And, because there's nothing else for me to do, I swim right for him. The suit drags me down, and I find myself wishing I had flippers, but the flotation works its magic, and I plummet down the curve of a wave, making a beeline for the tip of Bao's beak.

Bless him, he hesitates. He doesn't know what to make of this, of the lights and the noise and a tiny, very eatable creature swimming at him like he isn't the same size as the *Minnow*. His legs stop churning, and his eye narrows so shrewdly, so uncannily, that I almost spit a laugh into the NeoPacific. The distance between us collapses from hundreds of feet to nothing. I crash against his front, the armor warping horribly as it runs up against his knobby plating. The wind gets knocked right out of me, and my next breath comes in tinged with his horrible, wonderful carrion smell. I never thought the *stench* of a Reckoner was something I'd miss, but here we are.

Bao rolls his head, trying to fix his eye on me. I push off his chest and make it easier for him, swimming right for that spot I know I can grab easily.

I'm barely feet away when he opens his mouth.

In a panic, I pull the Otachi triggers again, raising my arm as he lunges for me. The lasers blast from my wrists and right into his eye. His only eye. His one good eye. Bao roars, but it's enough to stun him, to keep him in his place. The noise of his complaint hits my skull like a hammer, liquefying my thoughts.

I may be deafened, but he's blind. And he can't stop my instinct.

I lunge forward, my bare left hand outstretched, and this time my fingers find purchase in that ridge above his eye. With a groan, I kick myself upward, my foot slamming down on his eyelid, pinning it shut. His head snaps up, and I flail for another handhold before he manages to shake me loose. The muscles in my leg scream in protest as Bao tries to wrench his eye open.

I risk it—I grab for a line hook in the belt of the armor, unspooling the length of fiber and jamming the hook into the scales over his eye. Not a second too soon. Bao slams his head down against the waves, and I barely have time to suck in a breath before the water smashes into me, pinning me against him. My grip slips, but the hook holds true, and when he lifts his head again, I come up with him, choking and sputtering, and grab for the ridge. My dripping hair is plastered against my face, the helmet doing little to protect me from it.

Bao's eye snaps open. With a pull of my Otachi triggers, the homing signal flashes again. He tosses his head, and I fix my glare down his neck, where his ear sits. "Listen to me—" I start, but get cut off as he throws me against another wave.

When I surface, I grit my teeth and press against his

skull. "You stupid… little… shit…" I bellow at his ear. My breath comes in ragged, broken gasps.

I brace myself when I feel the rumble in his throat start, ready to lose my hearing all over again. But the noise comes out more a warble than a roar, and the muscles underneath my grip go slack. Bao blinks, tilting his head so that his eye points skyward, so that I can shift my weight to my knees. His gaze never leaves me.

"That's right, you vast idiot." I breathe. "Remember me?"

There's only one way for him to answer. I raise my arm, feeling his muscles shift as his eye slides in the wake of my motion. The seas around us boil and churn, and I curl my fingers slowly in the Otachi triggers. When they trip and the signal lasers fly across the NeoPacific, his eye runs down the line, the pupil shrinking as he takes in the harsh beams of light.

Bao's slow to start, every bit a terrapoid. First he stretches his neck forward, leaning out toward the Otachi's path. Then his forelegs start moving, churning with methodical, elegant strokes that carve through the water. I tilt the beam up, making sure his head stays above the waterline. Now that I'm tied to his side with no respirator, my life depends on it.

The waves roil around us as Bao picks up speed. He slices through them, unmoved by their commotion. I slip my free hand from the ridge, bracing against his skull and the embedded line hook, and pull a second line hook from my belt. With two lines holding my weight, I'll have my hands free to operate the Otachi. Once I have the second hook securely rooted in his scales, I brace myself. It could go wrong at any second, and what I'm about to do makes it even more likely.

I twist the Otachi triggers to *charge* and throw the signal out against the chaos of the NeoPacific.

He pauses. His blowholes flare, and his eye narrows. Every moment of his hesitation burns into me. It's too long—he used to take commands in an *instant*. He can't be the monster we need if he's unresponsive. I press my left hand against his skull, pleading for him to recognize the lights, the sound, or even the thoughts I'm directing at him.

I'm not ready for it when he does. He bucks forward, and I can't bite back the scream—first of terror, then delight—that bursts out of me. His limbs kick up a surge that catches me across the face. I spit the salt water in his eye and grin against the wind.

"Varma?" I ask, and the comm in my ear immediately snaps to life.

"You're alive, then?"

"Don't sound so disappointed."

He chuckles. "And I'm guessing the beast is under your command?"

I snap the Otachi over to the simple homing signal, and Bao slows after only a second of processing time. "More or less."

"Well, that was easier than I expected," he says. I squint against the horizon and pick out the sliver of the Splinter tracing lazy paths around the rising waves.

I laugh, shifting my weight against the sureness of Bao's skull. "Trust me, Varma. The work's only just begun."

18

From the navigation tower, I can barely see Bao's shadow on the horizon. He's been temperamental in the days since I led him back to the ship. Some moments I think he's genuinely bonded to the *Minnow*. Others I'm convinced he'll run.

So far I haven't felt like he'll attack us, but that's only a matter of time.

I've spent every waking minute with him, practicing his old signals, trying to get him back in shape, but it isn't enough. With no rewards to motivate him, he's grown sluggish, and I can almost hear him ask, *"Why should I?"* every time I throw a signal at him. He doesn't have any available targets to practice on, so our training is limited to simply giving him directions.

Which is what brings me to the captain's side today.

"I understand," Santa Elena says when I finish laying it

out. She slumps back in her chair at the navigation panel, her fingers tracing over the radio on her belt. "But you've come at me with a problem. A problem in your area of expertise. I need more than that from you. I need a proposal, at the very least."

My nails dig into my palms. "I… We've never trained Reckoners to fight like this. The only thing I can think of is actually hunting neocetes with him, but then I'd be creating some strange connections between eating and training that I don't want rattling around in his head."

She nods, her lips pursed.

When it becomes clear she's still waiting, I do my best to draw a breath without flinching. "I need ships. Ships for him to wreck. It's been too long since his first tug—I need to see that he can do it again. And if he's really going to be our weapon, I need to hone him."

Santa Elena leans over the navigation panel, her hair falling around her face as she twists the dials on the long-distance radio. "What you're saying is you need resources, correct?"

"Ships."

Her lip curls at my impertinence. "Fine. Whatever. Ships. Point is, we need them, and I've been waiting *years* to cash in on the favor Eddie Fung owes me. You ever been on an Art-Island, Cas?"

I shake my head.

The captain's grin could melt iron.

———

Artificial islands, I quickly discover, are nothing like their natural counterpart. Art-Hawaii 26 is built in a crescent, and only the sparsest greenery dots its surface. Within the crescent's center lies the harbor, where Captain Fung's ship, the *Crown Prince*, makes its berth. He's been kind enough to allow the *Minnow* to dock next to him, after assurances that we'll keep Bao from bothering his ships or any of the other ones docked there. The outer edge of the island is built with bladed ridges that dare any unwanted guests to run themselves up against them. The only way to set foot on Art-Hawaii 26 is through the horns of the crescent, each of which plays host to a wall of cannons.

As we pull up to the docks, I notice the anxiety eating away at Bao. The harbor is shallow, by far the shallowest water he's ever been in. He dives to the bottom of the artificial bowl, resurfaces, dives again, and resurfaces again, his blowholes flaring as he breathes rapidly in and out. Even with the signal beacon calling him, he begins edging toward the opening of the horns, yearning for the open sea.

I radio up to the captain and get permission to set him patrolling out in the deep waters. I have to do everything I can to calm his nerves—an uppity Reckoner is an unpredictable one, and he's already unpredictable enough as it is. I change over his signals, hold my breath when he takes a few extra seconds to process the command, and then release it as he turns tail and makes a beeline for the harbor's mouth.

Once he's clear of the horns, I join the captain and the other trainees on the main deck. As the docking arms extend to bring us into our slot, I get my first good look at Eddie Fung's palace.

I don't know what I expected, but it wasn't this. The compound rests at the center of the crescent, a beast of glass and steel. It shimmers in the afternoon light, and whatever doesn't catch the glare of the sun reflects the oceans around us, turning each surface a seething, electric blue. The *Crown Prince* slumbers in the slot next to us, so pristine and white that for a second I forget that Captain Fung is more than just an Islander prince. I'm about to ask Varma just how much piracy Fung engages in, but before I can open my mouth, I spot our host and his retinue striding down the docks to meet us.

Eddie Fung cleans up well. When we first met him on the Flotilla, he was dressed to blend in with the other pirates, but here in his kingdom, he's effortlessly changed into the smiling, polished look of a young prince. His pants are pleated, his shirtsleeves crisply folded up—Fung looks ready for a weekend at a country club, not anything remotely close to piracy.

Santa Elena smirks when she sees him, but there's something uncomfortable about her posture. She's fought her entire life for her living, for her stake in these oceans. Fung was given his place at birth, and from the look of things he's never had to struggle to keep it.

"Welcome!" he cries when he reaches the end of our gangway. Even from a distance, his smile gleams. The crew at his back might as well be his weekend companions, but for the guns at their hips. Santa Elena motions us forward with a twitch of her fingers, and we stride down the ramp to meet him. He offers a handshake to the captain, followed by a flirtatious grin at Chuck. I catch her nervous smile in the reflection of his mirrored sunglasses. He lifts his chin toward the horizon at the mouth of the harbor, where Bao's retreating shadow is barely a speck. "Magnificent animal. I accepted your request just to see him in the flesh, honestly."

"You accepted my request because you've yet to repay me for my generosity four years ago," Santa Elena replies.

"If I repay, it stops being generosity," Captain Fung shoots back, then laughs. Santa Elena joins him, but hers never reaches her eyes.

"Come along. I'll give you and yours the tour," he says, gesturing toward his fortress. "We have plenty of spare rooms if you want to sleep some of your crew on the island. Naturally there are parts of my home that are off-limits, but we'll go over that when we get to it."

That idea becomes more appealing by the second as Fung escorts us up the steps and through the estate's doors. The rush of cool air hits me like a wave, and I realize it's been nearly half a year since the last time I was anywhere near air-conditioning. I try to mask just how much I enjoy it. Varma doesn't.

The captain catches his blissful expression and rolls her eyes. "As long as you've got a radio on you, you're welcome to take rooms here, got it?" she says, keeping her voice low under Captain Fung's monologue about the island's construction. "Just don't get too comfortable. Desert me for Fung and I'll carve my name in your guts."

"Speaking of…" Swift mutters, raising her eyebrows as Fung curls an arm around Chuck's shoulders. Varma's grin falters.

Santa Elena's eyes narrow, but she stows the expression when Fung glances back at her. "Young punk," she growls, then pushes forward to our host's side. "Captain," Santa Elena says, smiling sweetly as she plucks his arm off her trainee. Several of his retinue have their hands on their guns before the word is out of her mouth. "We trust your palace is as nice as you say. But what about what we came here for?"

Fung doesn't miss a beat. "The ships—yes, of course! I'd assumed you saw them on your way in, but we can take our tour in that direction." He spins on his heels and points us down a narrow hall, his next breath already spent on the intricacies of his father's fueling business.

I watch Chuck carefully as he leads us out to the docks. She likes Fung—that much is clear from the way her attention drifts and lands, even from the rise in the pitch of her voice when she answers his questions about the *Minnow*. But I see her guilt too, the way she's constantly aware of where Santa Elena is and when the captain's looking at her.

Varma once said that Chuck chose the *Minnow* because the engine felt like home. But that was before Santa Elena sliced Code open and let him drain. Before the ship was hunted by the SRC, before our captain decided that we'd lead the charge in a fight against wild monsters the likes of which the NeoPacific has never seen. Maybe Chuck is smart, securing her way out now.

It's more than I've done.

The thought leaves a sour taste in my mouth that endures even as Eddie Fung leads our party out another set of doors and onto another dock. I glance down the line of sleek, silvery boats moored there, wondering where the junkers we're meant to wreck are. These look like Fung's personal fleet of pleasure cruisers.

"So," Captain Fung says, gesturing to the row of ships. "What do you think?"

At first I think he's asking Santa Elena, but Santa Elena is looking at me. Everyone's looking at me. "You... *These* are the ships?"

"Is there something wrong with them?"

"*Is* there something wrong with them?" I ask, forcing emphasis into my inflection. "You can't be serious."

Santa Elena swoops in before I make another misstep, wearing her best diplomatic smile. "They're perfect, Captain Fung. We never expected this level of generosity."

He waves a hand. "It's nothing. These old clunkers have been gathering barnacles for too long. Best to put them to good use."

I'm not the only one who seems to object to using luxury boats as Reckoner fodder. Beside me, Varma looks like he might throw up. Maybe it's the ships themselves—as a helmsman, he knows just how elegantly crafted they are, just how nicely they would handle. But what's more likely, I realize as he fixes a determined stare at Fung's back, is it's pissing him off that Fung was able to give them away like they're nothing. Fung's able to give us everything, it seems.

And Varma's imagining what Fung might be able to give Chuck.

I clap a reassuring hand on his shoulder, and his ever-present smile tilts into a grimace.

19

Later that evening, I inspect the abandoned yachts with Santa Elena in tow. I didn't ask the captain to tag along, but she followed me down to the docks when I announced my intentions to Fung, and it's not like I can tell her that I'd rather do this on my own. So I tolerate her presence as I climb up the narrow gangway and begin circling the deck of the first ship in the line.

I look for anything that might cause permanent damage to Bao. His beak is strong enough to crush metal, but any jutting sharp surfaces pose a threat to the delicate tissue in his mouth. Back on shore, we've had Reckoners get severe infections from slow-healing wounds on the tongue or inside of their cheeks. I don't want anything like that happening on a practice boat.

"Did you follow me here for a reason?" I finally ask once I've completed my check of the upper deck.

The captain smirks, leaning against the rail. She pulls a knife out of her sleeve and trails the blade over the varnish. "You've been wrapped up in the beast for a couple days. I figured it was time to check in."

"What do you want to know?"

"How much you told Swift when she visited you that morning." Of course. One of the other trainees must have ratted on us—I make a mental note to figure out which one later. Santa Elena twists the knife, skinning a chip off the rail. She cocks her head and flicks the knife again, carving off another slice.

"I didn't tell her anything."

"Don't lie to me, Cas."

"I *didn't*. All I told her is we talked about her prospects. Didn't say anything more than that."

"You expect me to believe Swift let that go?"

"I got her off the subject."

The captain's knife gouges into the rail.

"Turns out Swift was more concerned about how much you knew about..." I make a vague hand gesture. Santa Elena cackles, her eyes still on her carving. "Wasn't too hard to lead her away from asking the right questions," I continue.

"You're a work of art, Cas Leung," Santa Elena says with a smile. "I don't even know if I can take credit for it. I've seen the way you work with the monster. You're an expert at baiting—you always have been, even before you set foot on this ship. It'll serve you well in the future."

There's that word again. *Future*. Even the thought of it

feels sour and stale. The captain believes in it, from the way she talks. Believes that I have one, believes that it's tied to her boat. For all I know, she's right.

The captain keeps carving. I approach the rail next to her. Part of me goes live with tension at the notion of getting within her reach when there's a blade in her hand. The other part of me knows her reach has no bearing on my safety—if she can see me, I'm in range. Her expression remains blank, bored. I squint, trying to make out what the strokes of her blade have etched.

It's her name. I shift my gaze to the waters below us, biting back a smirk. Of course she'd be carving her own name into Fung's fancy boat. That's what she does—she takes things and slices them up until they're hers. She even inks her crew to mark them as her own, even if they might not stay that way forever. And suddenly, I don't want her praise. I don't want her to believe in me or my future. I don't want her knife in me for another second, etching herself into who I am as a person. It isn't enough that she's noble and brave, that she's fighting a good fight. I can't accept that part of her and ignore the rest, not when she's making me into her image. This isn't how I want to survive these waters. But it might be the only way I *can*. I make my own marks in the railing as my fingernails dig into the varnish.

"What's next?" I ask. I need the near future. The distant future's too crippling to think about.

Santa Elena pauses, sawing the blade back and forth in the L's path. "So far, none of the Salt have sighted any more of the Hellbeasts. Which doesn't sit right with me.

The Salt's been reporting consistent encounters—a new one was surfacing practically every week. Now they've stopped. I don't like it."

It sounds like something's changed. "Any word from fisheries?"

"The catch is worsening. It's already begun." She shrugs. "So the Hellbeasts are gone, but they keep eating. No idea what it means."

"Means we'd better train fast. Something's happening out there," I say, nodding to the mouth of the bay. "I'll push Bao."

"Do. I'll keep the channels open, keep asking questions. No rest until we know where we stand." She makes a few more vicious cuts into the wood, then leans back to admire her work.

There's one more question I want to ask. I can feel her waiting for it. "What was the favor?" I say at last, eyes fixed on the blade in her hand.

Santa Elena slips the knife back up her sleeve. "Four years ago, Fung was a precocious eighteen-year-old Islander prince who wanted to try his hand at the hunt. Little has changed, save for the age. He bought a boat, put together a crew, and threw himself out into the NeoPacific. Fucker had no idea what he was doing. And the first boat he tried to take…"

She breaks off, shaking her head, fighting the laugh building inside her.

"First boat he tried to take was armed to the teeth. He didn't realize that unescorted ships would be jacked up.

Nearly got ripped to shreds. We were patrolling in that area and picked up the battle on our radar. Neither of the ships were responding on Salt frequencies, so I brought the *Minnow* in to investigate. What I found was a complete clusterfuck. It took me five minutes to figure out which ship was the pirate and which was the mark—I mean, you've seen the *Crown Prince*. The ship Fung was in wasn't nearly as well equipped, though. By the time we started shooting, it was already starting to sink. We took down the mark for him, then scooped his crew out of the water. He offered me an exorbitant amount of money for his freedom. I turned him down. Money has its uses, but a man with his resources has far more. And you can milk a hanging favor for decades if you guilt them right."

I nod, and try not to make it too obvious when I push off the rail and step around her. There are more ships in the line to inspect, and I don't owe the captain any favors with my time. She lingers behind me, and as I make my way down the narrow ramp, I catch her putting some finishing touches on the name she's carved.

Santa Elena is nothing if not proud of her work.

———————

The training is slow, bitter work. The first time I taught Bao to take down a ship was a frantic affair. We had pursuit on our tail, and the captain wasn't doing me any favors then. Now, even with the threat of the Hellbeasts on the horizon, there's time to breathe. But the lack of danger nipping at my heels isn't what's keeping the training slow.

It's the fact that Bao, who used to be one of the fastest learners I'd ever trained, who learned his *charge* and *destroy* signals in less than a day, has regressed to the awkward, unsure movements of an adolescent beast.

I start to wonder if the wound that took his eye also did some damage to his head. Bao's main problem isn't even anything to do with the boats he's supposed to be wrecking. He keeps forgetting the *Minnow*. Reckoners are born with an innate need for a bond, which is supposed to be filled by their companion ship. But Bao's been flighty since his reunion with the *Minnow*, more beholden to his signals than to the ship itself. Every time he wanders, I worry that he won't come back.

He doesn't savage the first boat I set him on. He chews on it. With one foreleg he presses down on it, the metal shrieking under his weight, and then locks his beak around the ship's stern. He tests the ship's hull, flexing his jaw against it. I tug the *destroy* signal again, trying to get the point through his big dumb turtle brain. His jaw snaps tighter, and the hull crumples. Bao shrinks back, loosening his hold on the ship, his eye widening as he takes stock of what he's done.

The sight is so surprising that I end up doubling over laughing, which only confuses him more. He releases the boat, which immediately begins to sink, and noses his way over to the trainer deck. I wave him away with a flash of his *stay* pattern. This shouldn't be as funny as it is. If we're going to fight the Hellbeasts, we need to do it with a monster, not a wimp.

I call out the next boat and throw him after it the minute Fung's tugs are clear of Bao's radius.

This time, he does it right. His movements are still slow, calculated, hesitant, but he brings one foreleg down on the boat's stern, snaps his jaws onto the hull, and twists so hard that the metal shrieks when he rips it free. Another slash of his forelegs and half of the yacht plummets to the depths. I change over his signals, calling him to back off. He takes a moment to think, then releases his hold on the other half of the boat, letting it sink.

"Bring in the reward tug," I order through the radio.

The boat circles around, and I wrinkle my nose at the bloody carcass it drags in its wake, attached by ropes lanced through the tail flukes. It's a necessity, but it's a shitty necessity, having to hunt down neocetes to reward Bao for his good behavior. When I first trained him on aggressive signals in a single grueling afternoon, the promise of a reprieve was enough to power him. But with this slower, more consistent training, he needs food to drive his learning.

I considered trying to keep the bait alive, but I don't have that kind of cruelty in me—Santa Elena hasn't trained it into me yet. I told Fung's crew to make sure the neocetes have a clean, easy death, and they followed orders. "Cut it loose," I demand.

The crew on the reward tug loosens the lines, setting the carcass adrift. The animal's lungs are still inflated, keeping it floating even with no life in it. I swallow back my revulsion and set Bao onto it with a quick burst from the Otachi. He downs the wretched thing in one bite, throwing his head back to force it down his gullet.

Then it's back to work.

———————

By the end of the afternoon, I'm dripping with sweat and half-tempted to dive straight off the trainer deck and into the open sea. I turn Bao loose and restrain myself until the Minnow has docked safely back in Fung's harbor and I've had a chance to put away my equipment. I strip from my wetsuit down to my swimsuit and leap headfirst off the back of the ship, letting out a bubbled moan as the cool water sinks into my skin. I roll onto my back and float, keeping my eyes squeezed shut. With my ears under the water, I can block out the rest of the world. I can relax. I listen to the muffled rumblings of ship's motors, to the distant churn of the waves against the island's beaches, and let it drown out the constant noise inside my head.

But I can't keep my thoughts down. Now that training is over, now that I'm no longer distracted by a simple task, my head runs wild with a constant chant—*What next? What next? What next?*

The future's out to get me.

It's simpler with my eyes closed. With only white noise and the rocking of the waves, I can see my path. Train Bao. Solve the Hellbeasts. Unveil Murphy as the man who nearly killed an entire ocean. And then a gaping black hole after, where I'm swallowed into Santa Elena's world, carved up in her image, and set against the innocents in the seas I've been working since birth to save. The salt on my lips has never tasted so bitter.

"How's the water?"

My eyes snap open, and I let my legs drop. I squint against the sudden, blinding sunlight and find Swift leaning against the edge of the trainer deck with a beer in her hand. "What do you want?" I ask, wary. We haven't been alone together since that morning on the trainer deck. I've been too consumed by training Bao, and she's been… Has she been avoiding me? I have no idea where we stand—I don't even know what I feel beyond the way my heart starts racing.

She takes a swig of her drink before answering. "You weren't answering your radio." Swift nods to the lump of my discarded wetsuit, the radio still belted to it. "Captain told me to go down and check on you."

"Shouldn't you be radioing her back?"

"I did. Two minutes ago." She tips the bottle back again, smirking around the glass at her lips. When she swallows, she crouches and holds out the bottle so that I can see the label. "Fancy stuff. Craft. Fung brought a whole crate of 'em onboard after we docked. If you want one, you should go now—they're going fast."

I shake my head. "Not worth getting out. Water's too nice."

Those words shouldn't be dangerous, but they are. I see the flicker of Swift's intentions in her eyes, in the way her grip on the bottle tightens. I see her restraint, her confusion. Something in me hitches. I don't think I want her restrained or confused.

With two kicks, I glide to the trainer deck's edge. Swift rocks back into a sitting position and throws her legs out over the water, and I wind my fingers around a handhold beneath the deck's platform. A familiar sensation prickles over the back of my neck. We're teetering toward the cliff's edge, the crumbling precipice over Santa Elena's sea of secrets.

I step up willingly. "What's the captain trying to do to us?" I ask, keeping my voice low. Beneath my feet, the waters still glow warm from the ship's engines.

Swift leans out over her knees, her hair falling around her face. "It's always some sort of test. Not sure what it is this time—she couldn't possibly have known what the… situation is."

"I talked to her last night."

Swift's fingers tighten on the bottle. "What did you say?"

"Nothing more than what she wanted to hear."

"The fuck does that mean?"

My exasperation sharpens to a point. "Look at me." I wait until she's looking, until her eyes are fixed on mine. "She's playing us against each other—it's all part of this stupid power game she's created. No matter what, we lose, she wins, and the game goes on. The only way we stand a chance is if we're honest with each other."

Swift's brow furrows. "So be honest with me. What did you and the captain talk about?"

I freeze. I know it's bad. I know I can't take back my moment of hesitation, so I commit to it, lengthening the silence as I carefully consider the next words that come out of my mouth. No matter how tempting it is to unburden myself, I know the consequences for making this particular dive. The captain will skin me if I breathe a word about the way she's arranged Swift's future.

"She told me about how she saved Fung's ass four years ago. Funny story."

"You're shitting me," Swift growls.

"No, seriously—"

"Not the story, you jackass. I was *there*. I know what went down. You literally said we needed to be honest with each other and then dodged the question. I need to know what the captain has on me." She sets the bottle down on the edge of the deck, then clutches her head in her hands as she sinks her elbows against her knees. "Please, just… tell me what won't get you killed."

At least she understands what I'm up against. I nod, taking another second to compose myself. "The captain knows we're… involved. I didn't have to tell her, but I did sort of confirm it. Vaguely. She knows something happened on the morning after we set out to get Bao." I shift my grip on the handhold, twisting to face out into the harbor. My breath hitches, and I push off the ship, sinking onto my back again as I point my toes toward the mouth of the bay. There's a slight tug at my feet that I have to counterbalance with my arms to keep the current from dragging me away from the *Minnow*'s side.

When I slide my eyes open, I catch Swift staring. She blushes when she looks away, and I can't help the little scoff that rises out of me. She's seen me in so many other lights. She's seen me naked. She's seen me as a sobbing wreck. She's seen me beaten down, broken in pieces, and she's never been embarrassed to look at me. What makes now so special?

When her gaze returns, it comes with a wry smile attached. "There's no way out of this," she says.

"No way out of what?"

"You. Me. The vicious cycle where Santa Elena pits us against each other and makes us lie until our lips bleed."

"Right. Better ways of making lips bleed."

She grimaces, running a hand over the back of her neck.

"Do you wish there were a way out?" I peer up at her, my arms jellyfishing, the churning sensation in my stomach growing as I realize just how much her answer matters to me.

Swift's lips go taut. "There used to be other girls on this boat."

"And there aren't anymore?"

"Oh, they're still there," she chuckles. "And it'd be a far safer thing to go back to them. Captain never tried to use any of *them* against me. But… fuck, I don't know. I don't know what I want. If I'm really safe and free to go my own way…"

I like the way hope sounds in her voice, no matter how

false it is in reality. But before I can get too comfortable, she opens her mouth again.

"I'm supposed to choose myself first. That's what the captain teaches. She wants me to be ruthless. That's supposed to be the smart choice. And I don't know if I can make smart choices when I'm around you. So I don't know if we're ever going to make this work."

The water around me does its best, but nothing can combat the sinking sensation at my core. I know what this means, what she's trying to say. I close my eyes, swallowing before I dare say anything back. But keeping still, keeping silent when she's around—that's just as unbearable. "Swift?" I ask.

"Yeah?"

"You kind of deserve this." My eyes snap open as I throw up my arms and lock my grip around her ankles. She shrieks and thrashes, but not before I've yanked hard enough to topple her forward. Swift drops into the harbor waters with all the grace of a beached neocete. I push off her legs, trying and failing to keep my breath in my lungs as I dodge her flailing fists. The water mutes Swift's indignant shouts, and I swim deeper, enjoying—maybe a little too much—the distant sound of her calling for my blood.

When I surface, I barely get a chance to suck in a breath before she's raining down on me with a torrent of splashes and vicious curses. Swift seethes as I dodge her onslaught and backpedal with a few short kicks. "You little twerp," she finally hisses once she's calm enough to use her words in a less brute-force manner.

"Hey, equal footing," I shoot back at her as I spit out a mouthful of salt water. She shakes her head and swims for the trainer deck's edge with ungainly strokes brought on by her baggy clothes. When she hauls herself up and turns out toward me, I catch the outline of the tattoo on her chest through her drenched shirt, and in that moment I'm thankful for the chill of the water.

"I should probably… I don't want to answer the questions if the captain catches me in wet clothes," she mutters, scooping up her bottle. Swift turns her back and retreats. No pauses, no hesitations, no glancing over her shoulder. I'm tempted to get the last word in, but I don't know what it should be. So I just watch her go, waiting until I hear the trainer deck door close behind her.

20

Three days later, Lemon makes an announcement on the all-call for the captain and all trainees to report to a conference room on the second floor of Fung's compound. Everything about the situation sets me on edge, from the fact that we aren't meeting on the *Minnow* to the strange intensity of Lemon's voice, which rarely gets stretched beyond a flat monotone. Something big is going down, and as I hurry to the conference room, I feel a familiar rush of anxiety, like the days we were being hunted by the SRC.

But when I reach the room and burst through the doors, it's not an SRC armada that greets me, but a grim-faced Santa Elena with a laptop, as well as Fung, his batch of trainees, and Lemon. I sidle into the seat at Lemon's side, watching as the two captains mutter back and forth. "What's the deal?" I whisper to her, but Lemon gives a small shake of her head. Whatever the news, it's the captain's to deliver, not hers.

Swift's next to arrive. She resigns herself to the seat next to me, her scowl and slump letting me know exactly how she feels about it. Varma and Chuck come after, looking flustered enough to make me question the calculated interval between their appearances. When they slide into seats at the end of the conference table, Santa Elena clears her throat.

"The news isn't good, but I'm sure you lot guessed that," she starts. "This morning, we received a video call from the *Water Knife*. Their data places them a hundred miles off the Northern Republic of California's coastline." She plugs a jack into the laptop, and a display glows to life at the front of the room.

As soon as she plays the video, I feel like I'm going to vomit. The image is shaky, clearly taken from a phone, but even in the dawn's light I know what's happening. We're in the ship's navigation tower, and the deep bellows of a Hell-beast overtake the audio, so loud, so close that they max out the speakers. The deck of the *Water Knife* lurches, and Captain Kurosaki staggers into view. "Starboard guns, give it all!" she screams into her radio, then something in Japanese. "What the hell do you think you're doing?" Kurosaki snaps at the camera operator.

"Broadcast, Captain. Salt needs to see this," the operator replies. His voice sounds horrifically young.

"Good thinking, Chan," the captain says, slumping against the ship's control panels.

"Oh Christ, that's her lookout trainee," Swift groans beside me, and I take my eyes off the screen long enough to make sure that Lemon's okay. She shudders in the chair next to me, her fingernails digging into its armrests.

On the screen, Chan has shifted his camera so that we're looking out through the windows of the tower. The sea around the *Water Knife* boils, and I spot the glistening curves of a serpentoid Hellbeast rising and falling as the beast weaves around the ship.

My blood runs cold.

Serpentoids don't bellow. Their vocal cords aren't designed to dip that low.

Chan's camera tracks the serpentoid, then snaps across the sea to the *Water Knife*'s starboard flank, where a terrapoid monster twice the size of Bao cowers against the rain of bullets chugging out of the ship's guns.

"Incoming on port," someone shouts.

"All crew prepare for broadside! Helmsman, keep those engines spinning!" Kurosaki roars, and Chan's camera bobs up and down as he rushes to the other side of the navigation tower. The waves outside cut in a V-shape that I know all too well. The cetoid strikes the *Water Knife* with a thunderous crash, and the world onscreen tilts. Screams fill the air. Human screams.

The image shudders and shakes, the screen a blur of color. When it finally resolves, the camera's pointed at the ceiling. Chan's face pops into the frame as he scoops up the phone and swings it around, giving us a view of the navigation tower. Crewmembers cling to whatever they can, and in the center of it all, Captain Kurosaki stands tall, blood dripping from a cut on her forehead. "Engineering, report!" she coughs, then mutters another few words of Japanese.

I can't hear the garbled reply that comes through her radio, but when Kurosaki closes her eyes and inhales, I know exactly what it means. When she opens her eyes, her gaze lands on the camera. "Chan, give that thing to me," she says, and the image rushes to her side. She flips us to the front-facing camera and holds it at arm's length, running a hand over her mouth as she tries to compose herself.

"Brethren of the Salt. Or… whoever's listening. This morning, my crew sighted a serpentoid Hellbeast and gave pursuit. And, well… we found where they're all going." She tilts the camera out at the ocean, and murmurs rise from the trainees gathered in the conference room.

Around the *Water Knife*, the sea is alive with flukes and teeth and keratin plates. I start counting, but the constant seething movement makes accuracy nigh impossible. If I felt like I was going to vomit before, it's nothing compared to the way my stomach churns now. I should have suspected this. Should have had theories, should have warned the Salt to keep their distance. Going up against one Hellbeast— maybe the *Water Knife* could handle it. They brought down Uli, after all.

But against a pack, Kurosaki's helpless.

She turns the camera back to her face, but she's not ready for it—she's not a fearless leader, a pirate queen on her ship, in her rightful place. She's a woman scared out of her mind, struggling to keep her composure, and even as I see it, I feel part of myself recoil. But there's no dignified way to face this kind of death—there's only the quiet calm that she tries to wear as beneath her, the *Water Knife*'s limping engines sputter.

"Chan, how many have you sighted?" Kurosaki asks.

From off screen, Chan warbles, "Forty-seven individuals. So far."

She swallows. "Forty-seven of these beasts have banded together. Forty-seven pirate-born monsters. Some of them are young. Few of them are huge. A good chunk of them are—" Kurosaki cuts off as a clatter of gunfire rings out from the lower decks of the ship. "...aggressive," she finishes flatly. "Word from my engineers is the *Water Knife* will not make it out of here. So you had better fucking avenge us. Mark our coordinates. Stop this before our ocean pays the price." She closes her eyes and shakes her head. "I'm sorry for the part I had to play in all of this, and I'm sorry that I couldn't make my mark. Kurosaki out."

The silence that fills the room when the video stops is somehow worse than any of the nightmares on the screen. The image fades to black, replaced by an arrow twisting around in a circle, an invitation to replay the video that no one in this room wants to take. I break the stillness, leaning forward as I cradle my head in my hands. Forty-seven. Forty-seven, if Chan counted correctly. The number doesn't seem real. Doesn't seem quantifiable. It's around the size of the *Minnow*'s crew, but even if I assigned a beast to every person on our boat, I still couldn't conceive the scale of the Hellbeast pack.

It hurts to think of this many monsters born to people with no idea how to raise them, brought up in improvised conditions, and treated with none of the respect they deserve. There's no happy ending for beasts like them. They either grow until they've devoured the entire NeoPacific, or we'll find a way to kill them all before that happens. But with the Hellbeast population banded together, the latter seems nigh impossible.

The horrific reality of the pack sinks into my bones. When we made Reckoners, we made them emotional creatures. Needful creatures. Their brain chemistry was wired around a deep bond that would drive them to fight no matter the pain, no matter the consequences. I think of Durga, of the way she charged headfirst into the *Minnow*'s fire even as the cull serum was ripping her apart from the inside. I imagine the pups abandoned to a hungry world with that burning need inside them and nowhere to direct it. Nothing to love. Nothing to fight for.

Until they found each other.

"Cas…" Swift mutters next to me, but I don't want her concern right now. I want solutions. I want answers. I want Fabian Murphy carved open and tossed into the sea for what he did to these poor young beasts.

"Cas, your legs." Swift nudges my arm, and I realize that my fingers are wrenched into the flesh of my thighs so tightly that my nails have drawn blood. I let go, shaking my hands until they're loose. When I look up, I realize everyone in the room is looking at me.

"What?" I snap, and a muscle in Santa Elena's jaw

pulses. "You want me to bullshit some easy way out of this? You think I have answers?" I look around the conference room, desperate for an escape, but no one starts talking. "This is nothing we've ever faced before, from shore or from sea. This is new. This is *impossible*. A pack like this will burn through the NeoPacific in a matter of months. The damage they've done is already irreparable."

Fung looks like he's about to speak, but Santa Elena silences him with a twitch of her hand.

The quiet gnaws on me until my last frayed nerve shatters. I let out a sharp sigh. "Alright, fine—*fine*. If we're going to try anything, we'll need resources. Every gun we can get, every ship that will answer. If we could muster the whole Salt, what would that come out to?"

"Fifty crews, give or take," Santa Elena replies.

So we're roughly one pirate ship to every monster Chan counted. I close my eyes, trying to visualize how that would look, a pirate armada charging against a Hellbeast pack. All I can see is the way Bao's beak rips into Fung's yachts, the way his forelegs crush them, the way his claws shred through their hulls. If we run at the pack, there will be nothing left of us. These monsters are bred to sink ships, and even if only a handful of them are aggressive, there's no telling what they could do to a pirate fleet. It's more than a risk. It's suicide.

But if the pack goes unchecked, we're not just killing ourselves. The logical conclusion is clear—the pack would burn across the NeoPacific, devouring everything in its path. The monsters would eat until there was nothing left, until they starve themselves out and start eating each other. But by then, it'd be too late. The populations of neocetes, of whales, of fish would never be the same again. The Flotilla would starve. The other floating cities, the artificial islands, the shorebound pirate colonies. The SRC, NRC, and all the other states.

If the NeoPacific goes, we all go together.

"Bring them all in. All together. That's the only chance we have," I tell the captain, and relish the spark of pride shining in her eyes as she lifts her chin.

Fung shifts uncomfortably. "That might not be the best idea. Some of them probably bought into Murphy's trade. There'll be infighting before anything gets accomplished—they'll all be looking to blame someone for the way the world's gone to hell. Better to keep them separate. Spaced out."

Santa Elena shakes her head. "Then we'd have no control. The Salt needs more than just the ties that bind—we need focus to take this head-on."

"Captain, I have to object," Fung says, his eyes sweeping around the room—looking for dissenters on our side, I realize, as he zeroes in on the *Minnow*'s crew. "You yourself could be the target of it all—everyone knows you bought from Murphy."

"I wear my sin on my sleeve," she spits back, her eyes narrowing. "Where do you wear yours, *Captain*?"

The room goes deathly still. Fung's still dressed in his clean-cut, princely garb, but in this moment all I can see is the pistol he keeps holstered on the belt of his pleated slacks. The pieces of Fung's resistance fall into place. He's one of them—one of the pirates who bought into Murphy's trade, who paid good money for a stolen Reckoner pup. But he wasn't smart about it, not the way Santa Elena was. She made sure her pup was trained right. She has living, breathing proof of it. Fung has nothing to show to keep the Salt off his back. If they gather, if they learn what he's done, he'll be the first one they rip to shreds.

The first thing to move is Santa Elena's lips as she bares her shark-like smile. "The Salt will gather again. These oceans depend on it. And if any of them dare to forsake their sworn oaths, whether by turning on each other or by turning tail when we call..." She plucks her knife from her sleeve and throws it down on the mahogany table. Fung flinches toward his gun, but Santa Elena continues without batting an eye. "They'll have to answer to me."

There's only one captain in this room, and everyone knows it. The pretender nods, wiping his hands on his pants before he offers one to Santa Elena. As she shakes Fung's hand, I cut my gaze to Swift. She's rigid in the chair beside me, her hands twisted in her lap as she stares at Santa Elena, at everything she has to become if she makes it through this fight.

I look at Swift and see everything she stands to lose if she becomes it.

21

It takes nearly three days for me to find a free slot in the island's communications schedule. Every broadcast station is working around the clock to call the Salt in, ensuring that every single ship we can muster is bound for Art-Hawaii 26. It's left essentially no room for any other outbound calls. But I book an afternoon slot on a private station at last, and show up for the appointment ten minutes early.

The room is already in use by one of Fung's communications officers, who yells something in what I suspect is Tagalog loud enough that the door doesn't block the sound. He runs over his slot by a full two minutes, during which I stare at my watch and second-guess every single word I want to say, sitting cross-legged on the floor outside.

Whatever we're headed toward, there's a significant chance we won't walk away from it. Kaede Kurosaki's last moments still echo in my head—the fear in her voice, in her face, in the way she held the camera, and the way she stood tall despite all of it. She may have mounted a Reckoner head on the prow of her ship, but she faced the end with nobility and honesty.

And maybe it's time I started being a little more honest too.

"*Pasensya na*," the communications officer says when he swings the door open and finds me waiting. "All yours now."

The privacy of the room is overwhelming. Nothing but a computer at a desk, accompanied by a microphone and a lighting system for anyone doing visual broadcasting. The walls are coated with foam that dents nearly an inch when I lay my knuckles into it. I could break down, scream, cry—nobody would witness it. Not like the uplink café on the Flotilla.

I settle into the chair and pull up a fresh login screen. I fumble as I type, and it takes me three tries to get my password right before I'm staring at my inbox and the contacts listed down one side of it. Before I can let my fear, my nausea, my doubt overtake me, I slam down my cursor on the audio call icon next to Tom's name and bow my head as the speakers start to ring.

A minute of that repetitive, grating sound passes, and all the while I stare at my knees, at the marks my nails made in my thighs three days ago, at anything but the screen in front of me. He's not going to pick up. He knows better than to pick up. And just when I'm about to reach up and cancel the call, Tom answers.

"Cas?"

The words I had planned to say catch in my throat at the sound of my brother's voice. At the *hope* he radiates with the way he says my name, even if I'm imagining it. I inhale sharply, trying to find my starting place again. I really should have written it down. But all I end up saying, all that needs to be said at the moment, is, "Hi Tom."

He stutters for a minute, and I don't blame him. I came in with no warning, taking all the time I needed to prepare and giving him none. "You... You... *Why?*"

"I'm, uh... I wanted to talk," I say. The simple truths are the easiest.

On the other end of the line, there's a crackling pause as my brother breathes in.

I brace myself.

"Cas, what the fuck? No, seriously—what the *fuck* gives you the right to call out of nowhere, to—"

"Now hold on, you called *me* two weeks—"

"*You don't get to talk right now,*" Tom snaps. "I didn't join up with pirates. I didn't raise a fucking Reckoner for them. I didn't turn. And you're coming up on five months with the pirates, and you haven't seen fit to give us a single word until now—you just *call* like it's nothing? Did you even think about how I'd feel about this, or were you too busy frolicking through your fucked-up criminal world with your head up your own ass? Who the fuck do you think you are, Cas? Because you sure as hell aren't the sister I had who left on the *Nereid* five months ago."

It's my turn to breathe deeply, to sink into the silence

before answering. "I'm sorry. I don't know what else is worth saying to you, so I'll say it again: *I'm sorry*."

"You don't get to be sorry either."

"I read your e-mails." There's what could either be a scoff or a sharp breath on the other end of the line. "I *understand*, Tom."

"If you understand, why'd you wait until now?" he growls.

"Because I'm a coward. I'm scared and I'm weak and I'm every terrible thing you think about me. I couldn't do it when I had the chance a few weeks back, and I wouldn't have done it now, if I wasn't..." I don't know how to end that sentence, or if it even needs an end. He needs the whole story. It's his turn to understand. "Can you talk for long?" I ask, dropping my voice to a low mutter.

In return, I get the sound of shuffling feet and a door slamming. "Dad's out on a mission, and Mom's in the lab," Tom says. "I don't think she'll be back for a while." The screen flickers, and suddenly he's there, staring right into the camera. His desk is a mess of notebooks and textbooks, and I realize I've just interrupted him in the middle of his homework. The sight of something so normal, so distant, makes something rise up inside me like a wave, and all of a sudden the words I need to say won't come out. I force myself to look at his face and fight down the tears welling in my eyes. He's gotten a haircut recently, leaving it short and bristly, sticking up at awkward angles that he never tries to comb down. The video's quality is poor, but I suspect that the darkness on his chin is more than shadow. The idea of my little brother trying to grow out his beard nearly gets a laugh out of me. Nearly.

"Your turn," he prompts, gesturing at his screen.

I bow my head, blinking rapidly as I try my best to clear my eyes. I picture Santa Elena and the way she stands when she goes into battle, and I find myself straightening my spine to match. I click the video icon.

Tom's eyebrows rise as he takes me in. I watch him look me in the eye for the first time in five months, and it feels like the sixteen years before this never happened. After everything I've done, we're strangers to each other.

"I like the new hair," he says at last. "Suits… whatever else you've got going on."

"Thanks. The pup did half of it," I retort, and suddenly we're both smiling, just a little. Just enough. "I guess the beginning's as good a place as any to start."

I tell him about Durga's last days. He picked up bits and pieces of what happened from Mom, but when I tell him it was cull serum that tore her up from the inside, that the pirates had infiltrated our pens and poisoned her on shore, Tom's lip curls. "Fucking bastards," he snarls, and I agree with him, even as my thoughts meander guiltily over to how much I've forgiven Swift for it.

As I describe the pirate attack on the *Nereid*, his expression grows harder and harder, but he nods along as I walk through what happened when I was marched onboard the *Minnow*. "And the pill?" he asks.

It takes me a while to find the right words, to work past the horror inherent in remembering that moment. "I couldn't. Didn't. They threw me in a closet and it was the perfect opportunity, but I just couldn't force myself to… well, I almost did. I had it at my lips, and they walked in just then." *She* walked in just then, but I'm determined to keep Swift out of this story as much as I can.

So I move on to hatching Bao, to training him. Then to the months on the ship where I saw the way the pirates worked and lived, to the Flotilla and the world I saw there, the world we never get to hear about on shore. "Whole lives get lived on that raft," I tell him. "Every one of them innocent, but every one of them sustained on pirate-spilled blood. Whole lives that we ruin when we send beasts to kill with impunity."

He shifts in his seat, his eyes fixed on the papers spread in front of him as he mulls over my words. Several times he opens his mouth like he's about to say something, then breaks off, frowning. I let him think. Let him process. It took me months to wrap my head around the NeoPacific's complexities—I can afford to give him more than a minute.

"But you can't…" he finally starts. "You can't… just stand by while there are pirates hunting innocents. They're doing it to feed their families, sure, but that doesn't make it right. I still don't get why… why you…"

This is the part where I have to tell him, the part that determines whether my brother will be able to forgive me in the end. I look him in the eye and say, "Because the industry is rotten from the inside, and there's no saving it from the shore. Not after five months on a pirate boat, not while the man who's responsible for it all controls the strings of the entire Reckoner trade."

Tom blinks.

"Fabian Murphy's been marking viable pups as unviable, carting them off, and trading them to desperate pirates for a hefty cut. How do you think I would have sounded, coming off a pirate boat and telling people that?"

"*Murphy?* The guy's never got a hair out of place—how could he possibly be tangling with pirates?" Tom rubs at his head with both hands, his brow furrowed.

"That's his armor. That's what makes no one bat an eye when he tells them their pups failed criteria. But I saw him on the Flotilla. At the time it didn't make sense, but then I confronted the captain about where we'd gotten our pup and she told me up front. It was Murphy. It's all been Murphy." I sit back in the chair, pressing my fingers against my eyelids. "And now he's gone and fucked the entire NeoPacific."

An incredulous grin pops across Tom's face before he can take stock of what I said—he's never heard me swear that strongly before.

So while I've got him in a good mood, I delve into the events of the past month. First the cetoid in the Neo-Antarctic, then the cephalopoid at the Flotilla, and finally the transmission from the *Water Knife* and the implication behind it. More than forty of those beasts are running rampant in our waters, and as I keep talking, I watch my brother's face shift to match the horror I felt that day in the conference room.

"Last we heard, the pack was off the NRC coastline. So in a couple of days, that's... that's where we're headed."

Tom's jaw drops, and I wince. "You're *what?*"

I bite back the swell of emotion—I refuse even to identify what's rushing up my throat at the moment. "The pirates are coming together. Every last one of th—of us. We're going to go up against the pack with everything we have. And I don't know what's going to happen. I just know it's all we can do to save this ocean, so we have to *try*. So I had to try calling home too, just in case it's... it's..." It's too late to hold back the tears—I feel the swell, the burn, the leak of salt water out of the corners. But I'm past hiding it. I stare down the camera and let the tears fall where they will. This is the truth of me, and if it's the last chance I get, I want Tom to see it.

When Tom starts nodding, it feels like every weight inside me has lifted. "This... is a lot. I don't know what to think. I need time to work through it all."

"I wish I could give it to you," I say, my breath catching on the words. There's a sheen of something in his eyes too, something that makes me feel not so alone in this. "Look, I don't know what's coming next, and I don't know if I'll even live through it, but I know I owe you guys a better explanation. You and Mom and Dad. So please, just do me this favor—don't tell them anything yet. Don't tell them unless you're sure I can't."

Tom nods.

"I know it's early, but is there any chance you're ever going to forgive me for this?"

He looks right into the camera when he answers, and the thousands of miles between us feel like nothing in this moment. "I don't know, Cas. But you've got to believe that I'm trying."

He doesn't know what he's just said. He doesn't know what it does to me, but I think he sees a little of it. My shoulders go slack as I sink into the chair, an honest grin pushing past my tear-tightened cheeks. Tom's my brother, alright. And even if I never see him again, maybe there's hope for us yet.

22

After the call with Tom, I hustle down to the docks feeling lighter and more clearheaded than I've been since August. Even though my eyes are still red and swollen, I haven't stopped smiling. I know what I have to do. It's so ludicrously simple—it's been in plain sight all along. And if I'm right about my suspicions, then maybe, just maybe, we stand a chance against the Hellbeast pack.

When I board the *Minnow*, I spot Varma sunning himself in nothing but a pair of board shorts on the fore of the main deck. He tilts his sunglasses down when he sees me, his brow furrowing. "Another fight? Really?" he shouts. As I approach, his confusion deepens. "But… you're smiling," he says once I'm towering over him. "Okay, I'm not playing a guessing game with your weird love life. Give it to me straight."

"This isn't about Swift," I tell him, offering a hand. He

takes it, and I pull him up. "I think I cracked something, but I need a pilot and a Splinter to test it out. Want in?"

His smile twitches a notch wider. "Sounds fun. I'll go put on a shirt."

Two minutes later, I've donned my wetsuit, my Otachi duffle slung over my back and packed with the rest of my armor. Varma meets me at the aft Splinter dock, and I clamber into the needleboat after him, my whole body shaking with a kind of energy I haven't felt in ages. "Is it weird to feel this happy when your whole life's going to hell?" I ask as I pull the restraints over my shoulders.

"Nah, that's just optimism," Varma replies. "It looks good on you."

Before I have a chance to retort, he jams down the undocking button. The pneumatics jolt us sideways, and I bite down a scream as the Splinter plunges into the harbor. "I'm never going to get tired of that," Varma says the moment we settle. He spins the engines up and sets us in a lazy cruise away from the docks.

I slouch into the seat and unzip my duffle. As we prowl into the open waters of the harbor, I unsnap my restraints and start suiting up. Just days ago, this would have been a straightforward ride, a simple sprint for the maw of the crescent. But in the past three days, pirate boats from all across the NeoPacific have arrived. Fung ran out of docking slots on the first day, and the rest of them have been dropping anchor, haphazardly along the inner ring of the bay's curvature, creating a maze of hulls that Varma weaves through with a mix of reverence and caution. Brush up against any of these ships and we run the risk of being gutted before our own captain can get a word in.

I strap on my chestpiece, my fingers slipping on the clasps that hold it in place. Up until now, my training of Bao has been confined to the trainer deck—I haven't worn the armor since the day we brought him in.

"So, the plan?" Varma asks as we swing around the hull of what looks like a repurposed SRCese warship, its red and gold painted over but still visible.

I snap the Otachi onto my right arm. "Training as usual. With a fun twist."

"You're talking like the captain, and I don't love it," he deadpans, but he keeps driving. I pull my mask and respirator around my neck, set my helmet on, and roll my head back, watching the pirate guns pass above us like tree branches. All of these weapons, ready to carve into Hellbeast flesh. And yet the greatest weapon of all is lurking in the deep waters just outside the harbor mouth.

I set the Otachi to the homing signal the second we clear the horns. Bao surfaces a minute later, his blowholes trumpeting slightly as he lets out a stale breath. "Bring me up next to him," I tell Varma.

"Swear to me he's not going to take a swipe at my ride," he retorts. "Santa Elena will hang me from the nav tower if she loses another Splinter."

"On my honor as a pirate."

He lets out a faint *hmph*, just audible over the engines' whine, and twists the wheel. We glide across the smooth afternoon seas, drawing up along Bao's good eye. He watches us, his muscles tensing as the distance narrows. I double-check the armor's flotation, set my mask over my eyes, and then vault over the Splinter's edge. The NeoPacific plays a game of catch and return with my body, enveloping me before spitting me right back up as the floatation drags me back to the surface.

When I get my bearings, I find Bao staring me down, his eye skimming just above the ocean's surface. He tilts his head, bringing me into his shadow as he moves closer. I swim to his side and run a hand over the familiar holds in his skin and spikes. Beneath me, his muscles start to relax.

So I might be right about this.

"C'mon," I murmur, crimping my fingers in one of his keratin plates. "Don't you dare try anything." I let my arm take some of my weight, and a snort rings out above me as Bao's blowholes flare. I run the tip of my foot over the plates on his jaw, then slot my toes on a spiny ridge. His eye goes narrow. He remembers what happened the last time I tried this stunt.

"Varma, fall back," I hiss. "You're making him nervous."

"*I'm* making him nervous?" he retorts, the comm in my ear snapping with his words, but the whine of the engines grows focused as Varma spins the Splinter and retreats toward Art-Hawaii 26. Even though the distance puts Bao at ease, it winds me up more than I'd like. If things go south now, there's no easy escape.

I lean forward, pressing my chest against the side of his head as I shift my full weight onto him, and he responds just the way I want, rolling his head so that I'm lifted out of the water. His eye stays fixed on me, and I hold out my Otachi-clad arm, my fingers splayed to show him that I'm not going to give him any signals. The keratin beneath me creaks as his muscles slacken even more.

Next come the line hooks. I unspool the first line and jab the barb into his keratin plate, leaning back to test its hold with my weight. Once I'm certain it's stable, I pull a second hook from my belt.

Which is when it all goes to hell. Some distant noise—a backfiring engine, a discharging cannon, something else loud and sudden—cracks across the water, and Bao spooks. Before I have a chance to pull the Otachi, before I even have a chance to scream, he ducks his head, plunging beneath the waves. My instincts kick in, my mouth clamping shut just before I go under, but a half-breath does little good when I'm being dragged to the depths on a line attached to a sea monster the size of a warship. My ears pop, and I scrabble for my respirator, cramming the device into my mouth as the light around me fades. I let my lungs loose, and a cloud of bubbles bursts around my face. The device spins to life, my next inhale full of crisp, sea-flavored oxygen.

But I'm not out of the woods yet. He's dragged me deep, and if we stay down here for long, I run the risk of decompression sickness upon resurfacing. Already my ears are gearing up to pop for a second time, and I dig my teeth into the respirator's rubber as the pain in my head builds. I kick off the side of Bao's head, reorienting my body so that

I'm pointed along the line of his beak, and tug hard on the Otachi triggers.

The homing signal flares, and Bao falters beneath me. His pupil shrinks against the laser's brilliant light. I edge the beam closer to his eye, a warning that he can't ignore. He slows, and I twist the dial to the *stay* patterning.

He stops immediately.

"That's right," I grunt into the respirator. "Listen for once, you twit." I shake my head, trying to jar the pressure loose, then pinch my nose and blow to equalize. With my brain a little clearer, I find the second line hook dangling from my belt and root it into Bao's plating. Once I've regained my footing, I nudge him up with quiet bursts from the Otachi. We inch our way back to the surface slowly, pausing every twenty feet to give my blood a chance to breathe. The light grows around us until finally, finally we break into the sunlight. I spit out the respirator and suck down a gasp of unprocessed air, collapsing against Bao's head.

Another distant bang rings out, and the Reckoner hitches underneath me, his eye rolling wildly. I tug the Otachi, and the homing signal calms him before he tries to dive again. I have no idea who or what could be making noises like that on a peaceful island in the middle of the afternoon—all I know is that Bao's got beef with them.

A twinge of guilt curls through me as I remember what lies on the other side of his head. He's well within his rights to shy away from anything that sounds like cannon fire. But if he's going to be in the thick of a fight again, I need him to be better than that. I need him to be unshakeable. There's too much riding on it.

"You're okay, little shit," I croon against his plating, feeling just a little ridiculous. It shouldn't even be reasonable for a tiny human voice to calm a monster of his size. But I feel it—feel the tension fading beneath me. Because I've worked it out. I solved it.

Bao's emotional bond isn't to the *Minnow*. He's never treated it the way other terrapoids treat their companion ships. Even when she was too young and untrained to defend it, Durga used to nestle up to the *Nereid* like it was her favorite thing in the world. But Bao's hold on the *Minnow* has never been as tight, and I should have realized it the day he followed the sinking Otachi into the depths, leaving the boat behind for a simple signal.

He isn't attached to the ship. He's attached to *me*.

The ship didn't guide him through a tangle with three trained Reckoners. The ship didn't find him in the middle of a storm and scream in his ear to bring him back to what he once was. Normal Reckoners are taught by a rotating cast of trainers, making their companion ship the one constant in their lives, the place where their focus falls. But Bao had two constants—the ship and his trainer. His stupid turtle brain latched onto the latter and stuck.

Once I'm sure he's calmed, I prop myself against the line hooks, my toes dug in above his jaw and my weight balanced on the belt at my hips. Bao leans with me, tilting his head to accommodate the extra luggage hanging off him. A laugh bubbles out of me as hope takes root.

This just might work.

"Hey Varma?"

"Yeah?" he replies immediately. If he saw us go under, he doesn't sound phased. I guess he's optimistic too.

My grin turns wicked. "I'll give you a five-second head start."

He wastes three of his seconds trying to figure out what I mean. On two, he spins the engines until they shriek. On one, he streaks across the NeoPacific, his tail pointed squarely at us.

When my countdown hits zero, I twist the Otachi to *charge* and squeeze the triggers until my fingers pinch and burn. Bao's hesitation is momentary—present, but nowhere near the way he struggled when we trained from the *Minnow*'s deck. He lifts his head, lofting me higher as his legs send us careening forward. We pick up speed, and the sea wind breaks over my face. Its salt has never tasted sweeter.

Varma knows the game doesn't work if he goes in a straight line—no matter how massive, terrapoids can't close on a Splinter at full tilt. As we speed up, he cuts left and right, burning off his momentum until we're within snapping distance. He flashes a coy grin over his shoulder, then reaches into his gunner station and flips a switch. "Clip's disengaged, blanks are in," he shouts into the comm over the roar of the engines. "Ready for some fun?"

"Bring it," I reply, adjusting my footing in Bao's plates. He tenses, feeling the change. "With me, big guy. With me," I mutter.

The Splinter veers right, curving into Bao's blind side,

and I swing the Otachi to match, leaning up to peer over the crest of his head. Varma spins out, his guns pointed at us, and just as Bao's head comes around, he fires.

The noise of the blank shot cracks across the NeoPacific, and Bao's pupil dilates. He drops his jaw and roars, his fury barely shielded by my helmet and earpiece. I pull the Otachi triggers, flashing the *charge* signal out to our left, but Bao's focus is caught on the Splinter, on the source of the threat. He launches himself at the needleboat, and my earpiece snaps with Varma's sharp inhale as he rockets the Splinter just out of Bao's reach.

As the boat ducks into his blind spot, I flare the Otachi again, this time slashing the beams within inches of his eye. Bao jolts, then leans toward the line of the lasers, and my spine goes slack as he finally takes the command. Once we sink into the turn, I edge the beams back toward Varma, and Bao responds immediately. I can sense it beneath me— how his instincts are firing on all cylinders, how much he wants to wreck that boat.

But it's not boats he'll be wrecking if this all goes right, and I need that idea out of his head. So as soon as he's on the Splinter's tail, I say, "Varma, again. On his left this time."

Varma careens into a wide turn, his guns swinging their sight on us, and lets off a spray of blanks that snap and pop like firecrackers. Bao's head whips toward the Splinter, and I almost lose my footing—I have to drop my signals and clutch at his plates to ensure I don't slip. By the time I've recovered, he's charging right at Varma. I pull the *charge* signal again and point it to the right. A frustrated warble rolls out of Bao, but he swings in the lasers' direction, following me into his blind spot, trusting that I'm pointing him in the right direction.

A familiar rush washes through me. The power, the glory of being the most dangerous thing in these waters. Even the distant threat of the pack can't dampen it. If we can work him past his trauma, we might save these oceans. We might stand a chance after all.

I swing the beams back onto the Splinter's wake. "Again."

23

When we glide up to the docks, my smile matches Varma's. I keep trying to hide it, to settle my face back into the neutral mask I've grown accustomed to wearing on the *Minnow*, but I can't help it—I'm pumped up. As the claws snap around our hull and winch us up to the aft docking mounts, I shuck out of my armor with trembling fingers. With every piece that comes loose, my muscles rejoice. The adrenaline is wearing off, and the exhaustion is setting in. By the time the Splinter settles into its mounts, I have everything packed up in the duffle, ready for the inevitable training session tomorrow.

I left my radio on the trainer deck. I vault out of the copilot's seat and scramble over Varma, the good news burning inside me. I want the captain to know exactly what we've accomplished here. I want to scream it from the roof of Fung's palace.

But when I hear the thunder of running footsteps echo down the hall, my grin cracks in half. Swift skids into the Splinter dock, her hair wild. She gulps in a huge breath, then gasps, "Murphy. He's here. They found him."

My stomach turns. The noises that triggered Bao earlier—they weren't backfiring engines. And I ignored them. I got so wrapped up in training. I throw down my duffle and break into a sprint, blowing past Swift as I rush for the *Minnow*'s upper levels. The thud of Swift's and Varma's feet chase me through the ship and up the ladders.

I spot the crowd the moment I break into the sunlight. A seething knot of pirates parades from the island to the docks, marching a barefooted figure in front of them. As I rush down the gangway and throw myself headlong at the approaching crowd, I get a good look at the man who single-handedly destroyed our oceans.

Fabian Murphy has seen better days. His gray eyes flash wildly as he's shoved from all sides by hands and gun barrels, and he clutches his left arm with his right, staunching the flow of blood from a bullet wound in his forearm. He's clad in nothing but a t-shirt and silk pajama bottoms, like he was lounging before the pirates found him. When he spots me running toward him, he freezes in his tracks.

"What the hell is going on here?" I roar over the clamor, and the docks go still. A jolt of surprise runs through me—I didn't expect to be listened to. Before I can demand an explanation again, a familiar hand lands on my shoulder, yanking me back before I can charge at Murphy.

"They found him holed up in one of Fung's private

rooms," Santa Elena says. "Apparently he's been here since before the Salt convened, waiting for this all to blow over so he could make a clean exit."

"He can forget about that," one of the other captains chuckles, nosing his automatic into Murphy's back. "We're gonna hang this fucker from the docks."

The IGEOC agent's bulging eyes meet mine. "Please, Cassandra," he pleads. "Don't let them—" His next words are lost in a chorus of laughter that rises from the pirates surrounding him.

As the shock fades from my blood, I realize that I'm shaking under the captain's steady hand. It takes me an extra second to name what's doing it. Not fear—even if I weren't riding the high of being strapped to a Reckoner, the chemical cocktail in my head is nowhere near fear. No, it's like a *destroy* signal has been flared in front of my eyes. Pure wrath boils in my veins.

"I am a citizen of the Southern Republic of California. Under the laws—" But before he can finish, the pirates are laughing again. Murphy turns, seeking out the faces he knows. "Come on—Omolou, you can't... Stern, please?" He lifts his eyes imploringly to each captain. "Elena, I know you wouldn't—"

Her gun is out before he has a chance to finish his sentence. "You know nothing about me, Fabian Murphy, and you will address me by my full name or not at all." She levels the barrel between his eyes, and some of the pirates surrounding him shrink back.

No. Before I comprehend what I'm doing, I've stepped

217

into her line of sight, the barrel of her gun pointing right at my throat. The captain's eyes widen fractionally, but she doesn't let her cool mask slip. A familiar hungry spark lights up her gaze, the same look she wore when Swift took over in the fight to take down the cephalopoid. Santa Elena wants to see what I'll do next.

I grab the barrel of the captain's gun and rip it out of her grasp. She releases the weapon willingly, her hand dropping instead to the knife on her belt. "He's mine," I growl, low and serious.

Then I settle my fingers around the grip, turn on my heel, and point the gun at Murphy's forehead.

The world goes still. Everything slows, and in the space between two heartbeats, clarity tries to sink its claws into me. Isn't this what I'm supposed to do? Isn't this why I forsook the shore and threw away any hope of redemption?

Isn't this what the captain was supposed to shape me into?

Santa Elena makes no move to stop me. None of the pirates do. They must recognize that whatever is supposed to happen to this man, I'm the one with the right to dole out his justice. Murphy's shoulders sag, and he closes his eyes like he knows exactly what he deserves.

My finger itches for the trigger. I think of the devastation his greed has wreaked on these oceans. The thin catch, the way the fisheries will struggle for years to come. The untrained Hellbeasts, hungry for an ocean that can never sustain them. Kurosaki's crew and everyone else his bastard monsters have ever killed.

Electric green eyes. Santa Elena's knife. A laughing crowd at the captain's back, clamoring for blood. Femoral artery. Clean slice.

Justice.

My stomach turns. Every savage grin around me burns into my skin like a brand. I feel the steady pulse of that phantom *destroy* signal humming through my bones, but my hands start to shake on the pistol's grip. Three months ago, I watched a traitorous boy get dragged to the edge of the trainer deck and carved open in retribution for the way he had wronged us. And I fought tooth and nail to stop it, even though no one would listen to me.

That girl is oceans away from the moment I'm locked in. And just by being in this moment, holding a gun to Fabian Murphy's head, I know there's no going back.

The disgust surges up my throat with an impulse on its heels. I lower the captain's gun. Murmurs rise around me, but beneath them, there's the lap of waves against the dock's supports. The distant roar of the ocean. *No matter where I stand.*

The gun's such a heavy thing. The metal drags at my shoulders, but my shoulders have been strengthened by the weight of the Otachi. And in the end, it barely takes more than a flick of my wrist to send Santa Elena's pistol sailing end over end into the harbor waters.

I almost laugh to fill the silence that follows. What can they do to me? What can any of them do to me when I'm their best chance against the Hellbeast pack? I turn, expecting to see Santa Elena's teeth bared, expecting to see the calculation in her eyes as she figures out how to punish me for pitching her gun into the harbor.

But she's just staring at me. Her gaze is even. Hollow. Waiting.

"This does nothing." My voice comes out shaky, and I glance around. I half-expect to see the pirates with their guns out, shifting their aims to me, and my words get stuck in my throat when I realize that none of them have. Some of them are even lowering their weapons. The momentum of their revenge has broken.

They're listening.

"Killing him doesn't *do* anything," I choke at last. "We're pissed off. We're running out of time. We need to use that anger and that pressure, but not like this."

Santa Elena's eyes narrow. "Give me a solution then," she says. "What do we do with this man? What does *your* justice look like?"

I turn to Murphy. He clenches his wound tighter, his eyes shimmering as he stares right back, silently pleading for my mercy. It's less than he deserves. But death isn't what he deserves either. "The ship you came in on. Is it yours?"

He nods.

"And it's still on the island?"

Another nod.

I advance on him, squaring my shoulders and lifting my chin, trying to summon everything inside me that makes me look like the captain's favorite. "Get in your boat. Put this place to your back and keep running until you find somewhere where no one knows your name or what you've done. I promise it's going to be harder than it sounds. Word's spreading on these oceans, and I can't guarantee the same mercy from the next people who find you. Live out the rest of your miserable little life unknown. That's my justice."

Murphy lifts his chin, his eyes narrowing. He looks paler than usual, likely due to blood loss. But there's a dangerous spark in him, one that would have made me shrink back the last time I saw him. "And what about the rest of your life, Cassandra Leung?" he spits.

The captain's trained me into a passable liar, but I can't stop the slight hitch in my voice when I tell him, "I'll figure something out." I lift my gaze to the pirates that surround us. "You'll let him go, hear me? Or my beast might not be there when you need it."

Some of them nod, others glare, but none of them stop Fabian Murphy from staggering down the docks to a private cruiser that we all assumed was one of Fung's. No one makes a move until the boat's disengaged from the docking arms and spinning up its engines. I turn my back on the pirates, brush past Santa Elena, and make my way up the *Minnow*'s ramp, where Swift and Varma are waiting. Murphy's boat streaks through the horns of the crescent and out into the safety of open waters.

Once he's out of sight, I let the weakness in my knees take over, slumping against the railing of the main deck. A shadow crosses me as Santa Elena steps off the gangway. She gives me a small, taut smile that I definitely don't deserve. Her fingers are clenched around her radio. "Fung's locked up in his glass house for the moment, but he's ordering us all off the island before something goes sideways. We've got twenty-four hours to clear out—otherwise he'll turn the harbor guns on us."

"And once we're clear?" I ask.

The captain's eyes darken. "Thanks to Murphy, our situation is no longer stable. He apparently did a spectacular job of outing every single captain he sold to who's on this island. The infighting is going to start up soon unless we give the Salt a distraction. Which means it's best if we launch the assault immediately."

Any last drops of optimism inside me evaporate in a flash. I only just cracked Bao—we need more time to get him truly ready for a battle. But from the way the captain stands, one anxious hand on her empty holster, there's no way we're going to get that time. The Salt gathering was never a stable situation to begin with. Striking out against the pack is the only way we can salvage this mess.

I give the captain a short nod.

She moves like she's about to stride off, then pauses, leaning close. "Guns are replaceable, Cas," she murmurs. "You aren't."

Instinctively I try to twist her words into the hardness I've come to expect from the captain. My skill as a trainer— my *value*—isn't replaceable. That's what she means. But there's a flash of something softer in her eyes, something that tells me she meant exactly what she said. It guts me like a hooked knife, leaving nothing behind but a deep, persistent sense of shame. Santa Elena sweeps across the deck to the navigation tower. "Varma, with me," she says at the base of the ladder.

He turns to follow her, pausing only to glance between me and Swift and then waggle his eyebrows.

I should have let Bao eat him when I had the chance.

And then we're alone again, and just like every other time, it feels completely different. Alone with Swift is never the same thing twice. There's always something new in the mixture, some event that flavors the air between us. We don't have a "normal," I realize as I push myself upright on the railing. Maybe we never will.

"That was… that was a hell of a thing," she says at last. She stares at a point in the harbor—probably the spot where the captain's gun went beneath the waves—then raises her eyes to meet mine.

"I…" What am I supposed to say? I'm still trying to process what just happened, and the thing between us is so uncertain. "We made progress with Bao today," I blurt. "He might be ready."

Wrong answer. She turns, her shoulders squared, and makes for the ladder to the lower decks.

"I called my brother this morning."

That gets her. Swift spins back, shock written over her face. "You… How did that go?"

I give her a weak smile. I'm not entirely sure where it comes from. "There was some shouting. A lot of shouting, actually. Mostly from him, which I kinda deserve. And crying too. Mostly from me."

"Mostly?"

"Hey, I swear he had something in his eye."

She chuckles. Takes another step closer. The tightness in my chest lifts with every inch that collapses between us. I can't let hope start now, not with the Hellbeasts ahead. The question of the future, which used to be so terrifying, is now so utterly simple. The only future ahead of us is the one where we run headlong into that Hellbeast pack, and whatever comes next—I can't even think about it, can't dare to wish that it happens.

But because it's so far off and impossible, it's so easy to let this time be what it is, an awkward pocket between now and the moment that decides our fates. And in this little bubble, there's room for her coming closer. Room for her putting her arms around me, even though we're out in the open. Room for the small, desperate laugh that I breathe into her shoulder. I wind my arms as tight as they'll go, sinking into the solidity of her, the sureness in this moment.

The moment I remember what lies ahead, I feel her tense up as if she's been hit by the same thought as I have. Her fingers dig into my waist, and she whispers those familiar words: "Cas... what are we doing?"

But she's not letting me go. She's not pulling away. There's no room for secrets between us, no room for much of anything, but I'm not pulling away either. Her question hangs in the air, and I don't have a good answer for her. The only response I have is the push of my forehead against her shoulder as my knees get a little weaker. She understands—I can tell by the way she breathes in, sharp and sudden.

What breaks us apart at last is the snap of the all-call.

Santa Elena's voice announces that we'll be shoving off in an hour, and suddenly there's three feet between me and Swift, as if the captain's here instead of up in the navigation tower.

And just like that, we're going. The sound of the all-call fades, leaving the main deck eerily quiet. From deeper in the ship, I can hear the muffled sounds of crewmembers rushing to stations, getting the preparations underway. There are things both of us should be doing.

A look from Swift tells me we're better off doing them.

24

I lose track of time in the hours and days that follow. From the moment I arrive at our captain's side as we undock from Art-Hawaii 26, I'm expected to be on call for every single strategy meeting she convenes among the Salt. None of these meetings are in person—it's safer to leave each crew to their own ship after Murphy named names, but the trade-off is significant. Accomplishing anything involves a lot of yelling, a lot of repeating oneself, and a lot of swearing. At a certain point, Santa Elena's voice gives out and Lemon steps in, ferrying the words the captain rasps into her ear across the channels in a voice that's strikingly similar to hers.

I sit on the floor next to the communications desk, letting the captain's composition wash over me and jerking awake every time Lemon prods me at her behest. Santa Elena's painting a picture of a structured battle, but if I know anything about Hellbeasts, it's going to be anything but that. She wants formations, tiers of ships, attack patterns.

And she wants me leading the charge. I would have had far fewer objections before I discovered Bao's little secret about where his loyalties lie. Santa Elena's strategy has me front and center, strapped to Bao's head at the point of the blade she wants to use to carve the Hellbeast pack apart. Even if we win, I know it in my bones—there's no surviving this fight for me.

But maybe I don't deserve that, and maybe I'm okay with it.

To keep awake, I try to memorize the ships in the formation as we throw ourselves across the NeoPacific. The *Minnow* keeps to the center of the pack, making it difficult for Bao to follow us in the knot of hulls that press in from all sides. Constantly in our shadow is the *Crown Prince*. I was stunned to find that Eddie Fung had accompanied us when he shooed the Salt off his island, but when Santa Elena spots my raised eyebrows, she shrugs and says, "Fung only gets to own these oceans if they're still around after this." I resolve to be impressed enough for the both of us if she won't give him any respect at all.

Beyond a certain point, I'm useless, and the captain finally realizes it when it takes three solid pokes from Lemon to get my eyes open. The exhaustion I feel is set deep in my bones, and when Santa Elena relinquishes me, muttering something about my fortitude and the way it lacks, it's an honest miracle that I make it down the ladder from the navigation tower without seriously injuring myself. I peer at the overcast sky through blurry eyes as I cross the main deck. It looks like morning. I *think* it's morning. All I know is I need a bed, and I need it soon.

I don't make a decision about *which* bed that is until I find myself facing down the row of crew bunks. It'd be slightly easier to slump into my own room, the first in the row, but instead I stagger down to Swift's door, running my hand along the bullet-pocked, wood-paneled wall for support. I crack the door open, casting a sliver of light that cuts across the back of her neck, illuminating the Minnow tattoo at her nape.

Swift stirs in her sleep, and I slip into the room, closing the door quietly behind me. It's no surprise that she's here—like me, she's been run down by all the strategy meetings and prep. In the semi-dark of her room, I feel my way to the bed and sit on the edge, kicking off my shoes. She stirs again, rolling half-over. Her lips part like she's about to say something, but all that comes out is a brief hiss of air that isn't quite a sigh.

I collapse backward, her vinyl mattress crunching as my weight rolls over it. Swift reaches out and curls an arm around me, pulling me into her chest. I press my forehead against her collarbone. Her heart beats a rapid tattoo against my skull, and for a moment I'm fooled into thinking it's just like the way this started all those months ago—us in this bed, locked away in our little subdimension of the *Minnow*.

I slide one arm over her waist and lean into the illusion,

letting it cradle me until, at last, my exhaustion takes over and I go limp in her arms.

When I wake up, Swift's a step ahead of me. My eyes slide open, and immediately she pulls back, her chin dragging along the top of my head. "Time?" I ask. My voice comes out low and hoarse.

"No earthly idea," she replies.

"Good," I mutter in the instant before her lips crush over mine. Her kiss is slow, languid, her hand curling up around my neck as she pulls me deeper into it. A barrage of thoughts flickers through my head—*this can't happen, this shouldn't happen, this* has *to happen, I need this to happen*—before every last one of them is banished by the way her other hand snakes up under my shirt. I melt against Swift, my hips hitching as I roll to straddle her.

This could be the last chance we get. The last time we're able. Desperation drove the first time we kissed, and it's the thing driving us now. My hands find purchase in the pillow on either side of her head as her fingers skim below my waistband and then lower.

She reduces my vocabulary to a single word—just her name, over and over, until it becomes less than that, a series of jolting breaths into the cold air. I lose track of where we are, what we're doing, what's ahead. All that's left is impulse, need, and hunger. All that's left is me and her and the quiet murmuring between us.

I'm not afraid anymore, even though there's still so much unsaid, even though we still have secrets we haven't confessed, even though Swift's still a dangerous creature. I'm dangerous too in my own right, and I make sure she knows it.

We go slow. We take all the time we need, every second that's been left for us. I try to memorize her with my hands, every curve and swell of her, every ripple of her muscles, every careful way her mouth moves.

And she—

She tries to devour me.

25

The exhaustion wins again, for a little while. When I wake up next, Swift's still asleep, her back turned to me, her hands curled against her bare chest. I kick on the dim lights, rummage into her drawers, and pull on a clean shirt—a familiar striped one from the days when my only clothes on this ship came from her wardrobe. It hangs off my shoulder, and as I sit back on the edge of the bed, I find myself breathing in the smell of her that graces it. It feels a little ridiculous to be savoring a shirt when the living, breathing thing is sleeping just inches away from me.

It feels even more ridiculous when I realize she isn't sleeping anymore.

"Morning," she says, even though neither of us have any idea whether that's true. Swift pushes herself upright, a lazy smile tugging at the corners of her lips as she yanks on her discarded tank.

I'm not sure whether it's the best idea to grin back, but I do anyway. Fuck the solemnity of this messed-up day—whatever day it is. We're both probably going to be dead soon. Smiling's one of the few things we have left to enjoy.

But as I lean a little closer, the smile fades from her lips, replaced by something far more serious. There are words she's trying to conjure—I can tell from the strain in her eyes. Swift has never been good with words. And from the way she grapples with these ones, I know I'm not going to like them.

I wait.

She does too. She holds back until the moment when the words are on her tongue and she can look me in the eye at the same time. "I… I love you," Swift blurts, and even by the second word, she realizes that there's nowhere for this to go but down.

A horrible, sinking feeling rips through my heart, leaving a hole where the right words should be. Love is a promise. It's a word with the future in mind, and the future's anywhere but where my mind should be. And even though it kills me to admit it, I can't make the same promise. I don't love her. Or what I feel for her doesn't feel like it deserves to be called "love." Doesn't feel whole, doesn't feel right to give it a word that means so much.

What I end up saying is, "You shouldn't." What I want it to mean is, *You can't.*

Her face struggles to keep its armor. She drops her gaze to her knees, twisted in the bedsheets, and in this moment she looks so small, so unlike anything I know her to be. "I just… I wanted you to know before—" Swift's voice breaks on the thought. There's something nauseating about it.

"Look," I say.

She doesn't.

"When we go up against what's out there, there are no promises. No guarantees. You can't just say something like that like you expect…"

"Like I expect what, Cas?"

"Like you expect it to change anything."

It cuts deep. Her lips twist as she tries to keep her face neutral. "If we die out there, I don't want any secrets between us. I don't want to go to the depths with that on my conscience. I've got too many other regrets—I won't let this be one of them."

I press the heels of my palms against my eyes. "You want no more secrets?" I can't help the harsh edge building in my voice. "I'm about to die anyway—what's the point in keeping the captain's?"

Her breath freezes in her chest. I wait a moment, partly to be sure that she's stopped breathing, mostly to give her a chance to stop me. But she wouldn't, won't, doesn't.

"She's playing you, Swift," I say, low and quiet, because god knows what other ears are listening in. But I don't leave it at that—Swift deserves to know the whole truth, even though I can feel it shredding me to admit the secrets I've kept from her. "She's set up this whole twisted, convoluted system to goad you into being her perfect heir. The captain's carving you up in her own image, and she knows exactly what buttons to push to turn you desperately loyal."

I can't look at her for this next part. I turn away.

"The out you have isn't an out at all. She pulled strings to get your family into a stable situation. She'll hold that over you the instant you lean away from what she wants. Even the way she treats me—she's using me to bait you, by making you think I'm in her favor. She made me keep secrets and push you away and act... God, I don't even know where what she wants stops and what I want begins anymore."

The horror of what I've said hits me at the same time it hits Swift. All this time the captain's been slicing away at Swift, and only now do I see the truth of what I've been.

I'm the knife.

I push off the bed, gather my clothes in my arms, and make my exit without another word. Swift doesn't try to stop me.

I give up. The captain's won. I bought into her game, never questioning what I'd have to sacrifice to be her pawn. There's a reason she's held her place as captain for ten years. There's a reason I've gotten nowhere in the months since I came to her side.

I'm all boiling fury with nowhere to direct it. I storm to my bunk and change into my worst, baggiest, splotchiest clothes, making sure to throw Swift's shirt into the corner on the floor where it belongs. Barefooted and pissed, I slam the door behind me and make my way down to the Slew.

It used to be nothing but the captain's orders that could get me down here, but I storm onto the training ground without an inch of hesitation. No one else is here. I still have no idea what time it is, but the emptiness of the hold suggests it might be the middle of the night. The Slew is wrapped in the quiet drone of the engines, which echoes in the empty space. Suspended from the beams toward the fore of the ship is a set of punching bags. That's exactly what I need right now.

I don't bother to wrap my knuckles or put on gloves. I lay hit after hit into the sack in front of me, my skin burning with each punch I throw. A steady rhythm sinks into my muscles as I keep going, but no matter what, my mind won't clear. I strive for emptiness, for nothing but me and the punching bag and the metronome of hits. I fail. The bag is Santa Elena. The bag is every beast that could kill me today. The bag is my own stupid choices.

"Holy shit, shoregirl."

I pause, glancing over my shoulder. Chuck stands in the door of the hold, rubbing one hand over her eyes. Her wild hair is bound back in a plait, and the baggy clothes she wears suggest that she was in the middle of sleeping when I came crashing down here. "Sorry," I mutter, leaning into the cushion of the bag.

"No, by all means, keep going. See how many people you can wake up before one of us shoots you. If Varma gets his scrawny ass down here, we can start betting on it."

I roll my eyes, turn back to the bag, and keep hitting.

"Fine. Not like I needed sleep anyway." Through my pummeling, I hear her footsteps approach.

"There's no way in hell you hear this from your bunk," I growl through gritted teeth.

"Wasn't sleeping in my bunk," Chuck says as she picks up a roll of gauze and starts wrapping her hands. "Can't, tonight. Too much going on. It's simpler in the engine room."

I pause.

"And what's your excuse for making a racket down here?" she asks before I have a chance to get my own questions out. "You fuckin' hate training exercises, Cas. Something's gotta be really wrong."

It feels stupid to be confessing anything to her. Of all the trainees, Chuck's the one who's most distant from me. She's rarely alone to begin with, always joined at the hip with Varma, and I don't think I've ever had a conversation with her individually. "The captain's been getting to me," I mumble. I let my hands drop to my sides. "I kinda had an epiphany about what she's turned me into, and it came at a bad moment."

Chuck raises an eyebrow as she finishes off her left hand and starts on her right. When I don't elaborate, she nods. "Swift?"

"In the worst way," I reply, a bitter laugh on the heels of my voice. And because it's the middle of the night, and because she's a stranger, and because there's nowhere else for the story to go, I tell her exactly what went down.

When I finish, Chuck's all but forgotten the punching bag in front of her. "That's fucked as hell, Cas," she says, fidgeting with her wrapped knuckles. "You know, there's a reason Varma and I stick to the down-low. I mean, there's only so much you can control, feelings-wise, but... at least the captain doesn't pull that shit with us. I mean she'll game us against each other, sure, but she's never…" She breaks off, shaking her head. "I'm sorry, shoregirl."

"It's okay."

"Nah, for real. We give you two a lot of shit, and it probably didn't help what Santa Elena's done to you." She claps me on the back with enough force to send me staggering sideways. "We gotta stick together if we're gonna make it out alive."

Something sours on the back of my tongue, but I keep my face straight. There's no "if" for me. I already know I won't make it. But I can't let it dampen Chuck's optimism—there's too little of it to go around.

She turns to the next punching bag and lays one hit into it, then another. "C'mon," she says when she notices I'm still standing there. "If you aren't going back to bed, your punching needs work."

I swallow back a thousand objections. I'm due to die soon. Hand-to-hand combat doesn't help me in the fight against Hellbeasts. I blurted the captain's secrets, failing her in pretty much every way that matters, and a little more training isn't going to do anything to put me back in Santa Elena's good books. I'm better off getting more sleep, especially if it's as late as she says it is. But I lift my fists, mimicking her stance anyway. She nudges the set of my feet, lifts my elbows, and raises an appraising eyebrow at my raw, bleeding knuckles.

"I'll manage," I tell her.

"You're gonna fuckin' break your hands, Cas," Chuck

says. She ambles over to the equipment bins, pulls out a pair of gloves, and throws them at me. "If there's anything I learned on this boat, it's the difference between the necessary pain and the unnecessary. Put on the gloves, and let's get to work."

And that's exactly what I do.

26

I used to be able to hide in this room.

That was months ago, when I wasn't one of the captain's chosen few. There were days back then when the crew would gather and I'd tuck myself into the throne room's dark corners. With every eye drawn to the captain's magnetism, I was invisible until the moment Santa Elena chose to draw me into the spotlight.

Now I'm on the dais at her right.

The pack is at the edge of our radar, and the *Minnow*'s crew has gathered to commemorate the start of our captain's command. I look out over the sea of now-familiar faces. These forty people Santa Elena has scraped together from the fringes. These forty who won't all make it. A small pulse of relief hits me when I remember the under-fifteens are missing from the scene. The captain's left is empty—Alvares and the others are back on Fung's island.

I try not to look at Santa Elena. She stands before us, proud and tall, dressed in her best armor. Her fingers tap at her sides the way they always do when she's counting. I watch the fingers, not the woman attached to them. When they stop moving, that becomes impossible.

"Listen up!" Santa Elena shouts, and every spine in the room snaps straight. She lifts a radio to her lips, which Lemon has already rigged to blast across Salt frequencies ocean-wide. Every ship in the assembled fleet is listening in as our captain takes center stage. "A lot of you are probably wondering what you did to deserve this."

Some of the crew chuckle.

"Those of you who aren't are going to have to bear with me. Because this thing didn't start when one man took advantage of an industry too secure in its own power. It didn't start when he peddled his beasts to people like us, people those monsters were designed to destroy. It didn't start when we got desperate for a way to hold our own in the oceans we call home, the oceans *they* merely cross. If there's a place where this whole thing started, it's with the Schism itself," she roars into the radio, her voice echoing around the throne room.

Rumbles of assent weave through the crowd.

"We got left behind. Left to fend for our own in these oceans. Bereft of that inherent, birth-granted institutional advantage, that *citizenship* they enjoy on the shore. And when we came into our own anyway, they sent beasts to put us down. Now we stand on the edge of the abyss, on the precipice of our ocean's future, up against the consequence of those shore rats' choices. Today isn't just about saving the NeoPacific. It's about proving why it's *ours* in the first place."

My nails dig into my palm. No one can *own* the NeoPacific. Not us, not the shore, not the beasts in the water. But Santa Elena's words are working on everyone else in the room. Grins are out. Tattoos are bared. Hands are tight on pistol grips. She'll drag us into this fight if it's the last thing we do.

Which it likely will be.

In the planning of this venture, I told the captain over and over that we're signing our own death certificates by going up against a Hellbeast pack. Even with fifty pirate crews, even with the lighter craft, even with a monster of our own, we can't expect to walk from this. But those odds don't matter to Santa Elena—not when there's a chance for both the glory of saving the NeoPacific and the opportunity to make an example of the entire Reckoner industry at the same time. In the face of that, all I could do was twist the strategy to minimize casualties.

Fighting from Bao's back, there will be nothing I can do to head off my own death. Even with my armor on, I'll be at the mercy of monsters that weigh hundreds of tons. My aim, my part in the captain's master plan, is to take as many of them down with me as possible.

But I'll do it. I'll do it to save these oceans and the millions who depend on them. I'll do it because I'm the only one who can. I'll do it because it's the only good thing I can do.

"That'll be all. Take your stations," Santa Elena says into the radio. She snaps it off, then tosses it over her shoulder with a wry smirk at the assembled crew. "You lot," the captain roars, and the *Minnow* roars back.

My spine goes a notch stiffer. I remember being on the other side of this.

"You wear your loyalty on your skin. Show it to me."

Every Minnow tattoo on the ship flashes out in the low light of the throne room as incoherent roaring rises from the crowd. Varma's grin doubles, stretching the ink on his cheek. Chuck and Swift bow their heads—Chuck to expose the Minnow on her back, and Swift to do the same for the one on her nape. Lemon lifts her chin, baring the fish that slashes across her throat.

And I turn my ankle outward, feeling as if the ink is scorching into me the moment it hits the light. Even with the hate and despair brewing inside me, I can't deny the mark itself, the simple, permanent etching that numbers me among the captain's loyal followers. I chose this. I brought this on myself. And now I'm going to see it through.

Santa Elena's grin grows manic as she claws the collar of her shirt open, flashing the Minnow tattoo on the left side of her chest. The captain is *starving* for the fight ahead. She drinks in the room's frenzy for a moment, then yells, "Stations, all of you!"

We trainees hang back as the rest of the crew packs out of the room. There's no point in trying to make our exit when the doors are blocked by a throng of pirates all struggling to get where they need to go. As we wait, Santa Elena stalks down our line, looking each of us in the eye. She reaches me last.

"Captain," I say. She may always have the last word, but I'll be damned if I don't snatch away the first.

"Cas. You've honestly exceeded my expectations."

"You've exceeded mine." I hold her gaze, meaning every word. I played her game by choice. I let her teach me, let her grow me into the kind of person I needed to be, all the while carving me into her perfect tool. I lost. She won. And I respect that. If this is the last I see of her, I won't let myself be consumed by hatred or resentment. I won't waste the power of those emotions on a simple confrontation.

Instead I focus on her nobility, which isn't hard. Even if her methods were ignoble, she's here, leading the charge against the Hellbeasts. She brought the Salt together in defense of these oceans. There's honor in that, and I stick out my hand to let her know it.

Santa Elena shakes it. "There's a phrase you trainers use. Some long-dead language. What was it?" the captain asks, baring her best grin. Her hand's still clasped around mine.

"*E tan e epi tas,*" I reply, not missing a beat. "With your shield or on it." Come back alive and victorious or don't come back at all.

"Perfect." She claps me on the shoulder. "With it or on it, Cas."

I match her smile. What else can I do? I'm going to my death, and the captain's securing her immortality. If she wins this battle, her name lives on forever, as it rightly should. Santa Elena relinquishes her grip on me and pushes me toward the door. As I step off the dais, I glance back over my shoulder. Not at the captain—I've had my fill of her. But Swift has her back turned, facing Santa Elena as the captain addresses her with both hands locked onto her shoulders. All I get is the tattoo on the back of her neck.

My lips tighten. No goodbyes for us. No last words. Maybe it's better this way. I let my eyes skim over Varma, over Chuck, over Lemon. The last one catches me, her fingers twitching up in a tiny wave. I return it, grinning despite myself, and then I'm out the door.

The ship's sunk into a familiar chaos. As I make my way down to the trainer deck, I dodge crewmembers hauling out ammunition from the *Minnow*'s stores. Today there's no holding back, so the hallways are a mess of crates and shells and things Swift would be better at naming than I would. But once I've descended to the trainer deck's level, it all fades, leaving nothing but the hollow hum of the engines. We're idling, waiting for the captain's command to move forward, the pack still a league away.

My wetsuit hangs on a rack over the counter. During my first days on the ship, I'd press myself into the back corner of the room to change, shielding myself from any possible eyes. Thank god I've worked past that inconvenience. I strip, pull on my swimsuit, and then grab the wetsuit. On shore, I'd have a patch over my right breast with the logo of our stable. I almost wish I had something to replace it, but even with the ink on my ankle, I know there's no symbol that can represent where my loyalties lie. For now, my allegiance is to the waters, to Bao, and to my own beating heart. And I can wear that just fine with my actions.

The armor comes next. My hands don't shake as I strap

it on. Maybe they should. I pull the skirt around my hips, a grimace flickering across my face as I remember the first time I wore it, when Swift was the one tying it on me. There's a stutter in my heartbeat for the things I'm never going to have. I push through it.

Earpiece. Helmet. Mask. Respirator. And finally the Otachi. I lock the device around my left arm, since I'll be riding on the left side of his head. Even though it's my non-dominant hand, I've dual wielded enough to have my signals down. Just to make sure, I twist the dials to the homing signal and squeeze quickly. The signal flashes, and the brief pulse of noise through the bones of my arm lets me know for sure—I'm ready.

I stalk to the back of the deck, enjoying the weight of my armored footfalls, and jam down the door releases. All three cutaways roll up, and the scent of the sea floods in, sharper and clearer than ever. I move to the center of the deck and pull the triggers again, only loosening my fingers when Bao surfaces with a blast of stale air trumpeting from his blowholes. His hide's been streaked with bright yellow waterproof paint to make sure the Salt doesn't target him by accident. I don't bother trying to call him into the deck. He barely fit the last time we tried that.

Instead I dive off the back of the *Minnow* and swim to his side. As I find my handholds in his plating and clamber up next to his eye, I glance back at the ship whose decks I'll probably never walk again. The ship that's been a twisted version of home since that August morning. I close my eyes for a moment, letting the feeling sink in, then get to work.

Once my line hooks are securely anchored, I lean back against them, letting the tethers take my entire weight as I announce, "Bao's ready to roll. Orders?"

"Take him out and around," Santa Elena replies.

I switch my signals and set Bao in a wide arc around the *Minnow*, keeping an even distance between us and the other ships in the fleet. We're meant to be the arrow's tip of the formation, leading the charge. I glance back over my shoulder as we move out ahead of the *Minnow*'s bow. The ships behind are in motion, jockeying for waterspace as they move into the attack patterns Santa Elena and the other captains have sculpted. A distant command echoes in my earpiece, and a second later, the Splinters snap off the hull of the *Minnow* and drop into the sea.

I turn Bao back toward the fleet, leaning to watch as the Splinters scatter and join up with the other small craft deployed from the Salt boats. One of those boats has Swift in it. The rest of the trainees have positions on the *Minnow*—Swift's the only one out in the open like me. I try to pick her head out among the milling ships, but at this distance, it's impossible.

She'll be okay, I try to tell myself. She has to be. The captain has big plans—a grand destiny meant for her eventual successor. But that future can't start until Swift is safely on the other side of this day. I roll my shoulders, my fingers tightening on the Otachi triggers. My own future is forfeit, but maybe I can give Swift the one she deserves.

Across the fleet, the Salt gears up for war. Guns roll out, decks flush with crew, and the noise grows and grows. The

Kitefish, Omolou's boat, launches a sail into the atmosphere, the foils snapping out like gull wings as the crew on deck wrestle with the lines. The *Kettle*'s copper armor ripples and flexes, and Weis's *Sunburn* unfolds a spectacular array of heavy weaponry. These are the best hunters in the NeoPacific, and they're pulling out every trick in their arsenals.

Up on the *Minnow*'s deck, Santa Elena strides onto the bow. She scans the fleet, her hands set on her hips, and even from this distance, I'm absolutely sure there's that proud little smirk on her face.

Bao shifts underneath me. At first I think he's nervous on account of the ship arsenals prickling around us, but then I notice the way his eye rolls down, the way his body edges against my command to stay at the surface. I jam my respirator in my mouth just in case and grunt, "How're we looking on sonar?"

"Peachy," Varma replies from his position at Yatori's side in the navigation tower. "Pack's still at a distance, but they're closing. Engine noise must be drawing them in."

I relax my spine.

Then Lemon mutters, "Bogey."

There's a shuffling from the other end of the comm, then Varma says, "Shit, yeah—something's under us. About ten meters in length. Thought it was one of the light craft. Good eye, Lemon."

"What's it doing?" Santa Elena asks. She steps up to the tip of the bow, peering into the dark waters below. I press myself flat against Bao's head, feeling his muscles wind tighter and tighter. He swings his head back and forth, trying to get a lock on whatever's beneath us.

"It's… pacing," Varma says. "Running back and forth along our frontline. Looks either cetoid or ichthyoid—"

"Ichthyoid," Lemon interjects.

"Right. Anyway, it's just… back and forth. Doesn't look aggressive, just confused. It's too deep to hit it with anything, unless you and Bao want to chase it."

"Bigger fish to fry," Santa Elena says.

"Cap—" Lemon starts, but by then it's too late.

The ichthyoid blasts out of the water in front of Bao. Its jaws open wide, rows of dagger-like teeth glinting in the afternoon sun. But its trajectory isn't for us, for the plated monster at least ten times its size.

No, it goes for the monster standing on the bow of our ship. And it gets her.

Its breach carries it in a neat arc over the *Minnow*'s prow, its gaping jaw catching our captain across the midsection. Her hand twitches for her empty holster, but even if the gun were there, there's nothing she could do against four tons of Hellbeast. The captain slams into the railing—something snaps—and the ichthyoid wrenches its maw shut, dragging Santa Elena with it as it clears the boat and smashes back into the ocean with a colossal splash.

And then it's gone.

And so is she.

And the Salt collapses into chaos.

27

I'm numb. Something's been torn out of me, and I didn't know it would feel like this. All around me are the sounds of revving engines, of waves on hulls as the fleet whips into a frenzy. The formation's been forgotten. Voices shout on the comm, trying to restore order, trying to process what's just happened, trying to deny it. Beneath me, Bao lets out a confused gurgle, his legs beating against the sea as he strains to take everything in with his one remaining eye.

I think someone's calling my name, but I don't know what to do about it.

She's dead. She's really dead.

It doesn't seem possible. Santa Elena's untouchable. Nothing should be able to kill her, not even a Hellbeast. But I saw it happen. I watched that monster snap her, take her to the depths. I tug the respirator out of my mouth. My stomach churns, then empties. Bao flinches away from the smell.

"Cas," the comm in my ear snaps again. "Cas, come on, the *plan*."

I scoff. The plan, the strategy—it all hinged on having her at the center, barking orders, directing squadrons. I was only a cog in it. I only knew my part.

"Cas," Varma demands. "Pack's almost on top of us. We need you. No freezing up on me, okay? We're going to work it out, I promise." But even Varma, who's always so sincere, doesn't sound like he can keep that promise.

I pull Bao around to face the open waters, straining to see what's coming for us. My mouth is sour with the taste of whatever I had for breakfast this morning, which can't have been much. The roar of engines around me is overwhelming—I can barely hear the instructions being shouted into the comm, only the vague notes of Chuck, Lemon, and Varma trying to pull the Salt together. But some of the ships are breaking off, charging forward. The formation is dissolving.

And out ahead, the NeoPacific is starting to boil.

"Cas, *move!*" Chuck screams into the comm as the *Minnow*'s engines roar behind me.

I twist my signals and throw Bao into a charge, glancing back over my shoulder to make sure we're keeping ahead of the ship's prow bearing down on us. Light craft rush past, grouping into squads as they weave back and forth, their guns already extended.

The *Crown Prince* is the first to engage. One moment

it's speeding along, and the next a tentacle whips out of the water, latching onto its hull and dragging the ship. The light craft flock to it, guns blazing, shredding the tentacle to a pulp. The cephalopoid relinquishes, but not before another arm lashes around one of the little boats' hulls and yanks it underwater. I don't see what happened to the pilot—I don't think I want to. But it wasn't one of ours.

Something surfaces. I don't have time to register what it is, because one of the *Sunburn*'s fore guns lights up immediately, blasting a flurry of shells into it. The noise of the explosions makes Bao falter, but when I tug the Otachi again, he holds true to the path I've set. "*Minnow* tower, give me something to kill," I choke against the spray. All around, Hellbeasts are rising, punching holes in what's left of our formation.

"Hang on," Varma says. "We've got a lock on Andromeda." The biggest serpentoid we identified from Kurosaki's video. Swift came up with the code names for the beasts we know. "She's after the *Kettle*, with Squad Bravo in pursuit. Looks like they'll need backup."

"I'm on it," I reply, changing the signals. "Call the light craft off—I don't want any stray shots spooking Bao." I force his head up and scan the fray until I find the copper-tinted plating of Mallory's ship. A sinewy coil twists around its prow, tilting the *Kettle* forward. I twist the dials to *destroy*, level my arm, and pull the triggers.

I think Bao remembers how to do this. He veers for the serpentoid, jaw dropping open as a vicious roar rips out of him. I press flat against his head, winding my fingers around the lines that hold me in place. This part is all on him.

He strikes with his claws first, raking down Andromeda's body until they find purchase in her flesh. A scream rises from the other side of the *Kettle*, and the muscle beneath us spasms. Bao lunges and bites, and a wash of hot Hellbeast blood rushes up my legs. The *Kettle's* plating snaps outward, and the weakened beast drops her coils, freeing the ship.

I twist the dials and point the beams out to the side. Bao drags Andromeda with him, and the *Kettle's* engines roar to life as the boat pulls away. But with the *Kettle* out of her way, Andromeda comes after us with a vengeance. She rears out of the water, her arrowhead snout twisting around as she bares row after row of needle-like teeth.

I don't realize she's on Bao's blind side until it's too late. The shock of her impact knocks me to the end of my lines, and my armor's the only thing that keeps my spine from snapping. We plunge underwater. Bao's legs thrash frantically as he tries to shake her loose, but she's got herself locked onto his plating, and already her coils are starting to move. I jam the respirator into my mouth and fire the Otachi, urging Bao to wrestle against the constriction. He manages to wrench one foreleg free and carve down her body. It only makes Andromeda squeeze tighter.

But when she lets her jaw loose and rears back to readjust her hold, Bao senses his opportunity. He twists his head around, flinging me outward, and snaps, his beak carving into the soft flesh under her throat. Andromeda spills, clouding the waters that surround us. Bao's body relaxes as her coils do, and with a mighty heave, he shakes her off.

I point the Otachi overhead, and we surface like a cork shot from a bottle. At the apex of our breach, I lean out and scan the chaos that surrounds us, trying to find the *Minnow*. But it's lost in the fray. We're surrounded by the noise of explosions and gunfire, by guttural roars, by aggressive Hellbeasts going against Salt ships, by nonaggressive beasts meandering, watching the fight with curious, bulging eyes. A young cetoid drifts right past us, unthreatened by Bao's attention as he snaps his beak after it. Its blubber is almost nonexistent. The pack isn't just vicious—it's starving.

"Andromeda's down," I announce through teeth gritted around my respirator. "Tell me where I'm needed."

"Here would be nice," Chuck replies. "Got a terrapoid gunning for the *Minnow* that just won't go down. That nasty fucker twice Bao's size—Medea."

"I'm on it." I force Bao's head up and spot the *Minnow* at a distance, cutting a tight circle as it tries to outmaneuver a behemoth of a terrapoid. A flock of light craft follow, pumping shell after shell into her, but Medea's too well-armored for the weaponry to have any effect. Her outline looks familiar. She might be one of my mother's creations.

I urge Bao underwater for our approach. We dip down, the clamor of the fight fading to the muffled rumble of engines as we coast below the clash above. I ease him into a roll, tilting his belly skyward as we draw up under Medea's shadow. If she notices our approach, she doesn't mind it. Probably thinks we're part of her pack.

We correct her. I change the signals, and Bao lashes up with his rear legs, claws digging into the gaps in Medea's plating. But like any terrapoid, she's single-minded and tough as nails. Instead of fighting back, she continues on the *Minnow*'s tail, dragging us along for the ride. The distant rumble and flash of explosions above mark where the shelling hits her, and the waters above take on a hint of red. But she keeps going.

Until Bao bites down. He latches onto one of her largest keratin plates and snaps his head back, ripping it free. The waters foul with gore, and Medea's head whips around. I find myself face to face with a monster twice the size of the one I'm strapped to. And she's *livid*.

"Fall back, fall back, fall back," I growl into the respirator, my fingers fumbling on the Otachi, but Bao doesn't need any sort of instruction. He kicks free and scrambles for the depths, barely making it clear as Medea's jaws slam shut inches from his side. Her size gives us the upper hand in maneuverability, but there's no beating her speed.

Bao claws toward the surface, his eye fixed on the shadow on his rear. We break into the open air, and I lean hard, my weight forcing him into a turn that keeps him just out of Medea's reach. The second she surfaces in our wake, a blast hits her, fired from one of the nearby ships. The heat of the explosion fogs my mask, but it doesn't do anything to slow Medea down.

I can feel the thud of my heart against my armor. We might have bitten off more than we can chew. As Bao curves around the hull of a fast-sinking ship, I glance back over my shoulder and breathe a sigh of relief as I watch Medea's fury switch to the boat that took a shot at her. Some of her keratin plates have been jarred loose by the explosion that hit her. A hint of bile rises in my throat. I've seen this before.

But she isn't Durga. She's a vengeful beast that'll consume the NeoPacific if she's left alive. I shake the reluctance building in me and point the Otachi at her retreating bulk.

Then I hear the snort.

It's a small sound, nearly lost in the chaos of battle, but it makes my blood freeze. The monster that made that sound shouldn't be out here. It shouldn't even exist in the first place.

I turn around and face the simioid.

The sea ape's managed to latch onto Bao's back, clinging by its massive arms as it pulls itself across his plating. It's nearly nine feet tall, and its thick fur drips with water. Its lips are stained with gore, and so are its claw-like nails. A broken chain around its ankle marks where it used to be kept. But none of that's what frightens me most about it.

Even with its fur, I can see its ribs. This animal is hungry.

And it's looking right at me.

I keep absolutely still, my Otachi directions forgotten. With my line hooks anchored in Bao's plates, I'm pinned in place, strapped to his head. In the midst of the fear that clouds my mind, I remember one of Swift's myths. Prometheus, who brought the secret of fire to mankind, chained to the side of a mountain. Waiting for the eagle to eat his liver.

I lunge for the line hooks' release, and the simioid lunges for me.

I don't make it in time. It's on top of me before my fingers reach the hooks. The Hellbeast hits me like a freight train, slamming me back against the ridge of Bao's eye. He squalls in protest, his head swinging from side to side as he tries to figure out what's going on. It spares me for a second—the simioid scrabbles for a grip, giving me time to throw my arms up over my face, because I know exactly how these monsters attack.

In the next instant, my world rips open. The simioid's claws slash down my forearms, tearing through wetsuit and skin and leaving nothing but white-hot pain in their wake. I scream, trying to keep my arms raised, trying to block what's coming next.

I don't. Not fully. The next strike hits true, the simioid's claws raking down my face, ripping off my mask, snapping the respirator from around my neck. Shallower wounds, but wounds all the same, wounds that burn and bleed. My mouth fills with salted rust as I turn my head and jackknife my body. Anything to get away from the inevitable. But I'm still tied down. All I can do is brace myself for the next blow and pray it ends it.

Instead there's the familiar sound of a Splinter's gun-fire right in my ear, and suddenly the blood that coats me isn't entirely my own. Bao's head jerks away from the noise on impulse. I open my eyes a sliver, just in time to see the light fade from the simioid's. Its grip loosens, and it slides off Bao's side, dropping into the ocean. And before I close my eyes again, I catch a glimpse of the most beautiful sight I've ever seen in my entire life.

Her face is stained with blood and grease, her hair swept back by wind. Her Splinter looks like it's been to hell and back. But Swift Kent came for me. She tried to save my life.

I don't think it worked, but it was worth a shot.

28

Something's interrupting the throbbing ache that resonates through my core. First with a rough jerk that sends a wave of pain rolling through my body—or what's left of it. Then the dragging, up and over, my back scraping the whole way. I try to resist, try to grab something, but something grabs me instead.

"God damn it, stop moving," Swift growls, her hands slipping on my wrists. I try to open my eyes, but it's like a weight pins them shut. She pulls off the Otachi and peels back my wetsuit's remains. A moment later, there's pressure on the wounds, squeezing the salt water into my flesh.

I shriek through my teeth.

"Jesus. Okay. *Okay.*" Her fingers lift from my arms just long enough to sweep across my forehead, down my cheek, over the wounds there. "I'm trying, Cas. I'm trying—fuck." She wraps something around my arms, then lays strips of it over my neck. With shaking hands, she loosens my chest-piece, breathing a sigh of relief when she realizes the claws didn't make it much lower than my clavicle. Bit by bit, she pieces me back together until the throb is trapped inside my body.

I crack my eyes open at last, and I'm greeted by the sight of Swift holding back tears as she leans over me. One of her arms is slung around my shoulders, pressing me against her chest as her other hand skims over the hasty bandages she's applied to my wounds. I try to sit up, to see more, but she keeps me pinned. "What—" I croak.

"Don't you dare," she snarls. "I didn't patch you up just so you could rip yourself open again."

I twitch my fingers over the surface beneath me. Knobby. Scaly. It hits me at once—we're still on Bao. I roll my eyes to the side, and sure enough, there's one of my line hooks trailing over the edge of his head. The other lays limp across my legs. "The battle," I groan.

Swift's eyes lift to the horizon. "Still going." Her lips set in a bitter line that tells me everything about *how* it's going. I can hear the noise of it still—the roars and shrieks, the blasts and cracks, the rumble of engines and scream of rending metal.

"Medea?"

"Still out there."

"Your Splinter?"

She scowls. "Not as important."

I'm about to tell her the captain would disagree, but then I remember that the captain can't do much of anything anymore. We've lost Santa Elena. The Salt's in chaos. We're losing this fight. Even though it sends fresh agony racing through my body, I lift my arms. Swift tenses.

I take in the damage. Even with the bandages wound around my injuries, I can see how bad it is. The sight of so much blood—so much of *my* blood—pulls a harsh sob out of me. I drop my hands to my chest, feeling along the claw marks that run up my neck and across my face.

"Honestly, I think it's an improvement," Swift deadpans, but even she can't commit to it. I squeeze my eyes shut, trying to force back the tears. They come anyway. Swift cradles me closer, and I lean into her chest, feeling my blood seep into her jacket. "You're going to be okay," she murmurs against my helmet.

"I'm sorry," I choke. "I'm so, so sorry." There were so many things I could have done, if I had just thought this through. I could have saved us all. There must have been a way. And now I can't do anything to turn the tide in our favor. The NeoPacific will fall to these monsters.

At least Swift's here. At least I don't have to watch the end alone. In the mess of this battle, she found me. She shot the simioid. She…

She climbed on top of Bao. Bao, who's fidgety, who's got beef with Splinters, who'd just bucked a giant ape, let Swift swim to him, climb up his side, and cut me loose in the middle of the fray. And now he's floating at the surface, perfectly still. Waiting.

My gaze drops to the Otachi she pulled off my arm. It

sits beside us, its plating cracked, but the scars in it don't look too deep. "Does that still work?" I ask.

"Cas…"

"Don't… Just check it, *please*."

The magic word works. Swift shifts, reaching out to grab the Otachi. She sets the device on my lap, and I hold it still as she tries to press down on the triggers. It takes her a few tries to get it right, but when she does, the *charge* signal blasts out ahead of us. Bao lurches forward, and Swift flails to keep us on his head as I clutch the Otachi to my chest. Even as the pain slices through me, my lips twist into a grin.

We can still make something of this.

"Cas, this is nuts," Swift stammers. "I can't—I haven't been trained. I have no idea—"

"I do. Do what I say, twist the dials I tell you to, and point the beams when I order it."

"You're going to bleed out if you—"

"This isn't about me," I snap. The lacerations on my face twinge with the effort. "We can still fight. So we're going to save these goddamn oceans, Swift. Or we're gonna fucking die trying." I fumble with the line hooks on my belt, but she swats my hands away hard enough that I inhale sharply.

There's a pause.

"Let me get that for you," Swift says, unspooling a line and driving it home into Bao's plating.

It takes a few more lines to get me secure. My waist is firmly anchored against the plating on the top of Bao's head. Swift kneels behind me, my torso propped up against her legs. She hails the *Minnow* and reengages my comm—apparently they cut me off when I started screaming. Relief floods my veins as Varma's voice fills my ear, begging to know what happened.

Swift jumps on him with a string of colorful curses before I have a chance to explain myself. "But enough about me," she says once she's exhausted her vocabulary, adjusting the Otachi straps around her arm. "Where's the best place to turn the tide?"

"No one's been able to put a dent in Medea. She's sunk three ships so far, and if you ask me, she's getting better at it."

My brow furrows. "What is it?" Swift asks.

"We don't have respirators or masks. It's nigh impossible to take a terrapoid from the surface."

"What's that mean for us?"

I grimace. "Means we have to get clever about it. Give me the Otachi."

She leans over my shoulder, sticking the device out for me to inspect. I prop my elbows up on my stomach and run my hands over the dials, twisting and pulling until I have the signal where I need it. The pain is fading, giving way to numbness. I'm not sure if that's good or not.

"Try that. Find her and guide him wide around."

Swift pulls the Otachi with a familiar sort of hesitancy, the same caution I wore the first time I used them. The beam carves across the waves and the vibration of the signal buries into my aching wounds. I glance upward in time to catch the disbelieving smile that flickers across Swift's lips when Bao responds, lunging after the lasers' line. Her other hand digs into my shoulder—she doesn't have any line hooks to hold her down, so she's relying on me to keep her anchored.

I do my best to scan for Medea, but it's becoming harder and harder to keep my head up. Swift must feel me fading—she nudges my shoulder and says, "Got eyes on her. What next?"

I peer at the horizon, at the vague, bulky shadow in the distance, swatting at a ship's retreating tail. "Otachi," I mutter. She drops her arm, and I start twisting dials again. My fingers are sluggish and unresponsive.

"Had no idea how *heavy* these damn things are," Swift pants, propping her arm on my shoulder as I work. "And you used to wield two of them?"

"We can switch if you'd like," I reply, which gets an almost-laugh. I let my hands fall, and she lifts her arm again. "That's set to *destroy*. Point it at her throat, and hold on for dear life."

I watch her hoist the Otachi and aim the killing blow. Even though we're in the middle of a fight for our lives, a fight we're losing badly, a profound sense of right settles over me. The loss of our captain leaves a ragged wound in me, but the worst part of her philosophy died with her. We won't choose ourselves first. We won't be ruthless and selfish. Even if the dent we put in the Hellbeasts doesn't eradicate them completely, it'll make a difference. And with the fate of the NeoPacific at stake, any difference is worth this.

Bao explodes forward as Swift pulls the triggers, her free

arm wrapping around my chest as she clings to me with everything she has. I forget my own body, forget anything but the power of the Reckoner beneath me as he surges against the waves, closing the distance between us and the target with a ferocity usually reserved for hurricanes.

Medea whirls on us, the ship in her claws forgotten as she lets out a vicious bellow that blasts strands of saliva through the air. Bao lands one foreleg in her keratin plates and bites down, the movement jolting us so harshly that Swift nearly loses her grip. She releases the signal and wraps her other arm around me. Her wrists lock around her forearms as blood spurts from Medea's neck.

I wind my fingers tighter in the keratin plates beneath me, even though it won't do any good. Darkness is starting to seep into the corners of my vision, and I can feel the tension leaving my spine. Medea heaves in Bao's jaws. The world tilts as he's forced backward, but he keeps his hold. There's a slight jolt—I think his beak sunk in a notch deeper.

Swift buries her face against my neck, and maybe it isn't so bad that it ends like this.

Then the comm in my ear goes live. "We've got incoming on the radar," Lemon announces.

"Incoming?" Swift chokes incredulously. "*More* beasts?"

"No," Varma says, and I've never been happier to hear his smile. "Ships. A whole goddamn fleet of ships. Flying red and gold, each of them escorted, and mad as a triggered Reckoner. Cas, want to explain?"

Even as Medea twists and roars, even as her claws carve

into one of the plates on Bao's side, a giddy lightness over-takes me. I've definitely lost too much blood. I must be hearing things now, because what Varma described has to be an SRCese fleet. Those boats haven't been on our tail since November. There's no way. It can't be.

Whatever those ships are about to do, I don't find out. My eyes slide shut, the darkness overtaking me, and though Swift's voice is in my ear, pleading for me not to go, I slip into unconsciousness at last.

29

I wake to bright, artificial lights overhead. For a moment I fool myself into thinking I'm in the *Minnow*'s infirmary, but the ceiling here is higher and there's a curtain wreathing me that definitely wasn't there the last time. I glance down at my arms. An IV connected to a blood bag and something else—most likely painkillers—is hooked into me at my elbow. The hasty bandages Swift must have dug out of her Splinter's med kit have been replaced with strips of translucent gel. Beneath them, I can see the thick, ropy lines of the claw marks. I lift one hand, first as an experiment, then to run my fingers over the gel. Even with the extra layer, I can feel the swollen ridge that the wounds trace.

I'll have scars. But it's better than the alternative.

Stiff and aching, I follow the gashes up my shoulders and over my face and neck. These weren't as deep, but even with careful attention, they probably won't heal well. I wobble my jaw, and the cuts on my face twinge. There's a swell of something like regret building behind my eyes. Maybe it's vain to be upset, but I'll never look the same again. I glance around for a reflective surface, but there's nothing within the bounds of the curtain around me.

"Was that... Is she up?"

I recognize the voice behind the curtain, and I swear my heart skips a beat. There's a scuffle of movement on the other side, and another familiar voice replies, "Let's check." The curtain peels back, and a relieved smile breaks over Swift's features. "See for yourself," she says over her shoulder.

She pulls the curtain wider, and I find myself face to damaged face with my brother for the first time in six months. He steps around Swift and gives me the weakest smile I've ever seen him wear. I don't know what to say, and I don't think he does either.

So I start with the obvious. "You got taller," I groan, sinking back against the pillows.

"Sorry," he replies with a shrug. "You got—" He stops halfway into gesturing to my face, and it stings. I don't want him to go easy on me.

My eyes flick to Swift. "What happened?" I ask.

Tom answers. "I told Mom and Dad that Fabian Murphy was selling off Reckoner pups and that a pirate-born pack had formed in the NeoPacific. They believed me—it explained why Murphy went AWOL this fall and the ecological crisis we were starting to see. We got a satellite commissioned and tracked down the poor beasts. They called in the intel to the SRCese military. And it looks like we got here just in time."

In time to save my life, I think but don't say. *Not in time for a lot of other pirates. Not in time for Santa Elena.*

"Turns out a bunch of trained Reckoners was enough to turn the tide," Swift says, though I don't miss the way her lip curls at what my brother's just said.

"The pack is gone?"

Tom nods. "I mean, the aggressive part of the population's been wiped out, but... well, some of the others did slip through the cracks. Not sure what we're going to do about that."

I close my eyes, trying to let the news relieve me. "And how on god's green earth did all three of us end up here?" I ask. By all rights, I should be either dead or on the *Minnow*, Swift should definitely be on the *Minnow* after everything that's happened, and Tom's got no business being out in the NeoPacific at all.

Swift answers faster this time. "After you passed out, Bao and I took care of Medea—"

"—with help from the SRC," Tom interjects.

Swifts scowls. "The new ships turned the tide, and we were able to put down the Hellbeasts that fought back. And as soon as we were in the clear, I started begging. We don't have blood on the *Minnow*, you know. Not the kind of thing we keep on hand. And they weren't exactly thrilled at the prospect of giving medical assistance to pirates. Tried to argue the point that you weren't exactly a pirate, and that's when this one—" She gestures awkwardly to Tom. "—jumped on the line. And apparently they listen to this kid."

"Well, I said we could treat Cas. I didn't say—"

Swift rips back the curtain, and I immediately understand why she's seething. We're in the medical ward of an SRCese warship, and all of the other beds are empty. Because of course this fleet didn't come to help us fight the Hellbeasts. It came to fight the Hellbeasts and happened to find us there. "The rest of the Salt?" I ask, though I already know the answer.

"When they found out they weren't getting any sort of aid, they split. Didn't want to risk getting on the bad side of escorted warships."

"And the *Minnow*?"

She grins. "Would never leave one of its own behind," Swift says, smirking at Tom's obvious reaction to her words. "They're lurking in our wake, making repairs." There's something else she wants to say, something that hurts, something I'm guessing sounds like *They didn't know where else to go.* We don't have a captain. We don't even have a successor to the captain.

"Well, I mean, you can't go back over there until the doctor clears you," Tom says. "Provided they don't try to arrest you or anything like that."

My hand drifts to where my pistol should be, but of course I don't have it. "I just led an armada of pirates against a pack of ravenous monsters that would have consumed the NeoPacific if left unchecked. The least they could do is thank me." I pause, my woozy brain trying to catch up with whatever my next thought was. "But why are *you* here?" I ask, lifting a finger at my brother. "You're sixteen years old, for Christ's sake. You aren't soloing, are you?"

Tom grimaces. "They decided it wouldn't count as a solo mission, since I'm working with a fleet. There are other trainers here who are supposed to be my supervisors, but I'm assigned as the sole trainer to Isolde of the *Midsummer*."

"Right, but…" It still doesn't make sense. With all of the trainers in the industry, all of the trainers in the Southern Republic of California alone, why send a sixteen-year-old with no prior solo experience?

Then Tom looks at me, and I get it. I know exactly why he got on this boat. Why he must have fought to be a part of the mission.

"You came to get me," I say, and Swift stiffens, her fingers curling on the edge of the curtain.

Tom nods and takes a step closer to my bedside. "Look, it'll be very easy to pass off what you've done as coercion. Stockholm syndrome or something. We could get you back on shore with almost no legal consequences. Maybe you could even be a trainer again."

"And they… want me back?" I ask, gritting my teeth against the tide of emotion rising in my chest.

"Of course we fucking want you back," Tom bursts, running a hand through his hair. "Mom's been worried sick—she's going to jump on me for not calling her the instant you woke up. Dad… I dunno, he'll be harder to bring around, and he's across the ocean on a mission at the moment, but we can make it work."

I stare at my hands.

"Right, Cas? We can make it work?"

"There's... I..." I stammer. My gaze betrays me, flicking toward Swift before I remember not to do that. I only regained consciousness five minutes ago. I can't be making life-altering decisions. "I need to talk to the SRC. I mean, someone within the SRC. That first. Then..."

It's enough of a nondecision that both parties in the room relax. But I can't. Tom's just thrown a choice in my face that I've had no way of preparing myself for. I can go with him. Go home. Wipe my slate clean. But that would mean leaving Swift behind, leaving behind the life I built on the *Minnow*, leaving behind Bao, even—who knows what the IGEOC would do with him if I'm not there? After he fought so bravely and after all we've been through, I can't stand the thought of abandoning him a second time.

But I burned my life down and walked away once before. A horrifying part of me knows how easy it'd be to do it again.

I glance up at Tom. "You should at least call Mom."

————

My return to the *Minnow* gets more fanfare than it deserves. Despite the objections of the SRCese doctor, Swift and I depart in a light craft driven by one of the soldiers on the boat only a few hours after I wake up. With the blood transfusions complete and my wounds safely sealed by fresh gel strips, there isn't much else she can do for me, and the situation on the *Minnow* is more pressing than anything related to my health. My head still spins, both from painkillers and from the hour I spent shouting over an ornery SRCese representative on an uplink channel, and I'm struggling to stay awake, much less upright.

The climb up the exterior ladder from sea level to the lowest deck does its best to tear me open again, even with Swift at my side helping me gingerly up the rungs. I barely get a chance to catch my breath before I'm snagged by a pair of gangly arms. "Varma," I hiss, my ruined arms limp at my sides as the wounds on my neck scream in protest.

"Sorry, sorry, sorry!" he says, jumping back. "Got excited. Didn't realize."

Chuck slugs me on the shoulder, in case I was getting any ideas about special treatment. I crack a grin in her direction, and then raise a stiff, painful salute at Lemon, who hovers over her shoulder. Surprisingly enough, they aren't the only ones. A good portion of the *Minnow*'s crew is here to welcome me back. I even spot Reinhardt lurking—probably waiting to see if the gel strips are reusable.

"Throne room," I say. "We've got things to discuss."

Swift raises an eyebrow. "I'd tell you to get some goddamn rest for once, but..." She slings an arm around my waist and lifts my wrist around her shoulders with an exaggerated sigh. "C'mon, you lot. Let's let her burn herself out."

No one takes the throne when we file into the room. Swift sits me on the edge of the dais, and the rest of the trainees settle around us. I lean back against the leg of Santa

Elena's throne, waiting for the rest of the crew to make their way in.

When they do, Swift stands up, setting her hands on her hips as she surveys the crowd. "Been a lot of change around here," she starts, and a murmur of assent rolls through the crew. "It seems like there's something we have to work out—not just between the five of us up here, but with everyone on this ship. We threw in our lot for the futures of these oceans, and now the benefits are coming around. But that means we have a choice. We decide where we go from here, and we decide who leads us there." She glances down at the other trainees and shrugs. "I don't know how to go about it, but it's something we need to do." She sits back down on the dais, and nothing but silence follows her.

"Anyone?" Chuck says after a minute passes. "No one has any opinions?"

But I don't feel qualified to captain this vessel. And I don't think any of the other kids sitting next to me feel ready either. They've all been training under Santa Elena for years, but none of them anticipated having to fill her shoes this soon.

And it was supposed to be Santa Elena's choosing. She was supposed to live long enough to make a decision. In private, she told me she'd most likely name Swift as her successor, but it wouldn't do any good to bring that out into the open when the loss of our captain is so raw.

So instead I push myself to my feet, wobbling a bit as I steady myself against the throne. "The question of leadership isn't something we can sort out immediately. But we can start charting our course. There are obligations we have to fulfill. First on Art-Hawaii 26—we have to pick up Alvares and the other kids. But after that…"

I take a deep breath.

And I tell them the deal I've outlined with the SRC.

30

The road to the facility is rocky and winding, doubling the strange sensation of riding in a car again. After months at sea, every jolt over a pothole or a washboard feels like a punch in my lower back. I glance across the backseat to where Swift sits, staring out at the passing palms and scrub. It's twice as strange for her—she's never ridden in a car in her life.

Our driver is a bulky military man who's said maybe three words in the forty-five minutes I've known him. I can't tell if he's not talkative or if he's mad that he has to shuttle a pair of teenagers up the coast on "personal business." He drives, he doesn't get lost, and he doesn't say anything, even when we pull up to the facility. When he cuts the engine, I glance over at Swift. "Well," I sigh, "this is it."

I push the door open, the slashes on my arms stinging

from the effort. It's been two weeks since the attack, long enough that I don't have to reapply gel strips every morning, but the wounds have a nasty tendency to bust open if I strain them. The ones on my face have been healing better—not enough though. Varma likes to say I have "character" now, which is a weird word for scars.

Tom's the first one out the door. He beams when he sees me, and it makes my heart lurch just a little. I give him a quick hug, and he hugs back with a gentleness I never would have expected from him. When he steps aside, my mother is standing behind him.

I don't deserve the look she's giving me. I'm a traitor to her industry, partially responsible for the biggest crisis the Reckoner trade has ever faced. I joined up with pirates. I killed trained Reckoners. I was supposed to take that little blue pill my father gave me, the one that would have killed me and stopped all of this from happening.

But none of that seems to matter as much as it should when we're standing face to face. So I do what the captain taught me. I straighten my back. I look her in the eye. And I forget it all when she steps forward and folds me into a careful hug.

Mom's eyes fix on my scars, following the lines they trace over my face. "I wish you'd stay," she says, reaching up to cradle my jaw. Her thumb runs cautiously down the raw, nerveless ridge of one of the claw marks.

"I—" My voice catches in my throat as I spot a shadow in one of the facility's windows. Tom told me not to expect

Dad's forgiveness any time soon, and I wasn't surprised that he wasn't part of my welcoming party. But I know it's him, watching me now. Maybe someday, maybe soon, he'll see enough to make him step out from the shadows. Until then, I have to carry the distance like a knife in my gut and know that I earned it with the choices I made.

"I wish I could stay too, Mom," I say at last, bowing my head and taking a swipe at my watering eyes. "But there's unfinished business out there, and no one's better suited to take care of it." She's heard these words before. She'll probably hear them again. The IGEOC likes calling it "unfinished business"—it gives the impression that we're cleaning up a mess of our own making, rather than one of theirs. I glance back over my shoulder. "I brought along someone I'd like you to meet."

Hearing her cue, Swift steps out from behind the car and gives my mother an awkward wave.

"This is Captain Swift Kent," I say, and there's something about those three words that makes my smile uncontrollable. "She'll be in charge of the *Minnow* over the course of our commission. She's also responsible for saving my life." I leave off exactly how many times she's done it.

Mom's brow furrows. "You look familiar," she says. She really doesn't, dressed in her crisp new uniform with her hair halfway decent, but my mother must recognize Swift from the *Nereid*'s security footage. Mom takes an extra second to process the realization, then steps forward and offers a hand to her. "It's a very noble thing you're doing. Best of luck on your mission, Captain Kent."

Swift takes her hand and shakes it, and I know there's a part of her that still can't believe this is how she's received on shore.

Before the awkward silence has a chance to settle in, I jump forward. "I was actually—I mean, the captain wanted to see the facility. I was going to give her a tour, if that's okay."

Tom folds his arms, smirking. "You need help, or do you remember where everything is?"

I roll my eyes and grab Swift by the elbow. "Won't be more than a few minutes," I shout as I pull her away. I don't miss my brother's wink. He's seen me do this too many times before.

I lead the way down the narrow trail to the Reckoner pens. It feels weird to be walking these paths in civilian clothes, weirder still that Swift's following me. When we get to the concrete meridian that extends out into the bays, she stops. "Cas, what are we doing?" she asks.

I ignore her. There are eight bays in front of me, and one I know I have to go to. A magnetic pull draws me down the meridian to the last row of pens, the ones built for the biggest beasts we raise. One is occupied by a serpentoid that looks like it was in the Hellbeast fight, covered with raking scratches that no pirate weapon could produce. The other bay is empty.

As it should be. I'm all too aware of the shape of the ink

across my back as I sit down on the edge of the meridian, staring at my torn-up hands. Imagining the last time I was here. Feeling just how much has changed since then.

I don't turn around when I hear Swift's footsteps behind me. "This was her pen," I murmur.

"I know," Swift replies. The last time she was here, it was with a syringe of cull serum in her hand. Poor, simple, trusting Durga let her get too close, and that was it. That was what started this whole mess.

And now we're sitting on the cusp of another beginning. Tomorrow the *Minnow* ships out for the open seas with one mission—to track down and eliminate all of the remaining Hellbeasts. With Bao at our side and free rein of the NeoPacific, we're the perfect tool for the job. We're able to operate where state militaries can't, free from obligations to defend the citizens of the shore that make those militaries unable to spare any of their resources.

It'll be a long job. A difficult one. But if we do it right, we'll finally put to rest the disaster that Fabian Murphy started. The man himself has followed my instructions perfectly—no word of him has surfaced in the weeks since he left Fung's island. If there's any justice in the world, he'll never come back. Whether it's on some distant floating city, some inland mountain escape, or some uncharted island, he'll stay far away, trapped and harmless, for the rest of his miserable life.

Meanwhile, we'll reap the benefits of cleaning up his messes. It took nearly a full week of negotiation, but we've secured a hefty commission from the IGEOC to carry out our duty. Most of the negotiation was on my part, getting the *Minnow*'s crew to come around to working for the shore. Almost all complaining was put aside by the size of the offer. It's nowhere near a pirate take, but as an honest living, it can't be beat. If we're smart, if we're lucky, we'll be able to milk this hanging favor for a very, very long time.

Even better, it's enough to keep Swift's family looked after, and our open-ended assignment allows plenty of time to make stops at the Flotilla. Plenty of time to make stops in the SRC too. And anywhere in between, though our relationship with the Salt is a little shaky at the moment. Omolou's boat sank in the Hellbeast fight, leaving Lemon a free agent, but Eddie Fung was more than a little upset when Swift withdrew Chuck's offer and told him she'd be staying on the *Minnow* permanently. Chuck and Varma weren't upset at all.

Swift sits on the meridian next to me, her gaze fixed on the water as she rubs her thumb over the third line of ink slashed across her forearm. I've never asked her about the night she poisoned Durga, and I don't think I need to. She's haunted. That much is clear from the way she stares, from the way she won't look at me.

But I can't keep my eyes off her. *Captain* Swift Kent— because after all of the deliberation, we knew it could only ever be her. Santa Elena was right. Swift could be the greatest captain these waters have ever seen. And I can't wait to see that.

We have unfinished business, but we have an entire future to finish it. So I reach out and take her hand in mine, wincing as my wounds brush over her skin. She startles a little, then softens, her gaze finally flicking to me. I may not love her yet. I may not deserve to have her love me back.

But we've got oceans to cross. Beasts to hunt. Full lives to live. And I'm going to try.

The End

ACKNOWLEDGMENTS

This book almost didn't happen. The miracle that is you sitting here reading these words is the result of the efforts of so many incredible people, and all of the paper in the world wouldn't be enough to thank them.

So here goes nothing.

Brian Farrey-Latz, thank you for starting this journey with me. Mari Kesselring, thank you for bringing this story home to safe harbors. Profound thanks to the two Flux teams—can I call you Flux the Grey and Flux the White? Feels appropriate. To Mallory Hayes, Katie Mickshl, Sandy Sullivan, Bob Gaul, Megan Naidl, Joe Riley, and everyone else at Flux and North Star whose hard work makes dreams come true.

Thao Le, you wager of wars, lighter of fires, and beacon of hope—I couldn't ask for a better champion as my agent. Thanks for carrying us through the storm, and thanks to the whole team at the Sandra Dijkstra Literary Agency for your unwavering support for this little big story.

Tara Sim, I don't deserve you (or anything you put me through). Thank you for your wisdom, your friendship, your generosity, your incredible gift for storytelling, and all of those images I'll never be able to get out of my head.

Jessie Cluess, thank you for welcoming me to your

wonderful garbage city with open arms. There's no one I'd rather escape the clutches of Kettleman City with. Traci Chee, you're my favorite little old lady, and I'd be lost without your plot goddess powers. Thanks to Elizabeth Briggs, Audrey Coulthurst, Sarah Glenn Marsh, Roshani Chokshi, and all of the other members of the YA author community who form my salty pirate network. None of us sails these waters alone, and I'm so grateful for that.

Marisa Perez-Reyes, thank you for taking me to the ER in the middle of the night on the day I wrote only five words of this book—and, you know, for everything else too. Thank you Wop House for your wonderful weirdness that let my weirdness thrive. And it feels strange to thank an educational institution—especially one that put me through hell—but it feels stranger not to say thank you to Cornell for all of the little corners where I stole away to tell this story when I was probably supposed to be studying more.

Mom and Dad, I understand more and more every day what an obscene privilege it is to be your daughter. Thanks for a home where anything was possible with enough elbow grease, and sorry about the scientific inaccuracies (even the fun ones). Sarah, thanks for being my first creative collaborator. I can't wait to see where your amazing gifts go. Ivy, be good.

And finally, there's you. Whoever you are, you're reading this. You're with me. I can't thank you enough. This book almost didn't happen, but I fought for it, every step of the way, thinking of you here at the end. Thanks for finishing this story. Here's to many more horizons.

ABOUT THE AUTHOR

Emily Skrutskie is six feet tall. She was born in Massachusetts, raised in Virginia, and forged in the mountains above Boulder, Colorado. She holds a BA in Performing and Media Arts from Cornell University, where she studied an outrageous and demanding combination of film, computer science, and game design. She lives and writes in Los Angeles. She can be found online at @skrutskie on Twitter, or on her website, skrutskie.com.